BURNED BY LOVE

A FIREFIGHTERS OF LONG VALLEY ROMANCE NOVEL - BOOK 4

ERIN WRIGHT

WRIGHT'S READS

To my family:

Your support and love means the world to me. I'm sorry I've run off to see the country and wasn't at home for Christmas this year, but know that I was there in my heart.

And to Jasmine the Writing Cat:

Someday, I'll love another being as much as you love me. Thanks for all of the snuggles and help along the way. I'm sorry I include so many dogs in my books. I'll try to do better in the future.

AUTHOR'S NOTE, PART 1

Hi, y'all!

Burned by Love is the fourth novel in the Fire-fighters of Long Valley series, and there are another nine books currently published in the regular Long Valley series. I point this fact out because all of my books are written as stand-alones (the two main characters have a beginning, middle, and end to their love story, so you never have to buy a second book to find out how they work out their problems) but *Burned,* more than any other book I've ever written, brings in people from other books in the Long

Valley world. You'll soon see why that is, but I just wanted to say before you get started that:

1. *Burned by Love* is a standalone novel, just like every other book I've ever written; but
2. If you haven't read all of the other books in the Long Valley world yet (both the Firefighters and regular series), some of the side characters may not have as much meaning to you. So, perhaps you should go back and read the other books in the Long Valley world. *hint, hint, nudge, nudge*

Last bit of warning: *Burned by Love* goes back in time (to May of 2018) so if you just finished reading the third book in the Firefighters series, *Fire and Love* (which concludes in the fall of 2018), you might be confused when suddenly, people who were already together as a couple aren't together yet, or situations that happened long ago are now being repeated.

They're not actually on repeat, of course — they're just being told from Penny and Troy's point of view this time, and if I'm not mistaken, I think more than a few of you are going to be pretty surprised by how different that viewpoint can be at times. This is to be expected — every person in Long Valley has their own hopes and dreams and backgrounds and things they care about. Their reactions to the same situation are going to be very different, depending on that background.

So with that, please enjoy Troy and Penny's story. I hope it speaks to your heart like it did to mine.

CHAPTER 1

TROY

May, 2018

Troy Horvath had always been the quiet one of the bunch, and to be honest, he liked that about himself.

The way he saw it, it allowed him to sit back and take in the world, without being required to yack the ear off whoever was closest to him at the moment.

The way his aunt and uncle saw it, on the other hand, was that it allowed him to let the world pass him on by without even sparing him a second glance.

Actually, take that back — it made his *aunt* think it allowed the world to pass him on by without a second glance. His uncle had never said a word about the fact that Troy wasn't on the chatty side, at least not within earshot of Troy.

But then again, Aunt Horvath was (not surprisingly) a woman, and as far as Troy could tell, all women ever wanted to do was talk about their feelings, dreams, and desires, preferably all at the same time, and if a man didn't feel the same way, well then, there was something wrong with him.

Sparky was the only female Troy knew that didn't fall into the must-always-be-talking trap. She was content to just *be*, and didn't need him willing to discuss politics, religion, or the price of bananas down at the Shop 'N Go. Being the perfect female, all she wanted was for someone to pet her (preferably 24/7/365 if it could be arranged) and feed her doggy treats. He'd just adopted her a few days before, but they'd already formed a bond between them that was unbreakable. She trusted him with all her heart and soul, and after all she'd been through, that meant a hell of a lot.

As if she could read his thoughts, Sparky stood up and stretched, her back arching as her mouth opened wide, showing off all her pearly white canine teeth, and then she snuggled up against his legs, looking up at him with her soulful brown eyes. She was unabashedly begging for some pettings, and of course, Troy was happy to oblige. It wasn't hard to love on a dog that'd been through so much, but had somehow come out the other side sweet as pie. Her eyes closed in pleasure as her silky white tail began stirring up clouds of dust from the dirty cement floor.

He coughed a little from the dirt flinging through the air, but otherwise ignored it. He was used to working in dusty environments – his uncle's mill had dust floating through the air so thick, he could practically swim through it – so the dirty fire station floor didn't even rate a second glance.

No, what Troy was focused on was the

Dance of Desire happening right in front of his eyes.

He was at the monthly training session for the Sawyer Fire Department, and all of the volunteers (and the paid fire chief, Jaxson Anderson) were gathered at the station to learn better firefighting techniques or safety procedures or whatever else their brave leader wanted to teach them this time. Back when Troy's uncle was the fire chief, they didn't do *nearly* as much training as they did now, and it was certainly something that Troy could begrudgingly compliment Jaxson for improving since he took over back in January.

This training meeting was nothing like any other training meeting, though, because this time, a *female* was here.

In her typical, Georgia-Rowland-is-always-in-charge style, Georgia had voluntold the whole department that they were to be interviewed by a local reporter about the wildfire that had blazed through Long Valley over the last couple of days; a wildfire where Moose Garrett had saved her ass by breaking every rule in the book, and no doubt some that weren't written down, just for funsies.

Based on how Georgia and Moose were looking at each other right now, it seemed pretty damn clear to Troy that they'd done more than survive a wildfire together. Troy's hand stroked down over Sparky's silky fur as he watched the two pretend to be "just friends," even as the sparks that flew between them were so blindingly bright, he probably oughta go grab his sunglasses from his truck. Did Georgia and Moose think they were being sneaky, that no one was noticing that they were sending glances to each other that were bound to set the dry grass outside ablaze and start up a second wildfire? He knew that people in lust were oblivious, but surely not *that* oblivious, right?

Idly, he glanced away from the couple mooning over each other and checked his phone. This reporter guy was supposed to have arrived five minutes ago. How long were they gonna sit around and wait for him to show up before they moved on with their evening? It wasn't that Troy had anything he *needed* to go home and do – although it wouldn't hurt to do a load of laundry, and his kitchen could use a good scrubbing, none of that was pressing – but if given a choice between hanging out at the fire station and watching two lovebirds simper over each other, or being at home in just his boxers, watching a game with a beer in his hand…

Well, that choice was pretty obvious.

He tugged at the collar of his button-up shirt, wishing he hadn't bothered to change before coming to the meeting that night. Normally, getting dressed up in a collared shirt so he could go hang out with a bunch of guys in a greasy, dirty building for a couple of hours was *not* something he'd sign up for. But because of this reporter coming tonight – wherever the hell he was – Jaxson had put out the word for everyone to come dressed and cleaned up and ready for a photo shoot, just in case that was what the reporter wanted to do. Troy scrubbed at his clean-shaven jaw with a regretful sigh. He'd had a nice seven-day start on a beard going; now he'd have to start all over again.

Why Jaxson cared so much about what some dumbass reporter thought of them was beyond him. Uncle Horvath never would've stooped so low as to court the approval of the press. Chief Horvath focused on what needed to be done, and to hell with the rest of them. Jaxson seemed like a nice enough kid, but he sure had a lot to—

The air changed just then. The chatter of the men died away; even Georgia's giggle over whatever amazingly brilliant comment Moose had just made disappeared. Troy's head shot up as the crackle of electricity around him made the hairs on his neck stand straight up. Not a sound was heard in the cavernous fire station, other than the click of heels on pavement as the most gorgeous woman Troy had ever seen in his life came striding into the joint.

Holy

Shit

There were athletic, pretty women like Georgia Rowland. There were beauty queens like her cousin, Tennessee Rowland. There were cute, next-door-neighbor girls like Sugar Stonemyer down at the bakery, who Jaxson had started dating.

And then, there was this woman.

He rather felt like he'd been clobbered upside the head by a 2x4. Maybe a padded one, but there was *definitely* a 2x4 involved. As his gaze followed every slim curve of the woman's body – her long legs, her strappy high heels, her tight skirt, her styled blonde hair, her ruby red lips curved into a self-confident smile – he tried to make his brain work. There was something…

Something wrong here.

It was…something.

Oh yeah, why is this woman here?

Supermodels didn't tend to walk into a rural fire station on a Friday night just to hang out with a bunch of blue-collar guys and shoot the shit.

That just didn't happen.

The roar of surprise and lust in his ears finally died down enough for him to hear what she was saying. "Hi, I'm Penny Roth," she said as she shook hands with Levi Scranton, one of the guys on the force. "How long have you been a firefighter?"

He missed Levi's answer, too stunned to hear anything but the roar in his ears again. There was only one reason for this woman to be shaking hands with all the men and asking questions about being a firefighter.

But that meant…

His brain staggered to a stop. Seriously? This was the reporter? This paragon of beauty and legs and sparkling high heels was a reporter for the two weekly rags in the area?

Sparky whined and nudged Troy's hand, apparently not happy with the speed of his pettings. He looked down at her blankly for a moment, trying to remember what he was doing. Who he was. Where he was. Sparky whined again, and absentmindedly, he scratched her behind the ears, her tail resuming the rapid thumping of joy and pleasure at his touch.

His mind swam as he tried to put the pieces together – the reporter for the *Sawyer Times* and

Franklin Gazette was a drop-dead gorgeous woman. No spare tire around the middle; no balding spot on the back of her head; actually, no male qualities whatsoever. She appeared to be as feminine as they came.

It wasn't that Troy didn't think that a woman could be a reporter; it'd just never crossed his mind that she would be. The stereotypical reporter that Troy had imagined…

Well, that image was nothing like the woman in front of him, that was for damn sure.

She'd reached Moose and was now shaking his hand, chatting easily with him as Georgia looked on and glowered possessively. Even as Troy was busy trying to accept the truth of what he was seeing in front of him, he also found his mouth quirking up a bit with humor at the territorial look on Georgia's face. What, exactly, had happened up at Eagle's Nest when Moose and Georgia had tried to stay safe from the wildfire raging around them? It sure looked like they'd practiced some mouth-to-mouth resuscitation on each other.

And then, Penny Roth was walking towards him, and his mind went blank.

How she'd noticed him over in the corner, sitting on the tailgate of the water truck, accustomed — and expecting — the world to walk right on by, he'd never know. He wasn't used to being noticed. In fact, he counted on it, so her laser-focused gaze on him as she walked over… he just didn't know what to think.

Or perhaps it was the aforementioned 2x4, padded or not. He'd been walloped but good, and he wasn't quite sure he was breathing.

"Hi, I'm Penny Roth," she said again, reaching her hand out to shake his. He was frozen on the tailgate of the water truck, Sparky leaning against his legs and trapping him there even though he should be rising to greet her but moving didn't seem possible just then, except for his hand — thank God he could move it — so he raised it up and shook hers, and when their palms touched…

It was like grasping a bolt of lightning. Her gaze flared, as bright and brilliant as her smile, as they locked eyes. "Troy Horvath," he got out, wanting to hang onto her hand for the next six months or so. Just until he got used to the feeling shooting up his arm. Then he could let go.

But not a moment before.

Somehow, though, she seemed to be immune to this overwhelming desire to keep their palms pressed together to feel the electricity arcing between them, and instead pulled her hand out of his, dropping to her knees in front of Sparky to love on her. "Aren't you a sweetie," she cooed to Sparky, letting his dog give her face a bath while Sparky's tail swept up a storm on the dusty cement floor.

Troy was in shock. Moose was in shock. Levi was in shock. Every person in the room just froze, watching this unfold in front of them.

Sparky didn't like anyone except Troy. Not even Moose and Georgia, who'd saved her from the wildfire just two days ago, were freely allowed to pet her. As best as they could figure, she'd been beat by some sadistic son-of-a-bitch and now chose who was allowed within ten feet of her very, *very* carefully.

She didn't give out face baths easily. Hell, Troy'd just gotten his first one from her this morning. And here she was, loving on Penny like they were the best of friends.

His heart twisted a little at the sight.

Of course, it was good to see Sparky love someone else other than Troy. He was happy that it was happening. He was just in shock, was all. Nothing more than that.

"So, you're the one who saved Georgia from the fire?" the reporter asked, looking up at Troy, her eyes intense as she studied him from her kneeling position on the dirty fire station floor. She didn't seem to notice that Sparky was shedding white and black hairs all over her skirt and blouse, just like she shed all over everything else she came in close contact with. Troy had given up on being dog-hair free about an hour or so after he'd adopted her; it just wasn't gonna happen. Was Penny gonna be pissed when she saw where Sparky's fur was ending up?

He opened up his mouth to warn her, but decided to answer her question instead. This'd be a good test to see how much she really liked dogs; if she freaked out about having some stray hairs left behind, well, that'd tell him all he needed to know. Unlike Jaxson, Troy didn't believe he had to bend over backwards to impress the press.

He balled up his fist where her hand had slid into his, pushing the buzzing electric feeling away.

"No, not me." Troy finally managed a reply to her question – embarrassingly slowly but he got there – and jerked his head towards Moose, who'd followed Penny over to the water truck, Georgia trailing along behind him. "He did."

"I thought the dog was found up in the fire," Penny said, her brow knotted with confusion. "How did she end up with you, then?"

"She likes me," Troy said simply, shrugging his shoulders. *Just like she likes you* were the unspoken words left hanging in the air. Sparky loving on someone else...Troy was pretty sure in that moment, he could've been knocked flat on his ass with a feather.

Sparky did another swipe across Penny's face with her long pink tongue and Penny laughed. "How long have you been a firefighter?" she asked, continuing to pet Sparky as she looked up at him, ignoring the whole supposed reason for her being there – i.e., Moose and Georgia and the wildfire that'd burned hundreds of acres before nature had intervened and had kept the valley from going up in flames. Troy'd gone out on that call, of course, but by time they'd begun their work, nature had already taken pity on them and had reversed course.

You win some, you lose some, and sometimes, you're just damn lucky. Georgia had been the one to name Sparky; perhaps she should've named her Lucky instead.

Troy forced himself to focus on Penny's question. If he kept answering her ten minutes after she asked him something, she was gonna start to think he was slow in the head.

"All my life, it feels like," he admitted. "My

uncle used to be the head firefighter," he was choosing his words carefully, as carefully as he ever had, landmines waiting for him at every turn as he did his best to hopscotch across them. "So I began young. But he retired, and Jaxson—" he felt his tongue wanting to seize up but he got the name out without making an ass of himself, "—took over in January."

Out of the corner of his eye, he saw Moose and Georgia move away, and he wasn't sure if he wanted to thank them for it, or yell at them to come back. He wasn't supposed to be the one talking to the reporter; they were. They were the ones who saved the dog. They were the ones who lived through a wildfire all by themselves up in the wilds of Idaho. Troy'd had as much to do with all of that as he'd had helping Santa Claus deliver presents this last Christmas. But telling Penny to go talk to someone else, to go pin someone else down with her sparkling eyes, intent on drawing answers out of them…

He gulped.

"Your uncle was the fire chief, but after he

retired, they didn't choose you to be the next one?" she asked, the surprise clear in her voice.

He laughed a little at that. "It isn't a hereditary position," he said carefully, choosing each word before speaking it. He shrugged. "Plus, I didn't apply. I didn't want the job."

He heard Moose and Jaxson say something to the guys, and then everyone laughed. He hadn't heard what they'd said, but he was sure − absolutely sure − that they'd been discussing the two of them. He felt the tips of his ears go red. He wanted to shoot them a glare and tell them to back off, but pretending deafness seemed like a much safer plan.

Less talking was involved, anyway, which always made it a safer plan.

"What job do you have that is better than fire chief?" Penny asked, finally standing and swiping at the hair and dirt all over her clothes. She didn't seem pissed that she was filthy; she was just straightening herself out. Her curled blonde hair swung as she worked to clean up, and his mind paused on the idea of touching it. Would a curl wrap around his finger?

He forced himself to concentrate on her question.

Huh. What was her question again?

Job. She wants to know where you work, you dumbass.

"The Horvath Mill. The new one outside of town," he clarified. Sadly, the old one had burned to a crisp this past January after the mayor's son had thrown a cigarette butt into a pile of old rags and set the place on fire. Damn teenagers. That building was part of his family's heritage, and his heart still hurt at the idea of it burning like it did, leaving a shell of blackened bricks behind.

"Horvath, eh?" She slid onto the tailgate next to him, seemingly oblivious to the dirt and grime encrusted there. She was settling into place before Troy could stop her, so again, he snapped his mouth shut. The damage was done now, and hell, her elbow was brushing up against his. He could no more warn her to move than he could chop off that elbow. "Is the mill owned by your uncle, the former fire chief? Or by someone else in your family?"

Damn, she was quick on the draw. Family relations and who owned what and who was related to who was a constant struggle to keep straight in a small town, but Miss Penny Roth was apparently up to the task.

"Uncle," he said simply. It was the Horvath family mill, and as soon as Aunt Horvath could convince her husband to retire fully, it would be Troy's. None of their three kids wanted it, and since Troy'd been working there for most of his adult life, it just made sense for him to take it over.

And most importantly, it was what he was supposed to do. He always did what he was supposed to do.

"Do your parents live in town, too?" she asked as Sparky laid her head on Penny's lap and began begging for some attention. Troy sent his not-so-loyal dog a dark look of his own. It was good to see her feel comfortable enough that she would allow other people to touch her, of course, but did she have to go *that* far? Penny began absentmindedly stroking Sparky's head, scratching right behind her ears just like the spotted setter loved, and sure enough, Sparky's tail started flying again, dirt and hair going every which way.

"No, they live in Boise. I've lived here with my aunt and uncle since freshman year, though." He tried to quickly come up with a question to ask her so he could just listen to her talk and he could be free to retreat into blessed, comfortable silence, but she beat him to the punch.

"Have you fought a lot of fires, then, since your uncle was the fire chief? Is it an old hat to you by now?" Her eyes were pinned on him, a mysterious dark blue color that matched her shirt. He'd never seen quite that shade before, and wondered for a moment if she was wearing colored lenses.

He laughed uncomfortably. "Firefighting is never an old hat to anyone. Complacency is a good way to get yourself killed. But I have fought a lot of fires – both house and wild-fires." He was surprised by how many words were rolling off his tongue effortlessly, as if speaking easily to a beautiful woman – or anyone at all – was something that he did all the time. Did she know how strange this was for him?

Looking at her – beautiful, smart, outgoing – he was pretty sure she had absolutely no concept of what it was like to be trapped inside a body that didn't always cooperate.

"You guys are all volunteers, right?" she asked, bringing him back to the present. He nodded, and she continued, "I've always wondered if it was hard to find people to volunteer to risk their lives. Why are you willing to do this if you're not even going to get paid?"

"Volunteer doesn't mean unpaid," he hurried to tell her. "We get paid every time we respond to a fire. We just don't get paid otherwise. It is hard to find volunteers, though. People are busy with their own lives." He shrugged. It was understandable, really. He'd been raised to focus on the fire department and making sure that every fire was responded to no matter what, but he wasn't like everyone else, and that was okay. They didn't need a hundred guys to respond to every call-out; just enough guys to make sure the people of Long Valley were safe.

Anything beyond that was a bonus.

"Is fire chief also a volunteer position?" she asked.

He flinched. Without meaning to, she'd hit right on that sore spot with a hammer.

Looking at her, really trying to gauge who she was, Troy hesitated. Penny was part of the press. The press could say whatever they wanted; could twist his words and make him out to be a jealous jackass or a real gentleman. It was all in how she wrote it.

Could he trust her enough to talk about how virtually the entire town had been up in arms over Jaxson being made a full-time employee from day one, when Uncle Horvath had been a simple volunteer like everyone else? Last month, after Jaxson had saved Gage and Sugar from the Muffin Man bakery fire, the town had settled down a whole lot, seemingly forgiving Jaxson for being an upstart kid from the big city, there to raise their taxes and tell them how it was done in a *real* town, but for Troy, it still smarted a little.

Finally, he settled on telling Penny the truth, but nothing more. Personal feelings didn't matter anyway and certainly weren't newsworthy.

"He's a full-time employee," he said simply.

Penny raised one eyebrow in response to that, silently asking him to tell her the rest of the story, but Troy sidestepped the unspoken request. "Are you from Franklin?" he asked instead. He was damn sure she wasn't from Sawyer – if he'd ever laid eyes on her before, he would've remembered it.

Forgetting Penny Roth just wasn't something that happened.

"Born and raised," she said with a disgruntled sigh. Sparky let out a blissful sigh of her own as she snuggled deeper into Penny's lap, looking like a poster child for relaxation. With her eyes closed, the dog missed the second dark look Troy sent her way. Did she *have* to appear so at home so quickly? "I graduated in 2006,"

Penny continued, oblivious to the looks Troy was sending his traitorous dog. "You?"

"2000. Been here ever since. You?"

"Left town on graduation night." She shot him a laughing look. "Yup, I was one of *those* kids – attended graduation with my car packed to the brim with my stuff. I couldn't get out of here fast enough. Got my bachelor's in graphic design from a university down in San Diego. I —" She caught the surprised look on his face, and grimaced. "Being a reporter is just a temporary gig." She waved her hand dismissively. "I'm going to be leaving Long Valley soon, thank God, and heading back to civilization. No more living in a town where the most exciting thing that happens all year is the quilt auction, or when Mr. Cowell's cows get out and block the road into town."

Troy forced a polite smile onto his face, even as his heart sank. Of *course* Penny the Reporter wasn't planning on staying in the area. What part of the elegant, gorgeous woman sitting next to him looked like it belonged in rural, mountainous Idaho? Not those sparkling high heels. Not the frilly blouse. And certainly not her bright red lipstick. There wasn't a damn inch of her that fit in here, which would probably explain his overwhelming gut reaction to her. Of course he'd react that way. She was like no one else in the whole of Long Valley.

But now he knew she was leaving, and that meant she was untouchable. He'd be better off letting her walk away, no matter what the burning sensation in his palm where they'd touched was urging him to do.

He pushed off the end of the water truck. "Ready to go interview?" he asked, jerking his head towards the group of firefighters who appeared to be training on safety equipment. Georgia was still there, sitting off to the side at a decrepit desk covered with yellowed forms, patiently waiting around for Penny to ask her questions.

Penny pushed herself off the tailgate of the water truck also, a tight smile on her face, both of them ignoring the very humanlike groan from a disappointed Sparky. "Absolutely! I better get my job done, right?"

As they walked towards the knot of fire-fighters, Troy told himself that she wasn't the only one there who had a job to do. His whole purpose in life was to take over the Horvath Mill, nothing more, nothing less.

Dating the local reporter who was on her way out the door just wasn't in the cards, no matter how many 2x4's were involved.

CHAPTER 2

PENNY

*A*LL RIGHT, so she knew she was being dumb, but inquiring minds wanted to know: Did knowing that upfront make her more of an idiot or less of one?

She sighed.

Yeah, getting dressed up in her cutest skirt and her tallest heels and her lowest cut blouse to go to a grain mill (of all places!) sure wasn't a mark in her favor. Especially since the whole point of being there – a certain Troy Horvath – didn't even like her. There for a minute at the fire station, she'd thought he did, and then…

After practically throwing herself at him at

the firefighter meeting, he'd simply walked her over to the rest of the guys – well, and to Georgia – and had said she needed to interview them, then had slipped to the back of the group of men, leaving her with the unfortunate task of actually doing her job.

She'd interviewed Moose – *who named their child Moose?!?! Seriously, Idaho, this is getting out of control* – and Georgia as quickly as possible before making a fast exit, the stares all following her out the door. She'd worked hard on her piece back at the office, writing up an article with more heart and soul than she ever had before. Even Mr. Toewes, her boss and a normally unappeasable man, had told her it "wasn't bad."

She'd practically fallen over from such lavish praise.

Clutching a copy of this week's *Sawyer Times* in her hand, hot off the press, she made her way over to the front door of the Horvath Mill, ready to deliver a copy directly to Troy. Just as a way of saying thank you for his help. Nothing more than that. She absolutely wasn't hoping to get him to ask her out on a date.

Absolutely not.

She pulled the glass door open and walked into a wonderfully air conditioned office. She threw her head back and sucked in the cool air for just a moment, trying to bring her core temperature back down to normal levels. It was only May outside, but someone had forgotten to tell the thermometer on the wall. For a normally cool climate like Long Valley, the low-90-degree temps were an absolute killer.

"Can I help you?" asked an older woman sternly over the rim of her glasses, looking Penny up and down, clearly not believing that she belonged inside of a grain mill. She wasn't too far off with that assessment, of course, but Penny wasn't about to let that show on her face. Let the old woman think what she wanted.

"Yes, I'm here to talk to Troy Horvath, please," Penny said in her most polite voice possible.

"*Talk* to Troy?" the older woman repeated in disbelief. "You better be ready to do all of the talking," the heavy-set woman muttered under her breath as she pushed away from her desk and headed into the back, leaving Penny alone by herself up front.

Ignoring the dour woman, Penny walked around the clean, if totally plain, office that had all of the charm of a prison cell. Giving the place "that homey feeling" was not high on the list of priorities around here, that was for sure and certain. With nothing else to look at, she drifted over to the one picture someone had bothered to hang on the wall. In the center stood an older man, perhaps Troy's uncle, holding an oversized pair of scissors, poised to cut a giant red ribbon. He looked painfully out of place in the staged event, grimacing what could...*charitably* be termed a smile at the camera.

If one was feeling really, really charitable.

Further down the ribbon with his own pair of ridiculous scissors was a younger version of Troy. Unlike his uncle, he didn't even attempt to smile at the camera but simply stared at it levelly, waiting for the ceremony to be over so he could get back to work.

Looking closer, she was pretty sure they were inside of this office, although in the photo, someone had actually taken the time to decorate it with live plants and even a bouquet of flowers. This had to have been the grand opening of the new mill; nothing else explained an honest-to-God vase of roses on the front counter.

She wondered what made them move out here into the countryside to build a new mill, leaving the old one on Main Street to slowly crumble away under the onslaught of time. She'd seen the old mill on Main Street countless times as she'd driven through Sawyer on the way to Boise – she couldn't exactly miss one of the largest buildings in town – and had been sad to see it burn back in January. Now it looked even more decrepit, just waiting for a bulldozer to come along and put it out of its misery.

"Penny?"

His deep voice caught her off guard and

she spun in a circle on her heel, thanking her lucky stars as she did so that she wasn't a klutz. Spinning on the spike of a 3-inch high heel wasn't for the faint of heart.

"Hi, Troy!" she said breathlessly, the surprise of his appearance making her heart race. That, obviously, was the only reason her heart felt like it was going to thump right out of her chest.

Not because of the light blond stubble across his strong jaw.

Not because of the way his dark blond hair fell across his forehead.

Not because she could see the bulge of his biceps through the worn fabric of his dusty, dirty work shirt.

And absolutely not because even in her highest high heels, he was still taller than her.

It was a sad truthitude in Penny's life that it was difficult to find a guy who wasn't a midget compared to her − near impossible, really − and the height disparity only got worse when she wore heels. And since she loved wearing heels, she often went around the world feeling a bit like a skinny version of King Kong, towering over everyone around her, in danger of accidentally smashing the tiny people under her shoe without noticing.

Fine, that was a slight exaggeration, but only a very slight one.

And then, here was Troy Horvath. Even in her highest heels, she had to lift her chin just a little to look into his pale green eyes, eyes that were studying her intently, waiting for her to get on with it so he could go back to work.

Did she see a flash of interest in those gorgeous eyes? Or was she just wishing so hard for it that she was imagining things?

She took a deep breath and flashed her prettiest smile at him. It was now or never. "Hey, sorry for interrupting you at work. I didn't know your home address, so this was the only place I could think of where I could give you your very own copy." She pulled the newspaper out from behind her back and thrust it at him.

Slowly, he took it and unfolded it, studying the picture of him and Sparky in full color above the fold, Sparky's loving nature perfectly captured as she snuggled against his legs, looking up at him adoringly. The *Sawyer Times* was usually printed in black and white each week, unless an advertiser was willing to pay the upgrade fee to spot for a colored ad. When that happened, the whole newspaper was printed in full color. Penny had been thrilled to see that this week's newspaper got the color treatment – apparently some Dawson Black-horse cowboy was wanting to advertise a breeding stallion, so he'd paid the hefty fee to make it happen.

But what Penny cared about was that Troy's green eyes and dark blond hair and finely sculpted pink lips were going to be immortalized in full color for the rest of eternity, not to mention Sparky's pink tongue hanging out of her mouth.

It really was an awesome picture, if she did say so herself.

"I even mentioned the fundraiser you guys did last week," she said into the deafening silence when Troy didn't say a word, "and included how to donate money to help improve the radio system you guys use. It was Moose who'd told me that the system needed upgrading. Hopefully you'll get some more donations to help out…"

She trailed off miserably. Troy was still just reading over the article, standing there silently as she babbled on. She caught the smirk on the face of the older woman who'd sat back down at her desk, clearly giving her the "I told you so" look. Penny looked back up at Troy, confused. He *had* talked the other night. Not tons, but certainly more than just her name, which was all he'd said thus far today.

"It's even printed in full color this week!" She pointed at the large picture of Troy, front and center, as if he was in danger of missing it. "It's a lot cheaper to print in black and white, you see, so color is only used when an advertiser wants it for their ad, in which case they have to pay a lot more, and when that happens, then the whole paper gets the color treatment. It only happens maybe once a month, but I guess this week, a local horse breeder wanted to advertise his stallion in full color, so…there you go!"

This was going badly.

This was going very, *very* badly.

She'd told herself not to do this – not to throw herself at him and that was *clearly* what she was doing, wearing an outfit that would be more at home in a club on a Saturday night than in a mill, for hell's sakes – but she'd also told herself that she couldn't cover up her best assets, not if she was going to wrangle a date out of Troy, and now…

"Well anyway," she said cheerfully, *if* talking through a closed-off throat that was filling with embarrassment and tears could be considered cheerful, "I better head out. Got that quilt raffle to report on, you know. Crazy quilt raffles – so exciting! Can hardly stand the excitement of living in a thriving metropolis like Long Valley."

The sarcasm wasn't so much dripping off her words as pouring off them in waves. She flashed him a completely insincere smile. "Best of luck with the mill, and taking it over from

your uncle, and getting the radios for the firefighters. I'm sure I'll see you around."

She turned on her heel − even with her
throat almost completely closed off at this point
and her face stinging a brilliant red with embarrassment, she managed the movement effortlessly − and headed back for the glass front
door and the unbearable heat outside.

"Penny!" Troy called out as her hand
touched the cool metal bar of the door handle.
"Will you go out with me?"

She wrapped her fingers around the handle, holding on for dear life, and turned slowly
back to him.

CHAPTER 3

TROY

*S*HIT.

He'd really stepped in it now. Out of all of the dumb things that he could've blurted out, asking Penny Roth on a date had to be in the top five.

And dammit all, he was Troy Horvath – he didn't blurt things out. That wasn't a thing that happened to him. Ever.

Glenda had gasped quietly when he'd practically shouted the question, but he ignored her. She was a gossiping old lady who'd be sure to spread the news all over the mill by time the afternoon break was over, but Troy pushed that out of his mind for now. Since he'd been stupid and blurted out a question he had no right asking Penny…

Well, now he wanted an answer to it.

She turned back slowly towards him, and in those moments as he waited, the sweat on the palms of his hands surely smearing the cheap newspaper ink, he focused on keeping a poker face in place. That way, if she turned him down, the hurt wouldn't show. No reason to let any emotions show at all, really.

She looked at him across the tiny office, and then a huge smile split her face. He let the tiniest breath go, breath he hadn't even realized he'd been holding, at the sight. Penny Roth was gorgeous all the time, but when she had a happy, pleased smile on her face?

She was drop-dead gorgeous.

"I'd love to!" she said brightly. "Did you have something in mind? Actually," she said hurriedly, before he could speak, "if you don't mind, I've been looking for a date for the kickoff of the wine tasting and art walk in Franklin on Memorial Day. I have to report on it for the newspaper but attending a party without a date is…painful." She wrinkled her nose ruefully. "I promise to only take a few pictures before getting on with the date portion of the night. Does that work for you?"

"Absolutely," he said, thrilled that he hadn't had to come up with an idea of his own on the spur of the moment. He hadn't meant to ask Penny out on a date; he hadn't planned any of this at all.

Penny knowing what she wanted them to do? Priceless.

He snatched a business card off the counter from behind him and a pen, and handed them over. "Address, please."

"Of course!" she said, laughing as she scribbled an address in Franklin on the back of the card. "I'm glad you thought of it. I would've been waiting for you to show up, and you would've had no idea where to find me." As she handed it back, their fingertips brushed against each other and that same breathtaking sizzle of electricity shot through him.

This time, he knew she'd felt it, too. She sucked in a breath and they just stood and stared at each other and didn't breathe or move—

The phone rang, jerking them both out of their trance.

"Horvath Mill, Glenda speaking," said his ever-efficient receptionist behind him. At least someone was doing their job, since standing around and drooling over gorgeous women was certainly not part of Troy's job description.

He cleared his throat, tucking the card in his back pocket. "See you at five at your house," he said quietly, and headed back to work, ignoring the *clearly* interested look on Glenda's face as he walked by. She was still talking to the customer on the phone – Mr. Rawls, from the sounds of it, about a load of wheat he wanted to bring in – but that didn't keep her from eavesdropping on him at the same time.

Multi-tasking was absolutely something she

was good at, as long as at least one task entailed her poking her nose in where it didn't belong.

He couldn't find it in him to get upset over it, though. He had a date – a date with *Penny Roth*. He whistled under his breath as he got back to work.

CHAPTER 4

PENNY

S HE GRABBED TROY'S HAND and dragged him over to the wine tasting booth. Their passes – in the form of bright orange wristbands – entitled them to two small glasses of wine each, and she'd be damned if she was going to bypass the opportunity to drink on the company's dime. The pay wasn't exactly stellar at the newspaper, but there was the occasional bennie that came with working there, and being paid to cover the annual kickoff of the Franklin Art & Wine Walk was definitely on that list.

She stole a glance at Troy, the dark blond

five o'clock shadow along his square jaw giving him a scruffy, mysterious mountain-man aura that perfectly complemented his quiet, mysterious personality. She felt a jitter of excitement rush through her, spreading up her hand nestled in Troy's calloused one and shooting up her arm, setting off a whole flock of butterflies that had somehow taken up residence in her stomach.

Being there with Troy, feeling the pulse of the energy from everyone around them, feeling the winter stupor melting away as people began to enjoy the summer heat and longer hours of daylight and a total lack of any snow drifts in sight, something that sadly couldn't be said most of the year in Long Valley…

It made her giddy with excitement, and she hadn't even had any of that free wine to drink yet.

It was early, so the thick crowds that would show up in another hour or so hadn't made their appearance quite yet. It didn't take but a few moments to get to the front of the line, where Penny chose a pink moscato that looked delicious. Once her glass was poured, the gal working the booth looked at Troy expectantly.

"Same," Troy rumbled, and the harried worker quickly poured out another glass without blinking an eyelash. Penny, though, was a little surprised – she totally wouldn't have pegged him as a moscato drinker.

Huh. Well, just goes to show she shouldn't prejudge what a person liked to drink based on the thickness of the scruff on their jaw, right?

They moved off to the side, glasses in hand, and Penny turned to her date – she was on a *date!* – with a silly grin. "Cheers!" she said, clinking her glass against his and then throwing most of the wine back in one swallow. She wasn't much of a lush so downing that much wine in one go wasn't a habit of hers, but in her defense, it *was* a small glass. She was debating the merits of sipping at the remaining liquid and making it last or just finishing it off altogether when she looked over to see that Troy was simply holding his glass, not drinking anything at all. She tilted her head inquiringly, feeling a bit of heat start to flow through her veins from the alcohol.

"Ummm…do you not like moscato?" she asked him, completely confused. "There were other varieties back—"

"I'm the designated driver," he explained, and deftly poured his wine into her glass, refilling it almost to the brim. "I thought you could drink my wine for me." He winked at her.

Troy Horvath, winking. I wonder what Glenda would say about that.

Unfortunately, his flirtatious wink didn't completely wipe out the flush of embarrassment at her stupidity. Duh. Someone needed to be able to drive them back to their respective homes. "I don't know why I didn't think about that," she admitted ruefully. "Dammit, now I feel bad – I could've been the designated driver, you know. After all, I'm the one who's on assignment, so it really only makes sense that I stay sober."

Shit. She'd really gone and mucked this one up. She'd been so thrilled to have someone come with her to the event, and over-the-top excited about having that "someone" be Troy, that she just didn't think about the logistics of it all.

He shook his head and smiled slowly, a sexy grin that sent a shiver of lust through her. "You're a great writer," he said softly, yet somehow clear as a bell over the thumping music from the band up on the stage. "I'm sure you'll write a terrific piece, even with a little alcohol in you."

Huh.

Okay, so it turned out that she was *totally* susceptible to flattery.

She wasn't exactly surprised by this information; it was more that she just wasn't used to it. Mr. Toewes' assessment that the firefighter article "wasn't bad" was as gushing as the taciturn man had ever gotten with her. Ever since she'd taken the job at the newspaper, the community's feedback had mostly consisted of "helpful tips" on what she could do better next time (a main fav being that their picture should be more flattering – if she could just invest in a camera that took 20 years and 15 pounds off them, that'd be much appreciated. A close second was that she should definitely write up a long article every single week on the goings-on of their quilt auction / book club / chili cook-off / book sale / what-have-you, since it was *obviously* the most exciting thing to hit Long Valley since the advent of sliced bread).

So Troy's belief that she'd write a "terrific" piece, liquored up or not, was a nice boost to ye olde ego, that was for damn sure. She opened up her mouth to ask him what, exactly, his favorite part was of the article she'd written about him and the other firefighters, but decided at the last moment that fishing for compliments was going a little too far.

It really is too bad that it isn't socially acceptable to ask people to tell you how wonderful you are. I'd totally be all over that.

With a regretful sigh, she threw back all of the wine in her glass, promising herself as the warmth spread deliciously through her veins that she'd take it slow with the second round. "Why don't we get refills and then we can go scope out all of the artwork?" she asked, holding up her empty glass as proof of needing more. She was going to ignore the fact that she just downed two (smallish) glasses of wine in less than five minutes.

She wasn't a lush, really she wasn't.

The corner of his mouth quirked. "Sounds good," he told her and she promptly dragged him back towards the wine counter.

Life became a hazy, laughter-filled world after that. As they mixed and mingled in the crowd, she clung to Troy's arm, hugging his sculpted biceps against her side in what could be considered an overly possessive move, but with the buzz of the alcohol running through her, she just couldn't make herself care that she was practically throwing herself at him. As they mingled, they chit-chatted with a few people she'd interviewed for the newspaper; a couple of them even recognized Troy from the front page article.

Troy didn't say much as they wandered around, but then again, she didn't need him to. From what she could tell, he was a world-class listener – laughing, smiling, nodding, and making small noises at all the appropriate times. Normally, she'd suspect someone of zoning out if they were this quiet, but she thought of herself as pretty good at reading people, and that simply wasn't the case here. When he looked at her, he *really* looked at her. His eyes stayed locked on her so often, she kinda wondered if he was going to be in danger of running into other people since he didn't appear to be watching where he was going.

Her alcohol-tinged brain spun through the words she'd use to describe Troy Horvath to someone who hadn't met him. Quiet wasn't quite right. She looked up to see his pale green eyes locked on her, his intense gaze telling her that her every muscle twitch, her every sigh, her every wrinkle of her brow was being noticed, catalogued, and filed away for future use.

That was it – he was *intense*.

Intensely quiet, intensely focused, intensely *hot*.

Hmmmm…was that even a thing – "intensely hot"? Well, if it wasn't before, it should be now, she decided as she took another small sip of her wine.

They had begun to slowly make their way towards the art displays lining the sidewalks when she spotted Moose, Georgia, and Tripp – the guy from the credit union she'd met when she'd gone in to interview Georgia – all chatting in a group, and she began to head their direction instead. She raised her hand to flag them down when she realized, even through the pleasant haze of alcohol she was operating under, that something was wrong. Troy came to a stop next to her and they watched the threesome silently as Tripp stormed off, looking pissed, and then Moose and Georgia walked away in the opposite direction, not looking so happy themselves. Stranger than anything else was the fact that Moose was carrying what looked like a gallon of milk and a loaf of bread as they went. Had he been grocery shopping at an arts festival?

"I wonder what the hell that was all about,"

Penny murmured aloud, staring at the couple until they disappeared from view.

She felt as much as saw Troy shrug as he stood next to her. "No idea," he said quietly, his brow creased as he stared after them.

"Well, I should probably go earn a paycheck – let's go take some shots of the artwork," Penny said, and pulled him through the crowded streets towards Once Upon a Trinket. "My boss said to be sure to check out the display by Ivy McLain – apparently she's from Sawyer, and she's making it big. Have you ever met her?"

Troy nodded as they neared the office supply / gift shop / art gallery / chocolate store. Just like everything else in this tiny-ass town, Once Upon a Trinket served about 50 different functions. Penny sighed. She really needed to focus on getting back to civilization.

"She's younger than me, but I know of her," he said as they stopped in front of an easel. "With her red hair, you can't miss Ivy." Penny didn't know what he meant until she saw the large, framed author photo next to a stack of About sheets. Ignoring the information for a moment, Penny studied the picture of the Sawyer artist. She had a wide smile, brilliant red hair, and bright blue eyes that sparkled, promising mischief and laughter. She was, to put it bluntly, gorgeous.

Penny noted with a tiny shot of jealousy that Ivy's skin was clear of any freckles, which with her red hair, just didn't seem fair. Dammit all, Penny had loads of freckles speckling her body, and her hair was a natural brunette. Nobody knew that, of course – she looked dreadful with dark brown hair so she'd been dying it a sassy blonde for years – but the point was, she wasn't born with red hair, and yet she probably had more freckles covering her than this Ivy chick did.

Seriously, some people have all the luck.

"She's got some real talent," Penny murmured as she turned from the author pic to look at the paintings clustered in front of the store. On canvases large, small, and everything in between, Ivy had captured the scenery and vistas of Long Valley perfectly.

It was a truthitude in Penny's life that she wanted nothing more than to get out of this backwards town, but Ivy's idealized version of the area made even Penny reconsider – if only for a moment – her burning desire to live any-where but here. Franklin and Sawyer didn't have much going for them in terms of shops or people, but even Penny had to admit that it had an overabundance of craggy mountains and tall pine trees.

The brilliance of the colors, her use of space and dimensions...after the years that Penny had spent studying graphic arts, she could see in a glance that Ivy had a true gift, the kind of talent that other "gifted" artists would give their right arm for.

And then she realized something else: Ivy seemed to be obsessed with some dude Penny didn't recognize. Again and again, the same handsome, dark-haired cowboy appeared in almost every painting, sometimes as the focus of it, sometimes just in the background, but al-ways there.

Seriously, either the guy was her husband,

or her husband should be getting jealous – one of the two.

"Do you know who the guy is?" Penny asked, pointing to one of the paintings. "She seems to be…obsessed with him."

Kinda like me writing an entire article about you instead of Moose.

She decided to keep that comparison to herself.

Troy nodded. "He's the new extension agent in town. Took over after Mr. Snow retired. Doing a good job of it, too."

"Are they married?" Penny prodded. It wasn't that she needed to know any of this for her article – including the dating lives of the subjects of her articles wasn't exactly something Mr. Toewes encouraged – but dammit all, she was a woman. Of *course* she'd want to know all of the deets.

"Not that I know," Troy said with a shrug.

He was *such* a guy sometimes. A girl didn't paint roughly two million portraits of a guy if she weren't madly in love with him. Penny made a mental note to investigate this further.

"What did you say his name was?" she murmured, looking back over the informational sheet, trying to see if he was mentioned anywhere on there, perhaps as the inspiration for Ivy's painting career or something, but didn't see a guy's name anywhere.

It took a minute for Penny to realize that Troy wasn't answering her question. She looked up at him to find that he had a slightly...constipated look on his face. She shook her head, trying to clear it, and instantly regretted the movement. Shaking her head while wonderfully warm from wine wasn't her best idea ever.

Troy still wasn't saying anything. She put her hand on his arm. "Troy?" she said softly. "You okay? You look upset." She looked behind her to see if he'd just spotted something truly terrible, but all she could see were the crowds of people, wandering around as they laughed and chatted.

"I'm fine," he said abruptly, pulling her attention back towards him.

"Okkaayyyy…" she said slowly, not believing him one little bit but deciding to leave it alone. If he wanted to pretend he was fine, then she could pretend he was fine, too. Two could totally play that game. "So," she said, wanting to get back to the topic at hand, "do you know this guy's—"

"Want more wine?" he interrupted, holding up his glass. His almost empty glass. His hardly-worth-mentioning-let-alone-interrupting-her-about-it glass.

She looked from his glass to him, trying to figure out what in the hell was going on. It was hard to muddle through to any sort of conclusion since her brain was pleasantly mushy and happy and flitting from topic to topic like a hummingbird on steroids, but she tried to make it focus. Something was going on here, and she wasn't about to let it go until she figured it out.

Dammit. Because her brain was mushy and happy, she wasn't coming up with any smooth or sneaky ways of getting the info she wanted, so straight out with it, it was.

"So, do you hate the guy?" she asked

bluntly, holding her glass out so he could dribble the remaining drops of his wine into it.

"Who?" he asked gruffly, turning away to find a return tray to put his empty wine glass onto.

"Troy Horvath!" Penny snapped, and he turned back to her, shoulders tensed as he glared at her. "What has gotten into you?" she demanded.

"I'm fine," he repeated flatly. His face was flat, his eyes were flat, his emotions were flat. He had shut her out, as cold and hard as a slab of marble.

"Yeah, and I'm the king of Poland," she shot back. "Why do you refuse to say this guy's name? Do you turn into a pumpkin if you say it? Are you stuck in some sort of bizarre version of a Rumpelstiltskin spell?"

"Aust-st-stin Bishop, okay? And why do you care so much?" he countered. His face was flushed a little. Or at least she thought his face was flushed a little. She shouldn't have drunk so much wine. Maybe she was reading him all wrong. Maybe she was making a big deal over nothing.

And maybe she really was the king of Poland.

"Austin Bishop?" she repeated, ignoring his question. If he could ignore questions, then so could she. He nodded, scowling. "Thank you. I was just curious. Nothing more." She threw back the little bit of wine he'd just poured for her, handed the empty glass to Troy for him to put onto the discard tray, and then snapped a few pictures of the larger Ivy McClain paintings. It was a good excuse not to look at Troy for a minute while she tried to figure out what on earth his problem was, plus, there was the inconvenient fact that she really should at least pretend to do her job. She hoped idly as she turned the camera this way and that, trying to find a good angle that flattered the paintings, that the newspaper would be printed in full color when this article ran. Seeing these paintings in black and white simply wouldn't do them justice.

After taking enough pics that she could be

sure at least one or two would be passable, she slipped a copy of the informational sheet into her purse, knowing it would come in handy when it came time to write the article.

Unfortunately, she hadn't managed to make her brain come up with anything useful during the little interlude, which wasn't too surprising, considering the amount of alcohol she had buzzing through her veins, and Troy's unfigureoutable behavior.

Unfigureoutable...is that a word? It should totally be a word.

I think I've had too much to drink.

Sadly enough, though, now that she didn't have a camera to hide behind, she had a decision to make – did she push him until he told her what his major hangup was about saying Austin Bishop's name, or did she let it go?

Did she ruin the only date she'd been on in the past year just to satisfy her curiosity, or did she ignore the elephant in the room?

He held out his arm to her, forcing the situation. "Sorry," he mumbled, looking past her and into the crowds, refusing to meet her eye. "You want to look at other paintings?"

That was it? Just "Sorry, now let's pretend this never happened"?

She hesitated for a few endless moments before finally slipping her arm through his. She really should push him harder and figure out what his major malfunction was, and – more specifically, why he hated the name Austin Bishop so much – but…reality time: Her hormones were winning out.

She would never admit it out loud, of course, but it was hard to stay pissed at a guy as Brawny-Man handsome as Troy. If he ever asked her to do some truly heinous crime, like put the toilet paper roll on backwards, she was going to be hard-pressed to tell him no. She could only hope he wasn't some sort of criminal mastermind, because damn, would she be in a whole load of trouble.

With a silent sigh of surrender, she wandered arm in arm with him through the crowds. Some of the paintings were terrific, some were horrific, and some were…

"Did you get all the pics you need?" Troy asked as they stopped in front of an art display that seemed to mostly consist of metal spoons bent every which way and then nailed to a board.

…and some didn't even appear to be art.

Penny was a little surprised, honestly – it didn't seem like something she'd find in Long Valley but instead would be labeled "true art" by some pothead hippie in New York who'd wax poetic about how the bent spoons visually represented the way that consumerism was changing the world, or some such nonsense.

Just because she wanted to move to a large city didn't mean that she didn't recognize the pretentious bullshit that came with the territory.

Troy's question made her think that she wasn't alone in her less-than-overwhelming impression of this display, and a quick glance up at him confirmed that theory. She grinned a little to herself. Not exactly shocking that an Idaho farm boy wasn't finding a deeper meaning in a bunch of bent metal screwed to a board. And actually, it was a nice change of pace – some of the guys she'd dated in college would've tried to pretend that they understood the existential crisis of the artist who made this piece, instead of admitting that it looked like just a pile of junk to them.

"Yeah, I've got everything I need," she told him, patting her purse. "I picked up the info cards from some of the artists; I can call them and do some phone interviews, and have an article ready to submit by Wednesday at noon. Just another week in the life of a small-town reporter."

"Hey, at least you're not reporting on quilt raffles this week," he pointed out dryly, and she bust up laughing. Damn, Troy wasn't just handsome, he was also quick-witted. Where had these Sawyer boys been all her life? Her alcohol-soaked, squirrel-ridden brain instantly sent her back to her teenage years. When she'd been in high school at Franklin, it had been *so* uncool to date someone from Sawyer. Everyone knew it was where the hicks lived – the rednecks who had watermelon-seed spitting contests for entertainment, played the banjo with their toes, and were destined to be missing half their teeth by age 40.

Almost as if he could tell what she was thinking, he grinned down at her just then, showing off his pearly whites, all of which were still plainly intact. Her alcohol-induced ADHD brain, incapable of focusing for more than a few moments on any one idea, supplied the thought that she should ask him if he knew how far he could spit a watermelon seed, while also sending her heart into overdrive.

After all, he had a really, *really* nice set of pearly whites on him.

As her heart did its best to beat its way out of her chest, she silently told it to calm the hell down. No matter how surprising it was to find a Sawyer guy, of all things, to be sexy and handsome and enticing as sin, Troy was just a fun distraction until she could get out of this joint – nothing more than that.

And that wasn't something she could ever let herself forget.

CHAPTER 5

TROY

MAKING PENNY LAUGH…Troy wasn't sure if he'd ever felt as amazing as he did in that moment.

Bring it on – he could climb mountains or fly helicopters or beat the bad guy in hand-to-hand combat. He could do anything at all, because he could make Penny Roth laugh.

But what he *couldn't* do was stomach one more minute of looking at beat-up, twisted spoons. Was this one of those nutty big city trends that had somehow made its way to Franklin, Idaho? He would've never guessed it'd happen, except…here it was, so maybe his fellow Long Valleyians had gone and taken leave of their senses.

"Wanna get a bite to eat?" he asked her. Score points for being a twofer – this would allow them to get out of the twisted metal art section, plus his stomach was busily begging for a half a cow with a mountain of mashed potatoes on the side. He could only hope Penny wasn't one of those women who refused to eat in front of men lest they appear to be gluttonous and/or, God forbid, a real human being. He'd tried to be satisfied with the little cracker thingies with an even tinier pile of shredded veggies on top that they'd found as they'd wandered around, but the way he figured it, it hadn't been enough food to fill up a mouse, let alone him.

"I'm starving!" she said with a grateful smile. "I'd love to grab something to eat. Oh, have you tried the new Mexican restaurant in town? Their chips and salsa are just *awesome*."

"Haven't been there yet," he said, already starting for his truck, Penny in tow, happily leaving the twisted spoons display behind. "Heard it was good, though."

Once again, Penny was coming up with a terrific suggestion after he'd suggested something without having a firm idea in mind. Being around someone who knew what they wanted and weren't afraid to go after it...he could get used to this.

Other than that small hiccup where she'd insisted that he make a total ass out of himself, it'd been an awesome date so far. With any luck, she'd leave that topic alone and they could pretend it never happened and they could go on many more dates just like this one.

She was chattering up a storm about the new restaurant and how nice it was to have some place new to go to in town, and he nodded as he listened intently. He loved hearing her thoughts on the world; he *especially* loved the part where she didn't expect him to talk much. He was content to listen to her all day long. Hell, who wouldn't be content to listen to a gorgeous, intelligent, hilarious woman give her thoughts on the state of affairs in the world, the weather, and what should and shouldn't be considered to be art?

Being around her bubbly, happy, outgoing personality was pretty much a perfect fit for him. His aunt was always harping on him to talk more but he was a hell of a lot more satisfied with the idea of someone else filling in that gap so he could do what he did best – sit back, listen, and observe.

Observing Penny Roth was certainly easy on the eyes, no doubt about that.

Her ruby red lips stretched into a huge, genuine smile. Her skinny jeans, cupping her curvy ass. Her curled, bright blonde hair tumbling down over her shoulders.

Yup, observing her was probably the best idea he'd ever come up with.

At the restaurant, the waiter seated them, took their drink order, and promised to be right back with menus and the chips and salsa. As he headed off, Penny was looking at Troy expectantly, and he realized that he needed to come up with some questions to ask her so he could keep doing what he was quickly learning to love: Simply listening to her.

He scrambled around for a moment, until he hit upon it. "You hate living here, so why do you? Why not move?"

Another score for the twofer – not only did he want to listen to Penny talk, but there was also the true curiosity factor at play. Maybe if he knew what the answer was to this question, he could try to mitigate it or find a workaround or *something*.

She nibbled her full bottom lip thoughtfully which promptly sent his thoughts in a decidedly non-platonic direction, but before she could say anything, the waiter reappeared with the chips, salsa, menus, and drinks, bringing their conversation to a standstill. They perused the menus while munching happily on the appetizer. Penny was right; the chips were warm, lightly salted, and nicely crunchy, while the salsa was chunky with a bit of heat to it without setting his mouth on fire.

If the rest of the food was this good, he might've just found a new favorite in Franklin.

Finally, she shut her menu and set it off to the side. "My mom," she said simply, and it took him a moment to figure out what she was referring to. *Oh, her mom is why she's still living here.* "I had just received my bachelor's degree and had started looking for jobs to apply to when my mom called to tell me…" She sucked in a deep breath and then blew it out slowly. "She had breast cancer. She'd already hit stage four before she'd gone into the doctor's to get it checked out, because she's stubborn as a mule and kept ignoring all of the symptoms." The corners of her mouth quirked up at that one, but Troy was pretty sure it wasn't an indication of happiness. "I came straight home that night. The doc in charge told me bluntly that the chances weren't great that she'd last the year. Then—"

"Are you ready to order?" the waiter asked, yanking their gazes away from each other and towards him. Troy wanted to snap at the man to leave them alone, but the spell was already broken. Reluctantly, he ordered, anxious to get back to Penny's story. The man scribbled their order down and walked away with the menus tucked underneath his arm, *clearly* not realizing what he'd just interrupted. Troy made a mental note to not be as generous on the tip as he normally was as he looked back at Penny.

"And then?" he prompted her.

"Mom insisted that she'd be fine by herself, and I was free to go back to Washington or California or wherever was hiring. She's...independent. Stubborn. Hates to be a burden. I think if my mother's hair was on fire, she'd insist on putting it out herself. Accepting help is *not* her strong point." Penny popped a chip covered with salsa into her mouth and chewed thoughtfully for a moment. Was that guilt that was flashing across her face? "I believed her, and drove back to California. I think a part of me *wanted* to believe her, because it made my life easier if I did."

Yup, definitely guilt.

"I had my apartment and friends there – it made sense to me to try to get a job in the area before looking elsewhere. I was in the third – and last – round of interviews at this graphics firm that I'd been drooling over working at ever since I started in the graphics program in college, when one of Mom's friends called me. She made me swear on a stack of Bibles I wouldn't tell Mom where I got the info, and then told me that my mom was in serious trouble. She'd lost all of her hair, she was weak, she was throwing up a lot from the treatments, she wasn't taking care of herself at all, and from what this friend could tell, she had one foot in the grave. She told me I better come home or we were going to find my mom one morning, dead from malnutrition."

The server showed up just then, continuing his horrendous streak of bad timing, to deliver two steaming plates of enchiladas. Troy wasn't sure if he should thank the man for saving him from starvation, or strangle him for repeatedly interrupting them at the worst possible moment. After waving off his questions if there was anything else he could get for them – *just leave us the hell alone!* – Troy turned back to Penny. "And then?" he prompted her again, as he cut into his fragrant enchilada.

His stomach had started rumbling with hunger pains by this point, but he found himself almost as interested in Penny's story as he was in his food.

And considering how hungry he was, that was really saying something.

"So I packed up everything and moved back home," Penny said simply. "I didn't ask; I didn't tell her I was coming. I knew that if I did, she'd figure out some way of keeping it from happening. So I just showed up on her front doorstep one night and said, 'I'm here to take care of you, and you don't get to say no.' She was pissed at first – telling my mother anything, rather than asking, is a great way to get your head bitten off. But, as I told her, if she wasn't so damn stubborn, I wouldn't have to be so damn pushy. So really, this was all her fault. *Also* not something that she appreciated." Penny laughed ruefully, but Troy could see the pain in her eyes. He wondered how big this blow-up had really been between them. Without knowing anything about her mom, Troy didn't know if Mrs. Roth was a physically violent person, an emotionally abusive person, or just someone who didn't like being backed into a corner.

One thing he did know – he admired the hell out of Penny for refusing to be cowed by her mom's insistence that everything was fine.

Penny pushed her enchilada around her plate for a minute, took a small bite, then pushed it around some more. Either she wasn't actually starving like she'd claimed she was, or this story was upsetting the hell out of her. He felt a little pang of guilt for continuing to pepper her with questions when it was obviously not an easy topic to discuss, but on the other hand, she still hadn't gotten to the part where she explained why she was continuing to live in Long Valley. The way she was framing this made it sound like it'd all happened years ago. What was still holding her here?

"The next four years were a blur of doctor appointments, cooking nutritious meals for my mom, begging my mom to eat, holding her shoulders as she retched into the toilet...I feel guilty saying this, but there were times, in the dead of the night when I was bone tired and wanted nothing more than to sleep for a week but I had to get up and help my mother to the bathroom, that I wished that I'd never answered that phone call from my mother's friend. That's awful to say, isn't it? That's awful to feel. I just...it was draining. All of it. Constantly taking care of someone else for years on end, when that person isn't always the best at accepting that help...and then there were my friends."

She laughed bitterly.

"I thought I'd made lifelong friends in California – true BFFs. But those relationships couldn't handle the strain of what I was going through. No one wanted to discuss the differences between the various bedpans on the market and the updates that manufacturers should put into place. I can't begin to imagine why," she said sarcastically, and then heaved a deep sigh. "We were all just kids, really, but the difference was, they got to act like it. I didn't."

She shrugged, one thin shoulder movement with the twist of her mouth, and then,

"My mom had been declared cancer free once, and then it came roaring back with a vengeance, so the second time the doctors said she was free and clear, neither of us believed them. It had been so pervasive, so overwhelming, that the idea that it was really gone just didn't seem real. But she went in for her six-month check-up, and it was still gone. She'd started to gain her strength back, and the better she felt, the worse she became as a patient. We came to the mutual understanding that if I didn't move out of her house, she was going to kill me in my sleep, and I would deserve it."

This time, she laughed for real, and Troy's heart caught in his chest. He wondered for a moment if she knew how gorgeous she was; how distractingly beautiful her smile was. It made it hard for him to fully concentrate on what she was saying, but he forced his brain to anyway.

"But you didn't leave Franklin," he pointed out, a little confused. "Why not?"

She cut off a bite of her enchilada and

chewed, giving herself a moment to think through her answer.

"Because," she said finally, "I didn't believe the doctors. I kept thinking that there was no way that my mother was actually okay, you know? Not after how sick she'd been. I took care of her for four years. *Four years.* You just don't believe good news at that point. I expected her to pass away; that's what the doctors kept telling me. 'She's hanging in there for now – she's a fighter. But the chances of her being alive for another year is only 5%.' Things like that. Apparently, my mother is some sort of medical miracle. I keep telling her that she needs to start playing the lottery, since Lady Luck is obviously on her side. Anyway," she said, waving her fork dismissively, "I've been hanging around even after I moved out and into my own apartment, just in case she had a relapse. I got the job at the newspaper so I could have some money to pay my bills, and to give myself something to do other than call my mother every day and badger her about how she's feeling. Not that she'd tell me anyway, so usually I end up driving over and checking on her in person."

She took a drink and then pointed her fork at him seriously. "Otherwise, she'll tell me how amazing she's feeling, hang up the phone, and go right back to throwing up again. I watched her do that again and again with her friends over the four years that I took care of her. She is a phenomenal liar over the phone. *I* would almost believe her, and I knew the truth! But, the longer she's been doing okay, the more I have started to think that maybe I really can take a chance, and move back to civilization. I'd need to make a deal with some of her friends that they go over and physically check on her, not just call her to find out how she's doing, but I *almost* have faith that I can actually leave this one-horse town and get on with my life. So, I just need to find the right job, and then I'm out of here."

Troy nodded, keeping his face carefully schooled in a blank, neutral expression. Of course she was gonna leave. She'd told him that from hour one of meeting her. She hadn't hidden this from him. She hadn't tried to fool him into thinking she'd be there for the long term. She'd been crystal clear from the get-go.

He shouldn't have asked her out on this date. He shouldn't have blurted out the question of whether she'd go out with him.

He didn't blurt things out.

He didn't date casually.

He was never going to leave Sawyer.

She was never going to stay.

Yup, he was dumb all right. They didn't make 'em much dumber than Troy Samuel Horvath.

CHAPTER 6

PENNY

HEY WALKED OUT of the restaurant and into the cool of the summer night air. A shiver ran down her spine at the shock of the temperature change, and then another ran through her when Troy pulled her to his side, sliding his arm around her to protect her from the chilly breeze. "Thanks," she said through gritted teeth, determined not to let them chatter from the cold. It wasn't actually that cold – it was more that the temperature change from inside of the restaurant to outside had been so abrupt.

She looked up at him, the glow from the

street lamp hiding almost as much as it revealed. Much like it had been to talk to him, actually. She'd always been pretty open and free – *You could out-talk an auctioneer at a fire sale*, as her mother was fond of saying – but there was something about being around Troy that made her feel safe. Like she could tell him anything... even the truth. The truth about how hard it'd been to be her mother's keeper for four years. The truth about losing all of her friends because of it. The truth about feeling like life had passed her by while she'd been stuck in the slow lane.

So talk to him she did, but she'd also tried to get him to talk too, honest she had. But somehow, no matter what question she asked him, the topic was always turned back towards her. She felt a little guilty about that, looking back on it. She hadn't meant to monopolize the conversation so thoroughly.

She opened her mouth to ask him a question – to really get him to say something to her – when he opened up the passenger side of his truck and helped her inside, closing the door behind her like a true gentleman. The smooth-as-butter leather seats were a joy to touch, and so she decided that once he got in on his side, she'd ask him about his truck. Every guy liked to talk about their baby, right?

"You mentioned needing to find the 'right job,'" Troy said, sliding into the driver's seat and cutting her off without even meaning to. "What would that be?"

She hesitated. *Dammit.* Not answering a direct question seemed rude, but so did continuing to dominate the conversation.

Okay, fine, she'd answer this question and *then* ask him about his truck.

"I love art," she said as he pulled out of the restaurant parking lot and began driving in the general direction of her apartment. "I'm just really, really bad at it. I'm not saying that because I'm hoping you'll tell me, 'Oh no, I'm sure you're great – don't ever give up your dream!' but rather because it's the truth, plain and simple. Like that Ivy McLain chick you went to school with – she has *true* talent. Give me a pencil or a paintbrush, and I'll be lucky if

I can draw a decent stick figure for you. But then I discovered Photoshop, and I realized that I could be an artist with my mouse instead. So I got my degree in graphic arts, which basically just means that I'm wanting a job at an ad agency, at a print shop, at a magazine – anywhere that I can use my talent for layouts and space and fun fonts to create exactly the right image for a client. I may not be able to draw worth a hill of beans, but I have a good eye for how to use white space, how to combine fonts together, that sort of thing. It's not nearly as impressive as being able to draw or paint, but surprisingly, it's a lot more lucrative. What Ivy is doing – making money as an artist – is terribly difficult to do, and I'm impressed as hell that she can do it. I'm lucky that I enjoy creating ads and logos to help small businesses take it to the next level. Most people aren't lucky enough to be passionate about a career that also happens to make money."

Troy chuckled. "Too true. My uncle has always said that the mill pays the bills, but isn't much for feeding the soul. Well anyway, we're here."

Shocked, Penny looked through the front windshield to realize that they were parked in front of her apartment complex. "Wow!" she exclaimed, and laughed. "I guess I wasn't paying any attention at all."

And she hadn't asked him a damn thing about his truck. She'd done it again – yapped the whole time and didn't let him get a word in edgewise.

Before she could blurt out a question about his truck – *When did you buy it? What's your favorite feature? TELL ME SOMETHING SO I DON'T FEEL SO AWFUL ABOUT TALKING SO MUCH!* – he was already slipping out of the truck to come around and help her down. She was too late. If she randomly asked him a question now, it would be awkwardly obvious and weird.

She hadn't been like this around other guys. Why was she so off balance around Troy? Not helping one little bit, her nerves went into overdrive as she watched the handsome fireman walk around to her side of the truck. She wanted to kiss him. Did he want to kiss her? Was it going to be a peck on the cheek? Or a full kiss on the mouth? How far would she let him go? How far did she *want* him to go?

She felt like her insides had been tangled up into one giant knot, but before she could get them to calm down, before she could catch her breath and get her nerves to stop dancing, he was opening the door and holding out his hands to help her out of the oversized truck and then she was sliding down the front of him to the asphalt parking lot.

She hadn't meant to. She was innately graceful. She didn't tend to trip over her own feet or stumble while walking or…

…Or slide down the front of a guy, feeling every inch of his body, until she was standing directly in front of him.

Every. Single. Inch.

He sucked in a breath, his normally pale green eyes dark and unreadable in the moonlight, and then he was kissing her, burying his hands in her hair, tilting her head to the side as he plundered her mouth with his tongue. There was a tinge of desperation to the kiss, and even as she moaned and raised up on her tiptoes to give as good as she got, she couldn't ignore the worry building up in her. There was something wrong here. Something—

He broke away.

"Goodnight," he said, and then he slipped out of her arms, slid into his idling truck, and disappeared down the dark city street, his tail lights disappearing into the night. She watched him go, her hand pressed to her mouth, as the last of the happy alcohol haze that'd been warming her from the inside out disappeared along with him.

Why did that feel like a goodbye to her? Not just a goodbye for tonight, but a goodbye for forever? He wasn't actually going to walk away after that, right? Not after a kiss that poets would be writing about for years to come?

She turned and headed up the walkway and over to her fourplex, feeling off-kilter, off-balance, out of sorts. She didn't want to date a

Sawyer boy. She didn't want to stay in Idaho. She wanted to leave, and the sooner the better. So why would Troy's walking away tonight affect her? She wanted him to. She wasn't in a place where she could be tied down by a relationship, and especially not if that place she was being tied to was Idaho.

So why was she upset? She got what she wanted, right? An evening out with a handsome man, but nothing more than that.

She slipped into her house, leaving the lights turned off, and curled up at the end of the couch in the darkness, hugging a pillow to her stomach as she stared at her unlit fireplace.

Stupid Penny. I never should've gone over to the mill with that damn newspaper. I knew better. I knew it wasn't what I wanted out of life, but I did it anyway.

Stupid, stupid Penny.

CHAPTER 7

TROY

"WELL, you have to do *something* about it!" his aunt snapped, her patience with this well-worn topic clearly showing through.

Not that his aunt was particularly famous for her extensive amounts of patience to begin with.

"That mill has been in the Horvath family for generations," his uncle said stubbornly. "Even if that worthless fire chief let it practically burn to the ground back in January doesn't mean that we oughta just up and tear it down to placate a bunch of bureaucrats. Damn people need to keep their nose out of it."

"Those darn people," Aunt Horvath said pertly, correcting his swearing without directly scolding her husband, "are the city councilmen. This *is* their business. They don't want to see a pile of burned bricks on Main Street any more than we do. You can't blame them for wanting to make the town look nice."

"If they'd worry about something worth worryin' about, instead of just focusing on looks, we'd have a lot less problems in this town," Uncle Horvath grumbled. "They're a bunch of shallow fools, and they focus on stupid shit that don't mean a damn thing, instead of on what *really* matters. Just like when they hired that upstart from Boise who don't know how to run a firehose, instead of James. They oughta be sending that new fire chief those nasty letters instead of me, since he's the reason why my family's history's been destroyed." He slammed his hand down on the old scarred breakfast table to make his point.

Ah. Breakfast at the Horvath household. Always such a...

He looked at his arguing aunt and uncle, who'd move on to "discuss" whether or not they should become snowbirds that winter or stay in Long Valley. More like arguing full-throatedly, but his aunt liked to pretend that she never argued with her husband, so if asked, she'd declare it a simple discussion.

...Always such a contentious affair.

Without interrupting them, Troy stood and pressed a dutiful kiss to his aunt's cheek, carried his dishes to the sink, and slipped out the back door to head to his house, set up on the back forty of the property, leaving them to hash things out between them. Sparky, who'd stayed out on the porch while he was inside, padded along beside him.

Despite the fact that he literally once listened to them...*ahem* *discuss* the color of the sky in quite heated tones, he knew that they loved each other and if push came to shove, they'd lay their lives down for the other person.

But while they were both topside of the

soil, there was no reason to agree unnecessarily. That just might entail admitting that the other person was right, and Troy had seen them both twist themselves into a pretzel to avoid making such an admission.

He walked into the cool of his home and sucked in a deep breath of calm and peace. Although he loved his aunt and uncle dearly, and they'd been there for him when he truly needed them, it wasn't a stretch to admit that being around them could be taxing at times. For the sake of his sanity, he should probably quit eating breakfast with them every morning, but just the idea of telling his aunt that he didn't want to eat with her any-more made his blood run cold. She would be heartbroken, to say the least, and she would lament at length about how she didn't know what she did wrong to drive him away like this.

"At length" meaning at least the next ten years or so. If she really got butthurt over it, he could count on it being brought up for the next fifteen years.

No, eating breakfast with them was the least he could do, after all they'd done for him.

He slipped into his work clothes – Dickie jeans, a uniform shirt with his name embroidered over the breast pocket, boots – and clipped his emergency radio to his belt like always. Somebody had to answer every call, and make sure that the people of Sawyer were kept safe. He wasn't the fire chief, but he was a Horvath. Taking care of the town was what he was born to do. He may've been born in Boise but Sawyer was his home, and always would be.

As he drove to the new mill, Sparky in the bed of the truck, he mulled over the problem of what to do with the old mill. His aunt was right – they had to do something about it. Blackened bricks, windows broken, the sign proudly proclaiming *Horvath Mill – Where You Come For All Of Your Milling Needs* hanging drunkenly on one nail (his ancestors were industrious people, not creative ones)…well, it sure wasn't the badge of honor that it used to be.

At one time, it'd been the biggest and the

most technologically advanced mill in the Pacific Northwest. They ground wheat, oats, barley, and every other cereal crop; enough to feed the planet, it seemed.

But technology changed and the mill was no longer on the cutting edge. Then there was the fact that the mill was right there on Main Street, smack dab in the middle of summer tourist traffic and high school kids trying to get to school. It just wasn't ideal, and his uncle had made the business decision to build a second mill, one further out in the country, making it easier for tractor-trailers and farm trucks to get in to drop off and pick up loads. No more worrying about what the schedule was from the school district for that year, or when the hordes of tourists were going to start showing up.

Being a business decision – and a smart one at that – didn't make it any easier for his uncle, though. There was so much family and local history in the old mill. Tearing it down seemed almost sacrilege.

He looked through the windshield of his truck, surprised and yet not, to see the old mill in front of him. He was supposed to be going to work, not gawking over old family history, but…well, he was already there, right? Might as well look around for a minute and then get on to work.

He slid out of his truck, Sparky jumping out of the bed and happily sniffing around in the warm June sunshine. It was already a pleasant mid-70s at eight in the morning, which meant it was gonna be a scorcher today, no doubt about it. He really ought to get to work so he could start cleaning out the boiler room – always a hot and tedious job best done in the cool of the day – but found himself walking forward instead, studying the intricate brick work in front of him. There were large sliding doors on tracks that led into the interior, allowing trucks and semis to drive through, but above the blackened, weathered, broken wooden doors was an intricate pattern that the bricklayer had built into the mill.

This had always fascinated him – it was a *mill*. It was industrial. It was built for function, not beauty.

But throughout the building, there were patterns in the layout of the bricks, telling the story of a bricklayer who wanted to add beauty to an otherwise business-only building. Did his great-grandfather ask the bricklayer to do this? Or did he do it of his own volition? Troy had asked his uncle about it one time, and his uncle had just given him a blank look.

"What pattern?" Uncle Horvath had replied, straight-faced. The man had worked at the mill his entire adult life, and had never noticed a thing.

His uncle wasn't exactly the sentimental type, other than in his belief that if the Horvath men had wanted a mill in town, then by God, there should be a mill in town. The aesthetics were the last thing on his uncle's mind.

As Troy looked – really looked – at the old girl, he knew that neat patterns in the bricks or not, the city council was right to push his uncle to do something about it. Boarded-up windows, a crack running up one wall, blackened bricks, broken glass crunching under foot...

It was no longer the crowning jewel in the Horvath family legacy that it used to be.

He shoved at one of the sliding doors, cringing at the screech of ungreased metal, and slipped inside, Sparky padding along behind him, her nose glued to the ground as she took in every smell. Troy took a hard look around, comparing what he remembered to what was still standing. There were bird feathers and poop everywhere – the years of free grain meant that the mill had gathered quite a flock of fans, quite literally – but he tried to look past that.

What could it be used for, other than milling grain? It was such a big space – tall, long, wide, there was no dimension where it felt cramped for room. They could hoist semis up on lifts to do repair work on them, and still have loads of room to spare. Maybe his uncle could use this as the repair shop for the mill and their own fleet of semis.

But even as he conceived of the idea, he began to poke holes in it. There towards the end of using the old mill, the city had been getting grumpy with his uncle because of the semi traffic in and out of the place. It was only a block from the high school, and even his uncle had to begrudgingly admit that semis loaded down with grain didn't mix well with teenagers in a rush to get to school so they wouldn't be late for class. It only got worse during the summer break, with the loads of tourists coming through on their way to the lake or over to Franklin. Franklin was definitely the tourist destination that Sawyer simply wasn't, but on the other hand, you couldn't get from Boise to Franklin without driving straight through Sawyer. The more the tourist industry grew in Franklin, the worse the traffic grew in Sawyer.

All of the pains in the asses of dealing with tourists, with very little of the benefits.

That was Sawyer's lot in life, no doubt about it.

So maybe pulling in semis and working on them wasn't a good idea. Troy scrambled for another one. They could...

They could...

They could…

He had nothing.

Penny would probably have a great idea, or seven.

The thought popped into his mind, unbidden. Ever since their fantastic date a week ago, Troy had found himself thinking about the gorgeous blonde a lot more often than he'd meant to. It was hard not to think about her, though. Who could spend an evening with someone like Penny and then *not* dream about her? He knew she wasn't right for him; he knew she was temptation wrapped up in a bundle of seduction and topped with a big ol' bow of enticement. He knew that the smart choice was to walk away from her.

But that kiss…Good Lord, that kiss. He'd go to his grave, remembering that kiss. He'd told himself that he could have one kiss to remember her by – that there was no harm in that, right? – and then…

Well, he'd wanted more. A whole lot more. He'd wanted every inch of her and he'd known that she was his for the asking. If he'd wanted to go up to her apartment that night, she would've said yes. It was all there, in the way that she'd wrapped herself around him, the way that she'd moaned with lust.

He squeezed his eyes shut against the onslaught of vivid memories washing over him.

Did he *really* want to walk away already? Maybe he could be one of those people who had sex without any attachments. He could make her beg in bed, and then walk away. He could do that, right? He'd never tried to before, but there was no law etched in stone that said he couldn't. People did things all the time that they hadn't done before.

And while they were on their date together, he could ask her for her ideas on what to do with the mill, if she had any. Getting an outside perspective was a good thing, and her perspective − a woman from Franklin with a degree in graphic arts − would definitely be a lot more outside than his.

Feeling better already, Troy headed back to his truck, Sparky trotting happily alongside him, a spring in his step as he went. He decided to stop at Happy Petals on the way out to the new mill. What girl could say no to a gorgeous bouquet of flowers, and in yet another winning twofer combination, it also meant he could impress her without having to actually speak. A girl like Penny should be courted; he'd start out by sending her a bouquet of flowers, and then ask her out after that.

He whistled along happily to the newest Brad Paisley song on the way to Happy Petals, only a few blocks over. Carla could help him find just the right bouquet to impress Penny; she'd know what Penny would love.

A little loving, a little companionship, a little fun, and then Penny could get on with her life and he could get on with his.

This was totally a good idea.

CHAPTER 8

PENNY

$\mathcal{P}$ENNY STUMBLED into her kitchen, her jaw-cracking yawn causing her eyes to tear up so much, it was only an intimate knowledge of her tiny apartment that kept her from walking straight into the golden oak cupboards. Blinking through the yawn-induced tears, she riffled through her kitchen cabinets, finally finding the last Caramel Mocha Keurig cup to slide into place in her coffee maker. God bless Keurig – no more having to mete out coffee grounds and hot water while still 98% asleep.

She slumped against the kitchen counter,

eyes closed, waiting not-so-patiently for the machine to finish conjuring up its magic brew. She really needed to stop staying up so late but she had a new client – which meant she had a whole *two* clients now – who had wanted a mock-up for a new logo, and Penny'd wanted to impress the hell out of her.

The only way to grow her minuscule freelance graphic arts company was by word of mouth, and that meant giving 110% to each project she actually managed to snag. Penny didn't mind the hustle part of freelance work, but she also knew that realistically, it'd be a long time until she'd built up a stable of clients large enough to actually live off.

Her mind wandered down a well-trodden path, to the same answer she always came to when musing about her career choices: The most practical solution was to go to work for a large company where they'd already done all of that hustling, and focus on just the creative side of things. She had a metric shit ton of student loans that she needed to start paying on at some point; she'd kept putting them into forbearance because of taking care of her mom. But she couldn't ignore them forever, and they sure as hell weren't going to get paid with piddling, one-off freelance jobs, no matter how much the freelance world appealed to her.

No, what she *really* needed to do was spend some time looking at corporate jobs up in Seattle—

The Keurig beeped at the exact moment that someone knocked on the front door, scaring the shit out of her. Penny bolted upright, tugging instinctively at the front of her ratty bathrobe that she'd gotten for Christmas in the tenth grade, and had refused to give up even when it got so holey, it began to resemble a block of Swiss cheese more than a bathrobe.

She scowled at the front door, just a few steps away from the kitchen in her tiny apartment. Who on earth was at her door before nine in the morning? Anyone who knew her knew she wasn't a morning person, and to knock this early was practically guaranteed to get a Very Grumpy Penny answering the door.

She stomped over to the front door where

she peeked through the peephole to see a distorted view of a heavy-set woman dressed in turquoise from head to toe, lots of makeup, pleasant face.

Penny had *no* idea who she was.

She considered not opening the door; considered pretending to not be home. It was probably someone wanting her to attend their church that Sunday, and that was a discussion Penny wasn't about to have with a stranger.

But in the end, it was the turquoise that got to her. What missionary wore such a happy color?

She tugged the bathrobe tighter around her and pulled the door open. "Yes?" she said, squinting into the bright, way-too-early-morning sunlight. Who ordered the sun to be up at such an hour, anyway? Certainly not her.

"Hi!" the turquoise woman said cheerfully. "I have a surprise for you!"

Before Penny could tell the painfully happy woman that she didn't want or need her "surprise," whatever the hell it was, the woman pulled a stunning bouquet out from behind her back and thrust them into Penny's arms. "I love the ta-da moment," the woman said conspiratorially, leaning forward to whisper the information like it was some super secret she didn't share with just anyone. "It's one of my favorite parts of my job. Anyway!" She straightened up and pointed at the oversized bouquet that Penny was holding on to, more out of instinct than anything else. "There's a card in the bouquet – quite a handsome man was in my shop ordering these for you." The woman winked, a broad grin on her face. "Enjoy, and have a great rest of your week!"

The woman started back down the sidewalk before Penny could get a word in edgewise – a new one for her – and so she could only watch, open mouthed, as the bright, gregarious woman climbed into a turquoise van with *Happy Petals* emblazoned on the side, and drove off down the street.

Now there *is a business name that perfectly matches the owner.*

Before Penny's non-caffeinated brain could get sidetracked into imagining the perfect logo for Happy Petals, she looked back down at the huge bouquet in her hands. And "huge" was the operative word here – certainly the largest one she'd ever been given, and probably the largest one she'd ever seen in real life. This had to have cost someone an arm and a leg to send.

Troy?

He certainly fit the "handsome man" description but it'd been a week, and there'd been no sign of him. Not a phone call, not a Facebook message, not even a smoke signal on the horizon. She'd thrown herself at him once already – twice, if you counted the night she'd been sent to interview Moose and had instead interviewed Troy – and had made herself the very strict promise that she absolutely, positively wasn't going to do it a third time. If he wanted to go on another date with her, he could damn well make that clear.

Welp, it didn't get much more clear than this.

With shaking hands, she closed the front door behind her and carried the bouquet over to the kitchen counter, pulling the envelope out from amidst the blooms. *Penny Roth* was written on the front of the envelope in a spiky, small script, and she instinctually knew that it was Troy who wrote it. The turquoise-loving woman who'd handed this bouquet over probably used hearts instead of O's.

Heart going into overtime, Penny pulled the card out of the envelope. The same spiky, bold handwriting was on the card, confirming her suspicions about Troy being the one to write it.

Thanks for the amazing evening; I look forward to many more. Troy

Penny read it another three times, each time her brain refusing to believe this was really happening. Why the week wait between their date and this card?

He thought they had an amazing evening? *She* thought they'd had an amazing evening, of course, but when he hadn't contacted her…

Dammit all, she'd convinced herself that she'd moved on. It was a *good* idea for them to walk away from each other. They were going in different directions. And maybe she'd daydreamed about him asking her out on another date, but it hadn't been anything more than that. It wasn't actually going to happen. Second dates were like sliced mushrooms – if you waited too long to dig into them, they weren't worth going after anyway.

In Penny's experience, a week was well past that expiration date.

But these flowers! She picked up the huge bouquet from the countertop, seeing every kind of bloom and color under the sun represented in it. It was cheerful and lovely and all-encompassing – way more impressive than just a bouquet of red roses.

It was when she was staring at the card, lying on the kitchen counter next to her patiently waiting mug of Keurig coffee, that she realized that she didn't know what she was supposed to do next. He didn't give her his phone number. He didn't say to stop by the mill. There was no "next step" – just the idea that she was supposed to enjoy the flowers, and he'd get in touch with her later so they could go on more of these "amazing" dates together.

Not gonna lie, that felt a little weird to her.

She was a take-charge kind of gal. If she wanted something, she went after it. In Troy's case, she went after him twice. But now, he was going after her...kinda.

Or, more like that he was telling her that he was going to go after her at a future date.

Gah. Sawyer men. Why did they have to make this so confusing?

She picked up the bouquet and breathed in deep, the smell rushing through her senses, setting her nerve-endings on fire. These flowers were magnificent, exactly the ones she would've picked out if she'd been in the flower shop with Miss Turquoise.

Huh. Sawyer men. All right, so maybe they weren't so bad after all.

With a face-splitting grin, she grabbed her mug of life-giving liquid, and hurried to her bedroom. She had to step on it or she was going to be late for work.

Amazing evening...

Maybe at least one Sawyer man was worth keeping around.

CHAPTER 9

TROY

*S*TUPIDITY IN THE FLESH. *That's me.*

Somehow, some way, Troy had forgotten to actually ask for Penny's number. He had her address – home and work – but that meant driving over and asking her out.

In person.

By talking.

Out loud.

There were, as he saw it, many, *many* flaws to this plan.

He had an hour lunch break every day; he normally only took 20 minutes and would use it to duck into the employee breakroom to scarf down a sandwich, but today, he was gonna use every moment of that break and then some. Luckily, early summer wasn't the busy part of the year for the mill – there was the winter wheat coming in but it was otherwise quiet. Maybe he'd tell Uncle Horvath that he was gonna take an extended lunch. After all of the years of only taking 20 to eat and then getting back to work, his uncle wouldn't mind.

Probably.

He drove the 25 minutes to Franklin – the mill was on the far side of Sawyer out towards Franklin, so it wasn't the full half hour to get there, thankfully – breaking every rule in the book by texting while driving to tell his uncle that he'd be late coming back from lunch. He'd probably hear about it later, but this was worth it.

Hopefully.

He grabbed a box of chocolates from Once Upon A Trinket – adding hand-dipped chocolates to his arsenal couldn't hurt, right? – and then drove over to the newspaper building, hands shaking. Both the *Sawyer Times* and the

Franklin Gazette were run out of this same office; Troy had a vague recollection of going on a field trip here during elementary school but at the time, all he'd focused on was the loud thunking of the print machines running in the back. To an eight year old, they seemed like they were hungry – about to jump out and suck him in alive – so he'd spent most of the tour doing his best to stay behind the fat kid in his class, figuring that if the machine was gonna suck someone up, it'd go after the easy prey first.

Happily, everyone had survived the field trip, even the fat kid. He actually grew up to be a really nice guy, so Troy would take that as a positive.

He walked into the cool of the newspaper office, the dim lighting making it hard to see for a moment as his eyes adjusted. A bored-looking woman was sitting at the front desk, flipping through a magazine. "How can I help you?" she asked, but the polite, business-like inquiry didn't match her tone at all. She looked like she'd rather be doing almost *anything* but helping him. Filing her fingernails, chewing gum, setting her hair on fire…

Anything at all.

Just as he opened up his mouth to speak, she spotted the gaudily decorated box underneath his arm and instantly sized it up as a box of high-end chocolates from Once Upon A Trinket. She bolted upright and slapped the magazine closed, her face quite interested in whatever he was about to say.

The transformation was stunning, really, and it took Troy a second to regain his footing. *Just talk slowly. You'll be fine.* "Is Penny here?" he asked.

"No, she's out doing some interviews. I'm Shayla. Do you want me to take those for her?" She nodded eagerly towards the box.

Troy had to fight the impulse to hide the chocolates behind his back. "I'd like to write her a note and leave them both on her desk. Is," *breathe in*, "that okay?"

That was close. *'St' sounds — they'll get you every time.*

"Sure, sure!" said the young girl — she

couldn't have been more than twenty or so – enthusiastically. "Let me show you where it's at." She scooted off her chair and hurried deeper into the office, leaving Troy to play catch-up behind her. "How long have you known Penny?" Shayla asked over her shoulder, casual as could be.

He wasn't fooled one bit. He recognized a younger version of Glenda when he saw one. As soon as Troy walked out the front door, Shayla would be gossiping with every other employee about him and Penny, inside of sixty seconds.

Inside of thirty seconds if she was really on her game.

"Not long," he said.

That was not *nearly* enough information for Shayla, and she quickly moved to her next question. "You work out at the Horvath Mill?" she asked. She was at least observant enough to notice his work shirt with the company logo embroidered on it.

"Yup," he said simply, and then let the silence hang between them.

It was almost fun at this point. He could tell she wanted to take him by the shoulders and shake him – *GIVE ME INFORMATION!!* – but somehow managed to keep ahold of herself.

Barely.

"Well, this is her desk," Shayla said, gesturing towards a desk piled with more papers than the National Archives kept on hand. It was a wobbly looking piece of shit, and he wondered for a moment about its structural integrity with that much paper on it.

He pulled a blank sheet off a mostly used legal pad and plucked a pen out of the coffee cup that said, *I'm not bossy – I just know what you should be doing.*

He had to work not to snort out loud at how perfectly that fit Penny.

He looked up. Shayla was still standing there, watching his every move hopefully. She was probably thinking she'd read over his shoulder as he wrote out the note.

Not a chance in hell.

"Thanks," he said flatly, staring straight at Shayla, not moving a muscle.

With a disgruntled sigh, she flounced back up front, her skirt bouncing along with every unhappy stomp.

Troy could feel the eyes of a few of Penny's coworkers on his back, but when he not-so-casually looked around the office, everyone's eyes dropped quickly to their computer screens.

What did you expect – it's a room full of reporters, which are, by definition, nosy bastards.

Ignoring his audience for a moment, Troy quickly wrote down his number and a note that he'd forgotten to get hers previously, and then asked her to text him when she got off work. Hopefully she wouldn't find the "text" part of that weird. Everyone texted instead of called nowadays, right?

He slipped the note underneath the band of gold ribbon that the sales lady down at the chocolate store had used to wrap the box with, and laid it on Penny's keyboard – an easy decision since it was the only part of her desk that wasn't covered by something else. He'd been tempted to write, *PS Hi, Shayla!* at the bottom of the note, but wasn't sure if Penny would understand, or would get pissed about it. Better to leave sarcasm out of it.

With a nod to the receptionist, who was practically vibrating in her chair with impatience for him to leave so she could sneak back and read the note, he headed back out into the bright June sunshine, the glare off every shiny surface hurting his eyes after the gloom of the newspaper office.

And not a single printing machine tried to eat me, either.

With a grin of triumph, he slid back into his truck and headed back towards the mill. Not a bad save, all in all. After thirty-something years of watching every word he said, metering words out like gold coins – precious and rare – he'd found some workarounds to make it through life without it being painfully obvious that talking wasn't his favorite activity in the world.

Actually, he was probably only fooling himself – if he asked anyone in his family or at the mill if he liked to talk, they'd all probably piss their pants with laughter at such a stupid question.

But if he asked anyone in his extended family or at the mill if he *could* talk, they'd all say yes, of course. Only his parents and aunt and uncle knew the truth.

And with any luck at all, that would never change.

CHAPTER 10

PENNY

"LIKE, *REALLY* TALL," Shayla said, stretching her hand as high above her head as she could to indicate Troy's height. "But so quiet. I could hardly get a word out of him. How do you know him?"

Penny used her height plus her heels to tower a bit over the ditzy girl, hoping to intimidate her into shutting up. Shayla reminded her of Glenda, actually, now that she thought about it − both receptionists, both loved to gossip, both couldn't get Troy to talk.

They don't know him like I do.

Considering she and Troy had only gone on one date, that was a hell of a thing to say, especially since Glenda worked for Troy, but Penny instinctually knew it was true anyway.

Shayla continued on, seemingly oblivious to the fact that Penny hadn't answered her question. "Are you going to open up the note?" she asked excitedly. "And the chocolates? They only wrap a gold ribbon around the box when the *good* ones are inside. Otherwise, they use a silver ribbon."

"How do you know this?" Penny asked wearily, giving up on her idea of intimidating Shayla into shutting up – not something that usually worked anyway – and sinking into her office chair. Her feet ached. God, how she loved high heels. Unfortunately, she wasn't sure if they felt the same way about her.

"I worked at Once Upon a Trinket during high school. They always need extra help during Christmas and summer break. Eventually, they stopped asking me to come in and work for them, though. Their business probably slowed down or something."

Or they got sick of listening to you.

Penny decided to keep that theory to herself.

"Well, I'm going to get some work done," she said pointedly, staring up at the girl without blinking.

"You're not going to—" She broke off at Penny's pointed stare. "Fine," she grumbled and stormed back upfront.

Penny had to wonder if Shayla had already read the note Troy had slipped underneath the gold ribbon, but decided that for her sanity, she didn't want to know. Despite her professed nonchalance in front of Shayla, her hands were shaking as she pulled the note out and scanned it. After getting the flowers that morning, she'd spent her entire interview with Mrs. VanLueven that was supposed to be focused on her plans to grow a military support organization for returning soldiers, instead wondering when she'd see Troy again. By the end, Mrs. VanLueven had gotten more than a little snippy with her when Penny had asked her the same question three times in a row, and quite honestly, Penny couldn't fault her for it.

Daydreaming wasn't normally a flaw of hers. She was usually *too* focused on the world, what needed to be done, talking to the people around her, learning and growing…

No, she wasn't usually much for day-dreaming.

Penny,

I realized that I forgot to get your phone number so I could call you. I'd like to go out again. Maybe not to an event with quite so many beat-up spoons, though. Text me when you get off work.

Troy

And then his phone number.

"What did he mean by 'beat-up spoons'?" Shayla called back from her desk up at the front.

"I'm going to pretend I didn't hear that," Penny yelled back.

Blessed silence.

She slid the ribbon off the box and pulled the top off. Inside was an assortment of choco-lates that all looked good enough to eat.

Really? Good enough to eat? You know what you should do, Penny? You should write for a living, considering your amazing way with words.

She rolled her eyes at herself, and, dithering, finally chose a rounded dark ball with a few strands of coconut on top. Her teeth sunk into the chocolate and her tongue exploded with happiness. Coconut and dark chocolate – it was a combination for the gods.

Expensive hand-dipped chocolates and a huge bouquet of flowers, all on the same day, eh? Penny Roth, he may just like you.

She paused, her hand almost to her mouth with the other half of the chocolate ball of goodness.

What if he likes me too much? What if he's hoping I'll stay here?

She shook the thought off almost as quickly as it crossed her mind. She'd gone on exactly one date with the guy. It was a little too early to be worried about how they were going to make it in the long term. That was the kind of clingy bullshit that drove guys crazy. Now was the time to just go out, have some fun, and enjoy herself. Nothing else expected or needed.

She popped the other bite into her mouth and moaned a little with pleasure.

Yeah, she could get used to this.

CHAPTER 11

TROY

TROY PULLED UP to the old Connelly place, now owned by Wyatt Miller, and cut the engine.

Actually, now that he thought about it, Wyatt had owned this spread for probably a good fifteen years; Troy probably shouldn't consider it to be the old Connelly place anymore. *Old habits die hard, I guess.*

Wyatt had bought it off the auction block when Sheriff Connelly had lost it during that spate of shithole water years the valley had gone through. Hell, Uncle Horvath almost lost the mill at the same time because the farmers just weren't bringing in much grain to be threshed. You can't thresh grain that hadn't been grown, and grain doesn't grow if it doesn't have water.

It wasn't an equation that many were successful in getting around, and the local farmers weren't an exception.

When Wyatt had bought the place, Troy'd thought he'd acted like a hell of an asshole, going around and bragging to everyone that he'd do a damn better job of running the farm than Sheriff Connelly had. Wyatt wasn't much in the people skills department to begin with, and that round of bragging – when everyone in the area had been hurting because of the drought – hadn't won him any new friends, that was for damn sure.

But coming up on two years ago, the unlikeliest pair on the planet – the sheriff's daughter and Wyatt – had hooked up, and dammit all if it hadn't changed Wyatt completely, and all for the better.

In fact…

Troy squinted into the sunlight streaming through the windshield of his truck. Yup, there was Sheriff Connelly himself in the crowd, apparently ready to help with the move today. Troy'd heard that Wyatt and his father-in-law were getting along real nice nowadays, but still, it was a shock to the system to see it. After the fistfight the two of them had gotten into, Troy never would've guessed he'd live to see the day.

Sparky began whining in the bed of the truck, pulling him back to the present. She never jumped out until Troy got out of the cab, and she was getting impatient with his lollygagging around. She had four-legged friends to greet and humans to avoid, dammit.

"I'm coming," he grumbled as he slid out. The soles of his boots had barely touched the ground when Sparky took off like a shot, out of the bed of the truck and straight towards Ellie Mae, Wyatt's dog. They began busily smelling each other's asses as every dog in the world just loved to do, their tails wagging up a storm.

Ellie Mae was what could kindly be called a "farm dog" – there were so many different breeds in her, "mutt" didn't begin to cover it. Compared to her nondescript brown and tan shaggy coat, Sparky's breeding as a hunting dog shone through clearly. She had gorgeous lines and a silky white and black speckled coat that almost sparkled in the bright June sunshine.

Troy watched her closely, and saw the same thing he always did: Even in the midst of Sparky's delight of being around Ellie Mae, she was still carefully hanging back from the rest of the humans, watching to make sure no one came too close. Whoever the jackass was that lost her up in the hills – and had beat her into submission previous to that – deserved to burn in hell, no doubt about it.

Troy could only hope there really was a hell. It'd suck if Sparky's former owner got away with it all.

Sure that Sparky was okay for the moment, he wandered over to the back of the knot of people gathered around Abby, Wyatt's wife, clipboard in hand. "Everyone knows where the new place is, right?" she asked rhetorically, before continuing on anyway. "Up the road a mile and on the left. We're going to focus on getting the furniture down there today so we can get all of it set up and in place; boxes come down second. We can easily stack boxes around the furniture, but I don't want to have to rearrange furniture while also unpacking boxes."

Everyone chuckled politely at that, acknowledging the wisdom of her words. Stetson, Wyatt's youngest brother, looked over and saw Troy at the edges of the group. "Oh hey, Troy! Thanks for coming!" Everyone turned and said their hellos as Troy waved, pulling the edges of his lips up into what he hoped passed as a smile.

Being the focus of everyone's attention, even if it was friendly and welcoming attention…

He could finally breathe again when the group turned back towards Abby. "Juan is in charge of his room," she said, pointing at a Hispanic boy, already well on his way to being a heartbreaker at maybe 10 or 11 years old, "so any questions about it go to him. I'm going to be in charge of the kitchen and living room; Wyatt will be in charge of the rest of the house. Any questions?"

"Where do you want me to set up lunch?" Carmelita asked, standing next to Jennifer who was holding what appeared to be a poster child for adorable babies. Carmelita had been the housekeeper for the Miller family since Mr. Miller had been alive, and when Stetson had inherited his father's farm, Carma had come along with it, part and parcel. Troy had seen her around, of course, but mostly what he knew about her was that she was one hell of a cook. The fact that she was gonna be cooking today's meal as a thank-you to the volunteers for their help made Troy's stomach rumble with anticipation.

Hells to the yes! Coming out to help the Millers move from the old farmstead house to the new one Wyatt had built over the past year was looking like a better and better idea by the minute.

"Let's have you do it in the backyard of the new place," Abby said. "Do you need any help putting that together?"

"Only a man or two to set up tables," Carma said dismissively. "No one cooks in my kitchen except me."

Abby, wisely, didn't point out that the kitchen in question was hers, but instead just nodded her agreement. "Troy, Stetson, you help Carma set up the tables and chairs for lunch. Everyone else, let's go inside the old house and I'll point out the furniture that needs to be loaded up."

Troy hadn't actually been to the new Miller house yet, so he followed Stetson and Carmelita's lead in getting there. Once he stepped inside of the grand house, he sucked in a quick breath of surprise. *Damn.* Maybe Wyatt had ended up to be a better farmer than Sheriff Connelly, after all. He had to be kicking some major ass to be able to afford a house like this, anyway.

"I know, right?" Stetson said in his ear with a small chuckle as he stepped to Troy's side.

"Wyatt built a lot of it himself, though, keeping the costs down. They want a big house so they can foster-adopt a lot more children. Juan's such a great kid, I guess they figured they wanted ten more just like him."

It looked like it could house ten kids, with room to spare. Troy had heard that Abby couldn't have kids, so they were going the foster-adopt route instead. Damn impressive. He never would've guessed it of Wyatt Miller, of all people. Troy'd always liked Abby – how could you not? She was a sweet, hard-working woman with a backbone of steel – but still, he was surprised by just how good of an influence she was on her husband. Wyatt better be thanking the Lord every day that he found a woman like her.

"What are they doing with the old home?" Troy asked as he admired the river stone fireplace that dominated the north wall. Wyatt sure went for the dramatic.

"Selling it interest free to Jorge Palacios, his foreman, along with a little acreage. Jorge has been with him for years now, and with all of those kids and grandkids him and Maria have, Wyatt figured getting him into a real home instead of a double-wide was the best present he could give him."

Troy nodded thoughtfully. It was damn typical that the foreman of a spread lived in a double-wide on the place, free rent included as part of the job, but it also meant that they weren't building equity in land and homes of their own. To split off a piece of the property for Jorge to buy was a damn considerate idea.

Yet another change wrought in Wyatt by Abby, Troy was sure of it.

"Come, boys," Carmelita said in her light Hispanic accent, heading towards the back of the house where Troy guessed the kitchen was probably located. "Let us get set up in the backyard, then maybe I will feed you a little something before sending you back up to the other house, yes?"

Troy grinned at the back of her as the housekeeper moved without hesitation towards the kitchen, ready to get to work. He sure liked how she thought. The short woman was as round as she was tall, but there was a strength to her that clearly said she was in charge, and if you knew what was good for you, you'd do what she wanted, when she wanted it.

Troy had never been able to stomach simpering girls who said things like, "Oh, whatever you want," in response to virtually every question, and so he could instantly tell he and Carmelita were gonna get along just fine.

As Stetson and Troy carried tray after tray of food into the nearly empty kitchen, laying it all out on the granite counters for Carma, Stetson ribbed his housekeeper – someone, Troy could tell, who he considered to be a beloved grandmother – about outdoing herself this time. "You know what you should do, Carma?" Stetson asked rhetorically as he brought in a tray of empanadas. "You should open up a restaurant in Sawyer. Give Betty's Diner a run for their money. You would have people lined up around the block to eat your food."

As Troy set down a big bowl of fragrant, spicy salsa, he inwardly had to agree. The enchiladas, the salsa and chips, the empanadas…

he'd give his right nut sac to eat like this every day. Troy wondered for a moment about tackling the older woman and making a run for the front door with Carma tucked underneath his arm. She was damn short; he could probably make it to his truck before the alarm got out to everyone, especially if he knocked out Stetson with one of the cast iron pans beforehand.

"I am too old for such things," Carma said dismissively, but Troy detected a hint of longing in her voice. "And anyway, who would cook for you and Jennifer and Flint if I did not? You would waste away to nothing without me around."

"I could probably stand to lose a few pounds," Stetson said with a laugh, patting what appeared to be a perfectly flat belly. Troy wondered for a moment how it was that Stetson did stay so thin, with this kind of food surrounding him every day. He would have to wrestle a whole lot of calves to work all of this off. "And anyway, Jennifer knows how to cook." He paused for a second. "I think." Troy let out a bark of disbelieving laughter at that, and

Stetson turned to him with a grin and a shrug. "What? She's cooked a couple of times over the past few years, when Carma was stuck in Boise for an appointment or something. No one died. Well, at least no one worth mentioning. We just don't bring up Great Aunt Elma anymore."

Troy's belly laugh only grew in volume when Jennifer's voice chimed in behind them. She'd apparently come through the front door and had overheard their topic of discussion. "I'd take offense to that," Jenn said dryly, shifting Flint from one hip to the other without missing a beat, "except truth be told, I think Stets would divorce me within a week if he had to eat my cooking day in and day out. Not after he's been spoiled all these years by Carma. And anyway, between Flint and then the accounting firm I'm running with Bonnie, I just don't have time to cook three square meals a day."

"See?" Carma said dismissively. "Someone else will have to open a Mexican restaurant in town someday. This gives me the time to spend with my darling grandson." She held her arms out for Flint, who immediately lunged for his adopted grandmother, grubby fist waving in the air as he squealed with delight. Even though he only appeared to be a year old or so, Flint already knew which side his homemade bread was buttered on.

"Are you sure?" Jenn asked, eyebrows wrinkled with concern even as she handed the baby over. "It's a lot of work to put on a spread for so many people…"

"I am sure," Carma said firmly. "My boy and I will work together to make mole con pollo that will set everyone's taste buds dancing with delight." Troy bit back the smile that threatened to break out at that thought. The only thing Flint looked capable of helping with was producing more drool, but the matter was already settled. Carma had spoken, and so it'd be done.

"Now, you boys go and get the tables from the back of Stetson's truck and set them up in rows out back," Carma ordered them. "Jennifer, you can go help Abby with whatever she needs. We will be in here, getting things ready."

Troy and Stetson headed back out into the bright June sunshine, Jennifer trailing along behind them. "I noticed you didn't volunteer to learn how to cook," Jennifer said with a nudge to her husband's side. "You could cook dinner just as well as I could, you know."

Stetson turned back to his gorgeous wife with a snort of laughter. "You know I've never cooked a thing in my life. Carma always said that she would take care of it all, and you *know* how territorial she is about her kitchen. I'm not even sure I could boil water without burning the house down. Besides..." And then he was murmuring something in Jenn's ear and she was blushing and pushing at him even as she was raising her face to him to be kissed.

Rolling his eyes at the two of them, Troy hurried to the back of Stetson's truck to begin unloading the tables. He didn't need to watch the two of them mack on each other. Hell, at the rate they were going, there was gonna be a Flint Jr in nine months if they didn't knock it off.

Just then, a car pulled up, Declan piling out

and hurrying around to help his wife out of the passenger seat. Iris had been in a car wreck a while back and her mobility issues meant she preferred to get in and out of cars instead of trucks. It still struck Troy a little weird to see a farmer get in and out of a car instead of a truck, but it also spoke to Declan's love for Iris. Troy knew he couldn't imagine driving around town in a four-door sedan, for hell's sakes. At the intersections, he'd feel like a midget next to everyone else, sitting that low to the ground, not to mention that if he needed to get pert near *anything* done, he'd have to switch vehicles to do it.

Honestly, all three Miller boys…when they fell, they fell hard.

Iris straightened up, her hand on the hood of the car, and smiled up at Declan. "Thanks, dear," she said softly, lifting her mouth up for a kiss, a kiss that quickly became almost as involved as the kiss that Stetson had just been laying on his wife.

Huh. Watching the two of them, Troy immediately revised his stance on vehicle choices.

Maybe if the reward was a kiss like that, it wouldn't be so bad to drive a little car around after all, at least part of the time.

After what seemed like forever, the two broke apart, and Declan began escorting his bride into the house, treating her as delicately as a piece of blown glass. They'd just gotten married last month, and based on the way they acted around each other, the honeymoon wasn't anywhere close to being over.

"I can walk on my own, you know," Iris said scoldingly, but there was no heat to her words.

"But then what excuse would I have to leave my worthless younger brother and Troy to unload all of the tables and chairs without me?" Declan protested. He winked at Troy as they went past, and Troy grinned back. "It's about time Stetson shared Carma with the rest of us. I haven't had one of her handmade tortillas in so long, I've almost forgotten what they tasted like."

"I've been trying to talk Carmelita into starting a restaurant in town," Stetson said, holding the front door open for the pair to pass through. "That way, I'd be sharing her with the whole town. That's the kind of sweet guy I am. But Carmelita keeps giving me some line of bull...puckey," he stumbled over the words, saving himself from swearing just in time, "about her being too old to run a restaurant."

Troy raised an eyebrow at that. Was "bull-puckey" for Iris' sake? His wife's sake? Carmelita's sake?

He didn't have long to wonder.

"I heard that, Stetson." Carma's voice drifted out on the still summer air. "You must not use such language around ladies. Now, Iris, you come in here and I will have you peel some apples for me."

Iris and Declan disappeared into the cool of the house, and Stetson closed the door behind them with a guilty grimace on his face. "She has some scary-ass hearing skills," he muttered under his breath and then quickly glanced back at the closed front door, as if expecting to get scolded by Carma for saying that. Apparently, her hearing was only so good, though, because the closed door stayed silent.

Jennifer, Stetson, and Troy headed to the bed of Stetson's truck for another round of hauling. "Carmelita lets Iris help in the kitchen," Jennifer said, just a touch of disgruntlement in her voice as she tugged two folding chairs out to carry.

"That's because Iris can't help otherwise," Stetson said softly, "and Carmelita knows it. She is letting Iris into her domain so she has something she can do."

"Yeah," Jennifer said, the frustration in her voice melting away, "you're right. I'd rather never step foot inside of a kitchen again, than be forced to walk with a cane or with the help of another for the rest of my life. I really need to stop my whining."

Declan came back out just then. "What, still a whole bed full of tables and chairs to unload?" he asked, heckling his younger brother. "First I arrived late and then I took my sweet time escorting Iris inside, and there's *still* work to be done? Hell, why do I even keep you around?"

"Because of my charming good looks, of course," Stetson said with a huge grin. "Plus, I come equipped with a beautiful wife, an adorable son, and the world's most amazing housekeeper. You can't keep them without keeping me, too."

"Dammit, I hate it when you talk sense like that," Declan said, popping a kiss of hello onto Jenn's cheek. "Now, are you ready to actually get some work done?"

As they all went back to work, carrying the tables and chairs around to the backyard, Troy listened to the two younger Miller brothers flip shit at each other incessantly. Like every male under the age of 102, they were big believers in the, "If I tease you, then I like you – you should only start to worry if I'm nice to you," school of thought.

Based on the amount of ribbing they were doing, Troy was pretty sure they'd lay down their lives for each other.

Troy couldn't help the smile that spread across his face as he listened to Stetson heckle Declan about the spare tire he was starting to carry around the middle – total bullshit, of course, since Declan's stomach was just as flat as Stetson's. The Miller boys worked as hard as they loved, and fat just didn't dare settle onto them. Declan dished it right back, pretending to squeeze a love handle on Stetson's side and telling him that Carma must be fattening him up for the coming winter.

As much as Stetson and Declan teased each other, though – with Jennifer throwing the occasional jab in because, as she put it, she was the woman in the room and had to keep the two knuckleheads in line – they were content to work with Troy in a companionable silence. There was no pressure to talk; no questions; no "I'm just teasing" mean-spirited jabs because he wasn't chatting up a storm like the rest of them.

He couldn't help but wonder where else he'd find such a great group of friends; people who accepted him as he was. If he moved somewhere else, he'd have to start all over again, and who was to say he'd be as lucky the second time?

No doubt about it – he belonged in Sawyer. He'd known that for years, of course, but today was a hell of a good reminder of that reality.

But all of this just made him think of the one person he knew who didn't feel like Long Valley was their home – Penny. Not only did she feel like Long Valley wasn't her home, she wanted nothing more in life than to get the hell out of there. But she didn't know the Miller boys and by extension, the McLain sisters; Abby and her dad; or the adopted members of the family like Juan and Carmelita.

Troy stopped and quietly observed this branch of the Miller clan for a moment.

First, there was tiny Jennifer – Carmelita and baby Flint were the only ones in the whole group who were shorter than her, and that in-cluded Juan – kissing Stetson on his cheek by raising up on her tippy toes while telling him in a syrupy, gushing voice that he was such a "big, strong man" for doing all of this work today. Happily showing off for his petite wife, the cowboy posed for her in the typical body-builder style, shifting his weight from one foot to the other as he curled his biceps.

Declan, not to be outdone, was pretending to feel Stetson's biceps to test his muscle power and then shaking his head in mock disappointment at their puny size...even though Stetson looked like he could bench-press a steer just for fun.

Yeah, they're definitely brothers.

And then he mentally dropped Penny in among the middle of them, and knew she'd be laughing and chatting as she gave as good as she got. If Penny had been here today, she would've enjoyed the hell out of this, and not just because of the excellent Mexican food they were all about to eat, but because she'd fit in here. He was sure of it. She just had to realize that she could be happy here.

Welp, tonight was the night where he tried to prove that to her. He'd arranged it all already — after he finished helping with this move, he'd go home, clean up, head to Penny's, and do his best to sweep her off her feet. He was gonna follow a suggestion of Declan's, actually, who'd said that this particular date idea had worked wonders on Iris.

Just then, he felt the cold, wet nose of Sparky nudging the palm of his hand and startled, he looked down. She'd been waiting ever-so-patiently for all of the hubbub to die down before coming off the front porch, where she'd been quietly hanging out. She must've taken him just standing there as her cue that they were done, and now it was time to feed her some of that chicken she could smell drifting on the breeze. Even as he shook his head at her looking so forlornly up at him, her brown eyes liquid with desire for some of that Mexican food, he knew it was his fault for turning her into a beggar. She did eat her dog food, but only after eating all of the human food she could lay her paws on. Why eat dry dog food when there was meat to be eaten instead? She was no dummy.

He scratched her behind the ears and she happily wagged her tail, her tongue hanging out of the side of her mouth. She looked as happy and well-adjusted as any dog; the truth only came out when someone tried to push her boundaries by being too close to her when she hadn't given them permission to do so.

Oh.

Oh.

He could almost *feel* the light bulb pop on overhead.

As he stared sightlessly down at her, his fingers petting her even as his mind went a million miles an hour, he realized why it was that Sparky had accepted him from moment one of meeting him. Michelle, the local dog catcher, had even said it that day in the fire station – statistically, it was much more likely that an animal abuser was a male, not a female, so Sparky's instant acceptance of him had shocked everyone, even him. He was no dog whisperer. It was only Sparky that'd had this instant connection with him; this sure didn't happen with every dog he met.

But in that moment, staring down at her in the bright sunshine, pink tongue hanging out as she waited for him to lead them on to their next adventure, he saw himself in her. She was skittish around people, not sure who she could trust. She chose her companions carefully. Once she accepted someone, she loved them for life, but she trusted few at the outset. She'd been hurt – deeply hurt. To most, she was scarred, unusual, not like every other dog out there, but to Troy, that's what made her perfect. Her life experiences made her wary, but she'd known from the get-go that Troy knew what it was like to be hurt. She'd known from the get-go that Troy could be trusted.

Just like he'd felt around Penny. That night in the fire station, when Penny came over to interview Moose and Georgia but ended up interviewing him instead, he'd felt like a 2x4 had walloped him upside the head, sure. He'd felt a bolt of lust straight to his dick like he'd never felt before, sure. But there was something else – something deeper. It was ridiculous for him to feel this way – they'd only gone on one date. They'd only kissed one time. He knew almost nothing about her – was she a morning person? Or a night owl? Was she allergic to cottonwood trees? What were her thoughts on the politics of today's world?

But on another level, he knew *her*. He knew she'd be happy here…if she just let herself be.

It was up to him to show her how.

CHAPTER 12

PENNY

*P*ENNY SLID onto the cool, soft leather seat as Troy closed the truck door behind her and hurried around to the driver's side. He looked damn handsome tonight in his button-up shirt − no tie − and freshly washed dark blue Wranglers that did *amazing* things to his ass. Not that his ass needed any help looking amazing, but it apparently took the help when it was offered anyway.

He slid into the driver's seat and flashed her…a *nervous* grin? Was the stoic, quiet, unflappable Troy Horvath actually nervous?

That's it, I'm officially seeing things.

He put the truck into reverse and slung his right arm over the back of her seat as he backed the truck out onto the street. She cast around for something to say, and then remembered her line of questioning from the other night that she hadn't been able to pursue.

"This is a really nice truck," she said admiringly, and she meant it. She wasn't normally one for large trucks – she liked the gas mileage and maneuverability of her Civic – but this was a vehicle that fit Troy. She tried to imagine Troy cramming himself in behind the wheel of her car and almost snorted with laughter at the image. There was just no way his lanky, long, lean body would fit. "What brand is it?"

Troy shot her a laughing look. It was obvious he was surprised she hadn't been able to tell by the emblem in the grille. She mentally shrugged. All big trucks were just, well, big trucks. "Chevy," he told her. "A Silverado 3500 HD. 2017."

She nodded seriously, as if that all meant something to her. 2017...she was fairly sure that was what year the truck was made. And Silverado was the model? Maybe?

But…3500? 3500 of what? 3500 volts of electricity? 3500 pounds of strength? 3500 tiny squirrels running under the hood? 3500 people had a hand in making it? And what did HD stand for?

"You have no idea what that means, do you?" he asked dryly.

"Not a clue," she admitted easily. "I'm guessing Silverado is the model type, right?" He nodded, and emboldened, she continued. "I'm guessing it was built in 2017."

He laughed for just a second at that and then nodded again. "That's correct," he said, with only a small smidgen of sarcasm in his voice.

I guess I deserved that…

"I'm lost on the 3500, though," she admitted. "3500 *what?* 3500 running tigers, pulling your truck down the road?"

He laughed much, much harder at that one. "City girl," he finally said teasingly after he wiped the tears away. "No, 3500 is the size.

They simply picked that number." He shrugged.

"So it isn't even 3500 horsepower?" she asked. That was kinda what she thought it stood for, if she was going to be serious for a moment.

"Good Lord, no," he said, and laughed again. "That's the kind of horsepower a train engine would have. No truck can pull like that."

"Does it *weigh* 3500 pounds?" she asked. There seriously had to be some sort of reason for this number.

"Nope, it's a one-ton truck, so two thousand pounds. There's really no meaning to the 3500, I promise."

She screwed up her mouth at that one. She hated it when things didn't make logical sense. "All right," she said with a sigh, her voice clearly showing how put-upon she was.

But, Chevy's insane naming scheme aside, she noted that he was no longer stiff beside her, looking as nervous as a long-tailed cat in a room full of rocking chairs.

She would count that as a win.

"Thank you for the chocolates and flowers, by the way," she said, wanting to keep the conversation going before he could get nervous and clam up again. If she got him talking, maybe he'd forget that he hated it. "The chocolates were divine, and the flowers…I can't stop smiling, every time I look at them. Do you know the turquoise lady?" she asked.

"Turquoise…you mean Carla?" he asked, surprised, and then chuckled again. "She does wear a lot of turquoise…" he said musingly. "Never thought about it. Anyway, she's a year younger than me. You'll never meet a nicer lady. Everybody loves Carla. She took over the flower shop right out of college, renamed it Happy Petals, and has been there ever since."

"It was like 8:30 in the morning, I hadn't had a single cup of coffee yet, and she comes bounding up my front sidewalk, ringing my doorbell and hiding the bouquet behind her back. I almost didn't answer the door. I'm not much of a morning person—" He made a weird noise at that and she looked over at him, confused. "What?" she asked.

"Nothing, nothing." He waved his hand dismissively. "Not a morning person…" he prompted her.

She stared at him another moment, trying to figure out if she could weasel the answer out of him, and then let it go. "I'd stayed up the night before, working on a logo for a client, so it was going to be one of the slow-to-wake-up mornings. I'm waiting for the Keurig to brew up some magic when the doorbell rings. I look through the keyhole, and there's some chick standing there, and I'm thinking that she's there to pester me to attend her church on Sunday or something. Discussing religion with a perfect stranger is on my Top Ten List of Things I'd Really Love to Do, right behind 'stick myself in the eyeball with a cattle prod' and 'jump out of a plane without a parachute on,' so I'm thinking that I'm going to pretend I'm not home. It was the turquoise that got me."

"The color?" he said, clearly not understanding where she was going with this—

Hold on, just like she didn't know where they were going right now. Startled, she realized that they'd been heading towards Boise, but rather than making the 90-minute drive like she'd been assuming they were going to, they were instead pulling off on the Copperton exit.

"Yeah, the color," she mumbled distractedly, even as her mind scrambled to figure out what they were doing. Copperton? *Copperton?* Was this a joke? There were like twenty people who lived in Copperton, and that was only if you counted pets as people too. It was the very definition of tiny, backwards, arcane, redneck, smothering-with-its-small-townedness Idaho, where the 'fun' thing to do on a Saturday night was to go cow tipping.

She tried not to panic, but she was failing miserably. And she'd had such high hopes for Troy, she really, really had. He'd seemed almost normal, despite the fact that he was from Sawyer. She'd overlooked that fact. She'd decided to give him a chance, even though on the surface, there was nothing about him that made her believe they had a damn thing in common.

And then he pulled a stunt like taking her out on a date to *Copperton*.

"You okay?" he asked, his eyes flipping between the road and her. He'd obviously realized something was up, even if he couldn't tell what it was.

"Yeah," she said again, even as she scrambled to figure out what to do. She could…feign a broken ankle!

While sitting still in the cab of his truck, not doing so much as standing up, complete with her seat belt on.

She rolled her eyes at herself.

Okay, fine. She could…feign a stomach ache. A really bad stomach ache. A sudden one, a terrible one, with no choice but to go back home before she threw up all over the inside of his very nice truck.

She clutched her stomach but before she could see if her Oscar-winning skills were still

up to par, he pulled to a stop and cut the engine. "Are you sure you're okay?" he asked.

Moment of truth. Her hands were clutched
to her stomach. She just needed to tell him she
was feeling ill, and he'd take her right home,
she was sure of it. He was the kind of gentleman who wouldn't even blink an eyelash
about driving all over hell and back for no good
reason at all.

But something caught her eye and she really looked at their surroundings for the first
time since they'd taken the Copperton exit.
"Where are we?" she asked, all woe-is-me
faking instantly gone, and then grimaced. She
hadn't meant to let her cover slip so easily. She
just hadn't expected to see anything but a field
of cows in front of her.

"Train. Replica. C'mon," he said, and slid
out of his seat and hurried over to her side to
help her out.

"I can get out of a truck without you
needing to help me every time," she said, a
little more sharply than she'd meant to, pissed
at herself and taking it out on him. It wasn't

fair, and she knew it, but still, she was angry. She could be dancing at some nightclub in Boise tonight. It was a Saturday night; she had on a short skirt that showed off her legs; and she'd spent more time than usual on her hair. She looked good and she damn well knew it, and now she couldn't even manage to stay fake-sick for more than three minutes at a time and was gonna be stuck on a train, probably taking her somewhere so she could go tip cows.

"Yeah, but then I can't put my hands on your waist to swing you down," he pointed out, as if that was all the explanation needed. He also didn't rise to the bait – the testiness in her voice – and instead just sent a heart-stoppingly charming grin her way.

She tried to keep from grunting in annoy-ance, out loud at least. They started heading towards what she figured was the train station as she sorted through her options. She was walking now, so she could intentionally twist her ankle and fall to the ground. Maybe Troy would carry her back to the truck, and then she could at least enjoy the feel of his arms around her on what was most assuredly their very last date ever. Give her something to remember him by.

But Troy was already stepping up to the window and saying, "Reservations under Horvath for two," to the attendant behind the counter, and Penny could feel her second chance slip away. He'd made reservations beforehand. He'd spent money on this date. He'd tried to pick something that he believed she'd like.

It just turned out that he had terrible, *terrible* taste in dates.

He turned and put out his arm for her, and with an inward sigh of resignation and not just a little anger, she slipped her arm into his.

"You sure you're okay?" he asked as they strolled towards the platform.

"Yeah, I'm fine," she grumped.

She wasn't fine and she wanted to go home and she didn't want to get on a damn train and she didn't know why she was saying she was fine and—

It was the train conductor's uniform that

she noticed first. She wasn't what she'd consider to be a history buff, and she had absolutely no idea what an old-fashioned train conductor's uniform was supposed to look like, but still, this one was impressive. It sure looked real, all the way down to a gold chain connecting to a gold watch.

"Welcome aboard," the train conductor said with a large smile. "I'm Paul, and I'll be your conductor this evening. Watch your step, and come aboard." He moved to the side, gesturing them up into the train itself.

Whoa.

Penny's mind slowed and swirled as she went up the steps and looked around.

It was *gorgeous*. Dark wood paneling that showed its age, elegance personified. Rich brocade fabric covered every seat, and hung as drapes from the windows. She realized she'd come to a stop in the middle of the aisle, blocking everyone behind her, and with a start, began walking again, just in time to draw to a stop again. "Ummm…where are we sitting?" she asked, turning back to Troy who'd been escorting her from behind, like any gentleman would.

She wondered for a moment if he knew the urban legend behind why ladies always went first, and then Troy spoke, pulling her attention back to their seating arrangements. "2A and B," he said, pointing to a booth just a little further down.

She slid into place, feeling the richness of the fabric beneath her as she looked across the table to Troy, wide-eyed. "How long has there been a replica steam engine in Copperton, Idaho?" she asked, almost accusingly, like he'd been withholding this information from her intentionally. She knew she was being a little ridiculous, but seriously, though, how had she missed something this gorgeous? She wished she was wearing a hoop skirt and a big hat tied on with ribbons instead of a short skirt and high heels. Her modern outfit suddenly felt very out of place, and very tawdry.

"Didn't you come here on a field trip in the fourth grade?" he asked, puzzled. "It used to look more rundown, but it's always been here."

She searched back, trying to remember. Fourth grade wasn't exactly last week, but even so, she was sure that if she'd been here before, she would've remembered it. Even fourth-grade Penny would've thought this was pretty damn cool, despite it not having a single slide or swing set on it.

And then, a distant memory tingled just on the edge of her mind. Fourth grade was the year of Idaho history, and they'd gone on a lot of field trips that year, so it was hard to sort through them all, but...

"I missed that field trip," she said, pleased with herself that she'd remembered. "I woke up with a really bad stomach ache that morning," she felt a blush steal over her cheeks and hurried on before her face could become a flaming ball of red and then Troy would wonder why and she surely didn't want to explain *that* to him, "and ended up sick in bed all day. But it was a big, old, noisy train by all accounts, so I never really felt like I'd missed much. I had no idea it was like *this*."

"It didn't used to be – they remodeled it a

while back. A train lover dumped a lot of money into it. Some rides include a meal; some don't. I booked us for the meal package." As if on cue, her stomach let out a low rumble, and Penny shot Troy a laughing grimace.

"I didn't have time to eat," she said by way of excuse, even though that wasn't *technically* true. If she'd spent less time on her hair, she could've worked in a bite for lunch, but she'd wanted to look perfect, so…

Yeah, no time to eat.

"Hope the food is as good as the remodel was," he said, reaching his hand across the table to her and squeezing her fingers in his. The bolt of electricity that shot up her arm at his touch made her gasp. She gulped, hard, staring at Troy and he was staring back and she was wishing quite desperately that this polished, rich wood table was anywhere but between them because it was making it hard to do anything more than squeeze his hand back and—

"Welcome, welcome," the train conductor called out, breaking the arc of electricity between them. *Dammit.* She'd been about thirty seconds away from crawling across the tabletop and unbuttoning Troy's shirt with her teeth. As beautiful as this train was, she was really wishing that they'd spent time remodeling the sleeping cars instead. "Before we get going, we need to go over the safety procedures in case of…"

His words disappeared into a haze of lust as Troy brought Penny's wrist to his lips and began kissing it softly.

Oh, oh, oh, oh—

She wanted to let out a groan that could be heard halfway across the county, but instead, she squeezed her eyes shut, blocking everything out except where his lips met her skin.

That was, until his tongue met her skin.

"Oh!" she exclaimed softly, shifting on her seat, gulping hard. His tongue began tracing lazy circles across her sensitive wrist and she felt herself wanting to sink into the seat, languidly stretch herself out, and let Troy have his way with her, when she felt him softly lay her wrist down on the table. Her eyes fluttered open to see him sending a self-confident smile at her, a cocky grin that said he knew what she was thinking…and wanting.

There was a part of her who wanted to pretend that she'd been indifferent to the whole thing, but there was a more practical part of her brain that bluntly reminded her that she couldn't even manage to fake a twisted ankle while walking in high heels. Perhaps it was a good thing that she hadn't followed her teenage dream of going to California to be a movie star.

The train conductor finally quit talking about…whatever he'd been talking about, and the steam engine let out a long blast of its horn as it began to rumble down the tracks, giving Penny the perfect cover to not have to formulate a response to Troy's kisses. She turned towards the window and began admire the scenery instead – which really was beautiful – using it as an excuse not to look at Troy. He may be driving her insane with lust, but her gut told her there was something more than that going on.

He wanted more. Something deeper, something…

Something more than a fun fling to pass the time until she found a real job in a real town doing what she was really passionate about.

She kept her gaze focused on the rocky mountains and green pine trees and sparkling river passing by, not letting herself turn back towards Troy like her hormones were wanting her to. Should she confront him – put it all out on the table? Make sure that he understood what the deal was between them? She didn't want to ruin a perfectly wonderful date with a serious chat like that, but it wasn't fair for her to lead him on, either.

But I wouldn't be leading him on. He knows the deal. I told him that first night we met.

Feeling better about it, she turned back towards Troy and smiled. She must've been seeing things, or more like it, feeling things that weren't there. She was free to just enjoy a fun evening with a gorgeous man, no strings attached.

He'd been watching her closely, and when

she finally turned back to him and smiled, his shoulders relaxed and he smiled back. He was more in tune with her every frown, every sigh, every hand flutter, than any other guy she'd ever met. It made her feel loved...and a little creeped out, like her feelings were laid bare for him to examine, whether or not she wanted them to be.

A creepy love? A creepily loving man? No, that makes him sound like the next Jack the Ripper or something. He isn't that. He's just observant.

She wasn't going to admit to anything that she'd just spent the last five minutes contemplating, not if she didn't want to push him away. Guys didn't like it when girls got all clingy on them, especially not this early in the relationship.

No, it was better to pretend nothing at all was wrong.

CHAPTER 13

TROY

ATCHING PENNY'S FACE was like watching a play where all of the actors were mimes. He could see the expressions flit across her face, one after another, but he couldn't tell what they meant. He'd asked her probably a dozen times if she was okay because every muscle in her body had been screaming that she most definitely was not, but she kept promising she was fine, and at this point, he was a little worried that she was gonna get annoyed with the question.

That whole debacle aside, this date was going swimmingly well, if he did say so himself.

Her reaction when she'd gotten on the train… priceless. That wide-eyed wonder was exactly the same response Iris had had, at least according to Declan. There was something about the true elegance of a renovated train or home that appealed to the human spirit. *They just don't make them like they used to*…floated through his mind.

Not to mention the scenery. Looking out the window at the beauty that was only found in the mountains of Idaho, Troy smiled to himself. Yeah, he was pretty damn proud of himself, honestly. No one could look at that vista and want to move somewhere else. It just wasn't possible. He watched Penny carefully as she looked out the window, enjoying the view, and almost sprained his shoulder, patting himself on the back so hard. Yeah, this was a brilliant idea. He needed to send Declan a six-pack of beer as a thank-you for coming up with it.

Just then, the conductor stopped by their table to ask them how they were enjoying themselves.

"This is just amazing!" Penny gushed as

they swayed their way down the tracks. "How long have you worked here?"

"Ever since the new owners took over, about six years back now," the conductor replied, obviously proud of that fact. "I've always loved trains, so seeing someone restore this old beauty and bring her back to life…best present you could ever give me."

They began chit-chatting about the best – and worst – passengers he'd ever run across, and then what his favorite features of the train were, and just as they were getting into how many passengers rode the train in a typical month, a stewardess came by and told him he was needed back in the kitchen car. With a grin and a promise that he'd be back later, he headed towards the back of the train, moving easily despite the sway of the car, much like a sailor out on the open sea.

Penny turned back to him with a triumphant grin. "This would make a *great* feel-good story for the papers," she said excitedly, sipping at the wine they'd brought by while Paul had been chatting with them. "My boss loves it when I come to him with stories of my own, especially a local angle that hasn't been covered incessantly. Copperton is far enough away from Franklin that I'm going to say that it's probably been six years since anyone has written anything on this. We could do a follow-up – a *how's it been going, has it been worth it* piece. If I convince the company to run a large color ad in return that can run beside the article, it could be a real moneymaker for the newspaper, and lots of great publicity for the train. I love win-wins."

The stewardess came up the aisle just then, placing plates and silverware in front of each passenger, which saved Troy from having to verbalize any reply. But inside…he was damn excited. This was *exactly* what he'd been hoping for. Okay, maybe not that Penny would get an article out of the deal, but that she'd see that there really were fantastic activities and people, even in little ol' Idaho.

No reason to move somewhere else.

No reason at all.

CHAPTER 14

PENNY

THEY PULLED UP in front of her apartment complex, but instead of kissing him at the curb and him speeding off like his ass was on fire, this time she invited him up to her apartment. It wasn't a place she was particularly proud of – it was too small, too dumpy, and it was definitely *not* in the trendy part of Franklin. But, it happened to be the only place she could afford the rent in a tourist trap town like Franklin, so she took what she could get.

They stepped through the front door and Troy looked around quietly, assessing it. She felt defensive and opened her mouth to make apologies; to point out that finding an afford-able apartment in Franklin was like finding a unicorn sitting on your front porch one morn-ing, but before she could say any of that, Troy spoke. "I like the big windows," he said, nod-ding toward the front room windows, with the ever-so-inspiring view of the parking lot below. "Lets in lots of light." Even now, with the sun setting behind the Goldfork Mountains, there was still indirect light coming through, along with a front-row seat to a colorful sunset.

Those windows were the best feature of the apartment, and it struck Penny as so... *Troy* to look around and find the one believable com-pliment that he could give within seconds of walking in the front door. He was not only ob-servant, he was kindhearted and thoughtful. No doubt he could tell from her body language that she was touchy about how little pride she could have in such a place, and so he did his best to put her at ease.

She wondered again if all men from Sawyer were this thoughtful and she'd just missed it all growing up, or if Troy was some sort of mutant, even among his fellow Sawyerites.

So she did what she always did to say thank you to a cute guy – she threw herself at him.

Not using words, of course – she was no dummy. She used her body, because everyone knew that what men prized more than any-thing else was sex. Raising up just a bit – he was so damn tall, even with her in her high heels! – she wound her arms around his neck and pulled him down to her. She felt the fire spread through her veins as he gave as good as he got, not a moment of hesitation. Their tongues twisted and wound themselves around the other's as he thrust his hands into her hair, tilting her head so he could better access her mouth. She couldn't breathe or think; she could only kiss and fall into his world and then she was the one tilting her head to the side so he could kiss his way down her neck and the flames were only licking higher and higher…

"Penny," she heard, in some distant part of her mind, but it was far away and she instinctively knew she didn't need to worry about it. "Penny." It came again, and this time, the person meant business. She couldn't ignore them.

Her eyes fluttered open and in a daze, she looked up at Troy. "Penny," he whispered, stroking her cheek with his thumb. "So beautiful. So damn beautiful."

And then he was walking out the front door and down the steps to the ground floor and driving away and…

She sagged against the open doorframe of the front door, watching the taillights disappear, more confused than she'd ever been in her life. Why was Troy leaving her? The warmth of his kisses, the fire that had been licking over her body, took a long, long while to dissipate. When it was finally gone and she could truly grasp what had just happened, she was caught between stunned and pissed off. Did he not like her? Did he not want her? He'd said that she was beautiful – was he just trying to placate her? Who gives a woman chocolates and flowers and takes them on an expensive date on a restored steam engine and kisses her like he'll die without her...

And then walks away?

A cool night breeze swept up the stairs and across her body, finally pulling her the rest of the way out of her reverie. Numbly, she brushed her teeth, pulled on her PJs, and crawled into bed, staring up at the ceiling in the darkness.

If she lived to be 101, she would never, no *never* understand men, but especially men from Sawyer, Idaho.

CHAPTER 15

TROY

THE GOLDFORK MOUNTAINS were always gorgeous, but this time of year was his favorite. Troy loved these mountains when they were dusted with snow, when they were bright with the golds and reds and browns of autumn, but he especially loved them when they were green and alive in the heat of summer. When Penny had told him she'd never gone hiking up in the Goldfork Mountains during any season of the year, he'd made the instant decision that this would be their very next date together.

How had she managed to live in the Long

Valley area for so much of her life and yet never been up in the mountains? Where did she go to *breathe?*

He'd never understand women, not until the day he died.

Thank God he didn't need to understand Penny to enjoy being around her. She was like a finely crafted mystery novel, where the mystery was never actually solved.

Speaking of breathing…

He could hear Penny's breath coming in, in short gasps behind him, and he decided it was time for a stop at an overlook on the side of the trail. Give her a chance to rest up. Running her legs off wasn't a real good way to convince her that hiking up in the mountains was a fun thing to do.

She came up and stood beside him, sucking in deep breaths. He held out the water nozzle for his CamelBak to her and after a moment's hesitation, she reached out and began sucking down the cold water. Sparky, who'd been ranging further up the path, realized that they'd stopped without her, and with a whine, she headed back down to their side.

Poor girl. When Troy'd first stopped at the trailhead and gotten out, Sparky had stayed in the bed of the truck, whining, ears back, tail down. She looked *supremely* unhappy to be back in the same forests where Moose and Georgia had found her just months before. It'd taken some coaxing, helped along by the enticement of beef jerky, to get her to finally jump out. She still wasn't thrilled by their choice in hiking paths, but she'd calmed down some. As long as Troy, and to a lesser extent Penny, was there, she was okay.

"I didn't realize I was this out of shape," Penny said ruefully, letting the hose to the water pouch drop. "Please tell me the air is thinner up here or *something.*"

He chuckled at that. "We are quite a bit higher up here than down in Franklin," he reassured her. "This part of the trail is also damn steep. You'd have to be doing this almost daily to not be out of breath."

"You're not," she said, and there was more

than a hint of disgruntlement there. "You seem perfectly fine, and you're carrying the water and the food!"

"I carry bags of flour around for a living," he pointed out. "You carry a pen and a recorder. If I weren't in better shape than you to begin with, I would be after a month. And the same would be true if we swapped jobs."

She screwed up her mouth a bit at that, thinking it through. "Fair enough," she conceded. "Still, I think I need to get my ass down to the gym more often."

"Hmmm…" was all Troy said in response. *Your ass looks mighty fine to me!* was what he wanted to say, but it seemed…less than gentlemanly to mention that.

"Is that where Georgia and Moose got caught in the fire?" Penny asked, pointing to a craggy rock cliff in the mountainside further down the valley. The black burned ground was clearly visible, even from several miles away.

"That's it. That's also why Sparky isn't happy." Even now, the setter's ears were pinned back a little and her nose was wiggling in the air. She could smell the ashes drifting on the light summer breeze, still around months later. If they hiked over to Eagle's Nest, they'd probably find green growth poking up through the blackened landscape but from this distance, it just looked like a huge angry scar against the otherwise brilliant green of the pine forest.

"You sure have a better nose than I do," Penny said as she petted the loyal dog. Instantly, the rigidity in Sparky's body disappeared as she leaned against Penny's legs, tongue lolling, soaking up the love. "I can't even smell it; I can only see it. You lived through a hell of a lot."

"And the fire wasn't even…" He paused for a moment, almost saying, "the worst part for her" but luckily caught himself just in time. He knew he was getting more relaxed around Penny, but still, he couldn't believe he almost made that mistake. Making an ass out of himself in front of her sure as hell wasn't on his bucket list. "…How bad it got for her," Troy finished instead.

If he ever met the former owner of Sparky, he wouldn't be held responsible for his actions.

Hell, an ass whooping as bad as the ones the owner used to mete out to Sparky seemed like fair play to Troy. The asshole could see what it felt like to be beaten black and blue.

"I always thought my article might bring the old owner out of the woodwork," Penny said with a disappointed sigh. "I was hoping he'd show back up, wanting to claim his dog back. Then you guys could throw his ass in jail."

"Unfortunately, I can't imagine he'd be that dumb. The owner of Sparky also caused that wildfire. No one would want to be on the hook for the bill for putting it out."

"Dammit. You're right. I was just hoping he could get arrested for animal abuse. I didn't even think about the costs to fight the fire. He's *never* going to show back up." She sounded downright pissed off at the realization, and Troy could only nod in agreement. No matter how much it sucked, she was right.

He did smile a little at the fact, though, that they were both using the pronoun "he" without any real evidence that Sparky's former owner was, in fact, a male. Troy simply couldn't imagine a woman doing that kind of damage to a dog, and no doubt Penny saw it the same way.

Without even needing to talk about it, they began back up the path, this time with Penny leading the way. Troy's gaze followed her long pale legs up to the fringe of her cut-off shorts. She had the nicest pair of legs and the curviest ass he'd ever been lucky enough to lay eyes on.

He gulped.

The palms of his hands began to sweat from the torture of seeing her *right there* and not reaching out to touch her curves.

He remembered then what his great-grand-mother used to say at Christmastime when he was just a kid. They would hang up the bulbs together and then he'd want to bat at them or toss them around the house – he *was* a boy, after all – and she'd always say, "Perty, perty, but no, no," as she firmly but kindly pulled the shiny balls out of his hands and hung them back up on the tree, usually a little higher than they'd been before. Grandma Horvath was no dummy.

It was that memory that flashed through his mind just now because it's how he felt God was telling him to deal with Penny. *Admire all you want, but hands off the goods, buster.*

Huh. He wasn't sure why God would be calling him buster, but that was apparently how it was playing out in his imagination, anyway.

The bottom line was, Penny was the real deal. She wasn't a fling, she wasn't something to keep him occupied until the right girl came along. She was it for him, and if he didn't treat her with the respect she deserved by taking it slow, he could ruin it all.

So no matter what his dick was telling him to do or how much begging it was doing, he couldn't listen to it. He had to stay the course. He had to convince her that she felt the same way about him, and *then* he could let his dick lead him around all he wanted.

"So have I told you about the latest brouha-ha?" Penny asked over her shoulder, blonde hair swinging with every step. "My boss gave me the assignment this last week and I'm getting just as many phone calls from people telling me to drop the story as I am telling me to pursue it."

"Really?" Troy said, so surprised that his gaze actually left the curve of Penny's ass for a whole three seconds. Long Valley wasn't normally a hotbed of discontent and anger. "What's going on?"

"The county commissioners. They got the oh-so-brilliant idea that what we really need is a high-end ski resort just outside of Sawyer, up here in these mountains somewhere. Some developer's put a bug in their ear about it, and it's all that any of the businesses in Sawyer want to discuss. Except..." She paused for a moment. "Well, I guess it's any of the businesses in Sawyer that could get a boost from tourism that care. I don't suppose anyone out at the Horvath Mill has a strong opinion on the topic."

"I don't think so," Troy said dryly.

"The last disastrous stab at this happened while I was in high school and then off to college, so I didn't pay a lot of attention to it back then, but I've done a lot of research on it for this go-round and...well, I can see why there's such a division. When the last set of developers ran up that huge bill with all of the local businesses and then declared bankruptcy, that caused its own round of bankruptcies. Did you know five businesses in the valley went under because of them?"

"No," he said, surprised. He'd known that several hardware and lumber companies had shut down since they were the ones to get hit the hardest, but he hadn't realized the total was that high.

The previous company, Goldstone LLC, had used their status as the new ski development in the area to get a bunch of local businesses to give them overly generous lines of credit. The ski resort was supposed to rival Sun Valley when done, and everyone had wanted a piece of the action.

That was, until Goldstone ran out of money to actually make the ski resort a reality. One day, they were just gone, and they left a whole lot of unpaid bills in their wake.

Five bankruptcies from that…*damn*. He'd known it was bad, but not *that* bad.

Since Troy was six years older than Penny and a lot more in tune with the local business scene than she'd been in high school, he'd heard all about it, and honestly, the reverberations were still being felt in the valley all these years later. People were a lot more skeptical about developers moving in from the outside, for starters.

Even more surprising was that this was being discussed and he hadn't heard about it around the water cooler at work. Apparently Glenda was slacking on her self-appointed job to spread every bit of gossip as soon as she heard it.

"Stimson & Sons just barely reopened as Rustic Lumber Co this last year after restructuring their business and pulling themselves out of bankruptcy, so I went down and interviewed them first. They weren't happy to hear about this, to put it mildly." She laughed dryly. "They were talking about how the county commissioners better ask for a construction bond before anything really gets started, or they're going to be calling for some heads in the next election."

"Hmmm…" Troy murmured, thinking that through. He wasn't surprised to hear that the Stimsons took it like that. They weren't much for pulling punches, and if they had an opinion on a topic, then those opinions were voiced. The oldest boy, Phil, had absolutely no filter at all, from what Troy could tell.

"I went back to the county commissioners and told them what the Stimsons had said, and Commissioner Water just laughed at me. Told me the Stimsons were loud mouths, and they weren't about to take their marching orders from that bunch."

Troy chuckled a little at that. Commissioner Water was just as much of a loud mouth as the Stimsons were, so really, they just didn't like each other 'cause they tended to shout over the top of each other, neither of them any good at listening. People didn't like other people who were too much like them.

It was why he and Penny got along so well.

As far as Troy could tell, they had virtually nothing in common, which in his estimation, made them just about perfect for each other.

They hiked a little further along the trail in silence, hitting a patch of heavy woods, giving them a blessed respite from the burning sun. Even up here in the mountains, it had to be low 80s today, and doing the kind of exercise that they were, that easily made it a titch too warm for comfort.

"That's it, Troy, I can't stand it anymore!" Penny half shouted, coming to a stop and turning back on the trail to glare at him.

Shocked, he came to a complete standstill and stared at her, wide-eyed. She'd happened to stop right where the trail was sloping up-wards and with her ahead of him, it made them eye to eye for once. At 6'5", Troy didn't find himself eye-to-eye with people very often, and that, along with the out-of-the-blue anger from Penny, was making him feel more than a little discombobulated.

"What?" he finally said. She was breathing heavily from their strenuous hike, which made her perfectly proportioned chest heave in time with each breath. It was…distracting, to say the least, especially since he couldn't even remember the last time he'd gotten any, and he began blinking a few times, trying to clear the lust away enough to hear what she was saying, forcing his eyes up to her face instead.

"…never talk to me." She folded her arms across that delectable chest and glared at him.

Shit. He'd missed something important. Based on her anger level, something *very* important.

Welp, there was no way but forward.

"Who doesn't talk to you?" he finally asked after scrambling through his memory, trying to see if he could remember what she'd been saying, and coming up with absolutely nothing. She'd yelled at him out of the blue, and then her chest had been moving up and down rhythmically, and then she'd been talking about people not talking.

Her face reddened. "You!" she shouted. "*You* don't talk to me!"

Just then, Sparky came darting out of the

bushes where she'd probably been trying to score a bunny rabbit or something, and sat down on the dusty trail, whining as she looked back and forth between them.

"It's okay," they both said at the same time, leaning towards Sparky to pet her and calm her down. Troy jerked back at the death glare Penny was giving him, and decided to let her pet the setter. He needed every bit of brain power he could muster that wasn't being side-tracked by long legs or delicious chests to con-centrate on whatever it was that was making Penny pissed.

"We were talking right now," he pointed out logically. "The ski resort? The county com-missioner—"

"No, *I* was talking. *You've* said 'Not really,' 'No,' and in a real torrent of words, 'Hmmm...' I knew you were shy from the be-ginning. I thought it was cute that you were so shy, honestly. Tall, blond, mysterious...what wasn't to like? But it's been months, Troy, *months*, and all I ever get out of you are three-word sentences, if I'm lucky. I thought you'd eventually open up and start talking to me when you got more comfortable around me, but I'm starting to realize that was a fool's dream."

It was just about then that he started to get angry in return. "Now hang on a minute!" he challenged her. "You like to talk; I like to listen. Why mess with a good thing?"

"Because I can't date a stranger, that's why!" she shot back. "And that's what you are to me right now. A stranger. I know all of my own thoughts already, Troy. I don't need to hear myself say them out loud in order to know what they are, but what I really want is to hear *your* thoughts. What do *you* think about a ski resort being opened up just outside of Sawyer? I have no idea. You aren't telling me."

"You're angry because of a ski resort?" he asked, anger flooding through him. If that wasn't the damn stupidest thing he'd ever heard—

"Don't play dense with me!" she shouted.

He opened up his mouth to say *I'm not*

playing, but decided at the last second to keep that thought to himself.

"I'm pissed because I never know what's going on in that head of yours. You don't talk to me, Troy. Every date we go on, you listen and you nod and you let me get things off my chest, but I'm not getting your thoughts in return. That's how conversations work, you know, or at least that's how they're *supposed* to work. Is your whole family this dang blasted quiet all the time?"

"Only me," he snapped back. Why was she pushing and prodding at such a sore spot? Why was she hurting him so much? Couldn't she leave it alone?

"So I got the silent Horvath, huh?" she said sarcastically. "Lucky me. Does anyone else wonder why it is that you never string more than three words together at a time?"

"No, because they all know why!" he retorted, and then slammed his jaw shut so hard, he felt pain shooting through his head from it.

Shit, shit, shit, Troy. You've really put your foot in it this time.

CHAPTER 16

PENNY

*N*o, *because they all know why.*

The words kept repeating themselves, again and again, ricocheting around inside of her skull as they glared at each other, Sparky in the chasm between them, whining and licking her hand, trying to make everyone happy again.

"It's okay, sweetie, it's fine," she murmured distractedly, smoothing down the hair on the crown of the dog's head. "No need to worry."

No, because they all know why.

No, because they all know why.

That. Is. It.

She was going to get answers, and she was going to start getting them *now*.

"Troy Horvath, what aren't you telling me? I'm giving you ten seconds to spit it out or I'm walking back down this trail without you." She could hike back until she got into cell phone range, call her mother to come pick her up, go back to her apartment, and pretend that she'd never heard of Troy Horvath.

She could totally do that.

She totally didn't want to, but she could.

"I can't talk, okay?!" he shouted, his face red – from anger or embarrassment, she didn't know.

"You're talking right now," she volleyed back sarcastically. "So don't tell me you can't talk. That's bullshit, and you know it."

"You can be a real bitch-ch-ch," he bit out coldly. His eyes had shut down – he didn't resemble a person in that moment so much as a frozen wall of ice.

The pain stabbed through her at his words.

She never would've guessed that someone like Troy would call her that. *Never.*

And then it registered.

"You just stuttered," she whispered. He flinched at the word *stutter*, and she knew then what was wrong. "You *stutter*," she repeated in disbelief, torn between the shock of that revelation and the reverberating pain of him calling her a bitch.

He flinched again.

"Troy, talk to me!" she half-yelled, hysterical. "Is that what your problem is? That you *stutter* sometimes?!"

"Yes!" he thundered back. "I st-st-st-st-stutter. I can't even say the damn word. Are you happy now? Has this been *fun* for you?" He sneered the words, the pain on his face and in his voice deep and real and raw.

"Fun? *Fun?* Are you insane?" she spat out. "Of course this isn't fun! But at least I'm getting some answers, and that's more than I can say about the last couple of months! You're like my damn mother. She forces me to show up on her doorstep and insert myself – unwanted – into her life to take care of her and then gets all pissy about it when I do, but it's her being so damn stubborn that *makes* me do it. You were all proud of me when I did that with my mom; where's that pride in me now? It's only okay if I'm pushy if I'm doing it to someone else? Well, dammit all, Troy, I need answers, and if the answer is that you stutter, well fine, you stutter. It's not the end of the world."

"Easy for *you* to say!" he thundered back. "*You* haven't spent your whole life watching every word you say, worried you're gonna make a fool out of yourself. Words are *your* friends, not mine."

They stood there on the trail, glaring at each other, breathing heavily, Sparky whining, the babble of the mountain brook muted, hard to hear through the thundering in her ears.

Finally, quietly, "You're right," she whispered. "I don't know what it's like to stutter. I'm an extrovert. I love people; I love talking; I love all of it." He started to speak and she held up her hand to stop him and he fell blessedly silent again. "But Troy, that doesn't mean that I will happily do 99% of the talking from here on out. I can't have a relationship with someone who I don't know. I don't care if you stutter. I don't give a rat's ass if you stutter on half the words that come out of your mouth. But I *do* care if I can have a true relationship with you, and that means communication. *Two-way* communication. Tell me about it – tell me about stuttering. What causes it?"

"They're not sure." He was staring off over her shoulder, not meeting her gaze, a muscle in his jaw ticking away like a little time bomb.

She wanted to shake him by the shoulders. Here she was, trying to meet him in the middle, apologizing for what she said, but there he was, doing it again. Seriously, it was like he was trying to piss her the hell off. "Do they have any guesses?" she asked, each word deliberate and quiet, trying to keep calm but not doing a real great job of it. She wanted to learn, but he had to talk to her.

"Maybe genetics. Maybe not."

She counted to ten, breathing in and out slowly and deliberately. "Troy," she said as calmly as she could, "I want to learn. How can I learn if you won't tell me anything?"

"Google works real well," he said sarcastically, finally looking at her when he said it, but the fury in his eyes and his voice…it was like a slap to the face.

"Google works real…that's *it!*" she shouted. "Take me back home. Now! Drop me off in Franklin and never call me or text me or send me flowers or chocolates again! I'm done with you. I was *trying* to understand you. I was *trying* to learn, and all you can do is be a sarcastic asshole. Well, you can go be a sarcastic asshole on someone else. I'm *done.*"

Her eyes were filling with tears as she pushed past Troy and stormed down the trail, anger pulsing through her, making her want to shove him, hit him, yell at him.

Dammit all, she'd been falling for him, but apparently she didn't know him – not the real him. She never would've thought he would act like this. It just went to show that she really didn't know him at all. She'd been stupid, stupid, stupid…

It was the tears that got her in trouble.

They blurred the world in front of her and she must've stepped on a loose rock or something because she was suddenly sliding on her butt down over the rocks and dirt, and the brush and weeds were tearing at her legs and arms, and she was yelling, yelling with pain but she didn't know what she was saying, only that the world started tilting and whirling around her and the sky was below her which wasn't right at all and then she came to a stop but she couldn't breathe and dust and dirt were coating her tongue and mouth and throat and she was coughing, coughing, rolling over onto her side and gasping for air…

"Penny, Penny, oh my God, Penny!" Troy was pulling at her, and like a limp rag doll, she found herself in his lap, still hacking and struggling to breathe. There was something in her mouth then, and she heard Troy say, "Take a drink, nice and slow. Suck on the tube. You're gonna be fine. Swallow…swallow…"

The pure mountain water soothed her throat, washed out her mouth, and she sucked at it greedily then, wanting to wash the grit out of her mouth. "Be careful," Troy murmured. "Not too quick. Easy does it…"

Finally, when the water bag was drained and she was only sucking down air, she lay back against his chest, breathing in and out slowly, trying to figure out what she'd hurt, where she'd been scraped up. Sparky's whine of concern finally registered with her and she struggled to open her eyes, wanting to reassure the sweet dog. She got her eyes open to find Sparky just inches away from her face, soulful brown eyes begging Penny to be okay.

"I'm all right," she whispered, stroking the dog's silky white head and instantly, Sparky relaxed, her tongue lolling out of her mouth as she plopped herself down and snuggled up against Troy and Penny.

Penny laughed – just a little – at that, and the ice was cracked – just a little – between them.

Not broken, just cracked.

"If someone came along just now and found us sitting in the middle of the trail, they'd sure be laughing at us," Penny said, embarrassed, scrubbing at her cheeks, trying to wipe away the evidence of her tears.

"Let 'em laugh," Troy said harshly. "I don't give a damn. Are you okay? That was a real bad fall." He was stroking her hair away from her face, pulling strands out of her mouth and nose where they'd gotten sucked in during the tumble down the hill.

"Yeah, I'm fine," she said, her cheeks stinging red as she tried to pull away, but Troy stopped her as easily as a giant would capture a kitten. "I'm fine!" she insisted, but still, Troy wouldn't let her go.

"Let me look," he said, brushing at her scalp, checking for bumps or tears in the skin. "You could've really hurt yourself."

Sparky, sure now that the danger was over, dropped her head down on her paws and closed her eyes for a nice snooze, still cuddled up against them, her weight pinning Penny into place. *You're not helping*, she wanted to tell the dog, but she closed her eyes and submitted herself to Troy's ministrations instead. He felt his way up her arms and legs, checking for any broken bones but other than a few deep bruises, she was in the clear.

Finally, he had nothing left to look over, and so he simply cuddled her against his chest where she listened to his heart thump, beating a steady rhythm against her cheek.

"I'm sorry," he whispered into the stillness. "I'm not used to talking a lot. I don't mean to push you away."

She cuddled closer to him, not wanting to move out of the circle of his arms. It was safe here. "In case you haven't noticed," she finally replied, minutes later, "I like to talk. It's my schtick, you know? My bag." He chuckled at that like she'd meant for him to, and she smiled as she melted a little deeper into his arms. "But I can't be the only one to *ever* talk. That's really one-sided, even for a chatterbox like me. I want to know what you're thinking. I want to know your opinion."

"I get that. I like hearing your thoughts, so...it makes sense you'd like to hear mine."

"What letters trip you up?" she asked, snuggling against him, wanting to stay safe in the circle of his arms. After the yelling and the tumble down the hill, she wasn't quite ready to face the world.

"Not letters, sounds," he said, correcting her. "C-h and s-t. I can sing them but I can't say them."

"You can *sing* them?" She laughed, shocked. "Is that a joke? Are you joking?"

"Not even a little," he said solemnly. "No one knows why, but people who st-st-st-stutter," he swallowed hard and then kept going, "only do it while talking. I can sing every word I want without a problem."

"That's wild," she said, scrambling to come up with a hypothesis of why that'd be true and coming up empty-handed. It just didn't make sense.

"Did you know B.B. King was afflicted? Talk about singing your way through it. And

Elvis Presley. His wasn't as bad as B.B. King, but it was there."

She stared up at him, open-mouthed. "I had no clue," she said softly. "No clue at all."

He shrugged. "I looked online for info one time. Found a lot of singers. Too bad I can't carry a tune." The corner of his mouth quirked up for just a moment. "I used to talk... well, more," Troy continued. "Before I moved to Sawyer to live with my aunt and uncle. I've never been a ch-ch-chatterbox," he swallowed hard, "like you, but I did talk. But that's why I moved here. I got into too many fights."

"You?" she gasped. She never would've guessed Troy – quiet, gentle, giant Troy – would get into a fight with someone.

You also didn't think he'd call you a horrible word, either, and the pain of that memory shot through her, hard and bright. She was going to give him a piece of her mind about that, just as soon as he was done telling her this story. She didn't want to sidetrack him or, heaven forbid, stop him from talking.

But as soon as he was done...

"Me," he said with a small smile. "Kids would make fun of me for not talking right—"

She noticed his substitution there – *not talking right* in place of *stutter* – and wondered how many times a day he said something other than what he wanted to say, to avoid the land-mines littered around the English language. It had to be exhausting.

"—and so I'd hit them." He shrugged. "It wasn't like I could yell back – at least not without maybe messing up some more words and making it worse – so I let my fists talk for me. After a while, I got into fights because." He shrugged again, as if "because" was a real rea-son. "Eventually, I became the troublemaker. Down in the principal's office every other day, at least. My parents thought that a small, rural school would get me away from the bad crowd I was running with. They didn't want to face the fact that I was the leader of that crowd."

"Hey, you just said c-h without stuttering!" she broke in to tell him, thrilled. Maybe he was getting better over time and just didn't know it.

"I did?"

"School! You said a small, rural *school*."

He shook his head sadly. "It's the sounds, not the letters. C-h sound. School is really an s-k sound."

"Oh." She sank back down into his lap in defeat, and snuggled her head against his chest to listen to his heart thump as he talked. It was soothing and she soon found herself never wanting to move again.

"When I moved to Sawyer," he said, starting his story up again, "I decided not to talk any more than I had to. If no one knew I..." He waved his hand. "You know. Then no one would tease me, and I wouldn't get into fights anymore. It was a fresh beginning for me, and I wasn't gonna throw it away. After a while, even my family forgot that I used to talk more. They got used to me saying almost nothing, and I got used to fading into the background. That night at the firehouse, when you noticed me...I was shocked. I didn't expect you to. I was off to the side, and that was on purpose."

"Not notice you?" She laughed at the ridiculousness of the idea. "You were the very first person I noticed when I walked into the building. All tall and lanky and handsome, and of course, you were the only one there with a dog by your side, so obviously I'd spot you. But even if you didn't have Sparky there, I wouldn't have walked on by. A girl just doesn't overlook someone like you."

"Girls do all the time," he pointed out in an I'm-being-reasonable voice.

"I doubt it!" she said, wanting to laugh again but stifling it instead, trying not to hurt his feelings. He was *such* a guy sometimes. "Troy, if a woman isn't paying attention to you, it's because she's blind. I think you're just not picking up on the signals. If I hadn't come over with the newspaper to the mill that day, would you have asked me out on a date?"

"No," he admitted softly.

"I think you've probably been breaking hearts all over this town and don't even know it."

He looked at her skeptically and she popped him a kiss on the lips. "I'm a girl. I know these sorts of things. Trust me on it.

Speaking of being a girl…" She drew in a deep breath and looked him square in the eye, not allowing herself to get sidetracked by how damn handsome he was. "If you call me a bitch again, I walk away, and you never see me again. This is your only warning."

His eyes flared and she wondered for a moment if he was going to dump her off his lap and walk away right then and she was already starting to get pissed at him when he whispered, "I'm sorry. I was angry, and I didn't mean it. I will never do that again."

"I was beating on your sore spot with a sledgehammer," she said ruefully, "so I think we call it even this time. But never again."

"Never again," he repeated, and this time, it was his turn to lean forward and pop a kiss on her mouth.

He stood up, dislodging Sparky who let out a disgruntled sigh at being disturbed, and then with a shake of her coat, her tail was wagging and she was ready to go again. Troy held out his hand to Penny, helping her to her feet and pulling brush and sticks out of her hair while she brushed at the dirt and pebbles embedded in her skin. She had some light scrapes – road rash, as the younger version of her would've called it – up the side of her right leg that she hadn't even noticed until now. They began to sting, surprising her with the strength of the pain washing over her.

Just like a two year old who doesn't cry until he sees his momma, these damn scrapes didn't hurt one bit until I noticed them. Making me into a wimp over here. She decided she wasn't going to give into the pain and ruin the afternoon with Troy.

Well, ruin it any more than it had already been ruined.

"Do we want to keep going?" she asked, nodding towards the trail she'd tumbled down. "You promised me a beautiful lake at the end of this hike, you know." Plus, maybe she could wash her scrapes off in the lake and let the icy cold water numb the pain a bit.

"Sure," he said, and she could tell he was a little surprised that she was still up for it. She set her jaw stubbornly. She wasn't going to let the pain show, dammit. They began walking again, a little slower this time as Penny watched each step carefully.

"So, does everyone in Sawyer know that you stutter?" His shouted response from earlier – *they all know why* – still stung a little. Everyone had been in on this secret. Everyone except Penny. Did they all just assume she knew? Or were they watching her, to see how long it took her before she figured it out...if she ever did.

"*Hell* no," Troy said, and she could tell he was shocked that she thought that. She felt... slightly better to hear it. Not so ignorant. "My mom, dad, aunt, uncle, and three cousins. No one else knows. At least, they've never said anything if they have."

"You have three cousins?" She didn't know why she was surprised by that. He was allowed to have relatives. She just hadn't heard him mention them before.

Which brought her right back to what had caused their fight to begin with. The list of things she didn't know about him was probably longer than the list of things that she did.

"They're like siblings to me since I don't

have any siblings of my own, and because I've lived with their parents since junior high. But they've all moved away. None of them love it here like I do. That's why Uncle Horvath is giving me the mill instead of to his own boys. Neither of his boys want a damn thing to do with it. One's moved back East and the other's in the Air Force. Actually, Bryce should be getting out soon, or at least he's at the re-up-or-get-out point. I should ask Aunt and Uncle Horvath if they know what he's gonna do. And their daughter, Jessie, is down in Texas right now. Working for a small mom-and-pop oil company, doing their books. She never really worked at the mill; my uncle is old school and it wasn't a place for women in his mind. I think if a woman ever joined the volunteer fire department, Uncle Horvath would have a heart attack on the spot."

"Why does your uncle care if a woman is on the fire department?" Penny asked, confused.

"He used to be the..." He hesitated, and Penny remembered then.

"Fire chief," she supplied.

"Yeah," he said, and flashed her a grateful smile for not forcing him to say "chief."

"Damn, if you can't say *chief* without stuttering and your uncle used to be the chief, that must've been awkward."

"Not really," Troy said cheerfully. "I got away with calling him Uncle Horvath and no one blinked an eyelash at it."

Penny bust up laughing. "You are sure creative," she said admiringly, stroking his stubble-roughened cheek with her thumb. "You have to think and rethink through every word you say, and do it all without missing a beat."

"You'll notice I don't say a lot," he pointed out. "That's on purpose. It's tiring to talk. Words don't flow. They get st-st-stuck between here," he pointed to his brain, "and here," he pointed to his mouth. "It's easier to not say anything at all."

"Thank you for talking to me," she whispered, staring him straight in the eye. She wanted him to *feel* how grateful she was. "It means a lot to me. I don't expect you to become Mr. Congeniality, but I do need *some* give from you."

"Aunt Horvath wants you to come over for Sunday dinner," Troy said, apropos of absolutely nothing. "She's dying to meet you. You two can discuss my failings in depth. She is always telling me that I need to talk more."

Ah. That's where the connection was at.

"It sounds like we can commiserate together." Penny flashed him a teasing smile and he rolled his eyes.

"Here's something you can commiserate about," he said with a wicked gleam in his eye, and scooped her up in his arms and began carrying her towards the lake.

"Troy, put me down!" Penny half-yelled, pounding at his shoulders…

But not very effectively as she was saying it all through bouts of laughter. She really needed to work on being more convincing.

"Oh, sorry," he said, totally not sorry, and pretended to drop her.

She squealed and threw her arms around his neck. "Troy!!" she yelled.

"Shh…you're gonna dist-st-sturb the squir-rels," he said as he waded into the shallow water.

"It's freezing in there, isn't it?" she asked, ignoring the stutter. The sooner he realized that it wasn't a big deal, the sooner they could move on with their lives.

"May-ay-ay-be," he finally got out around chattering teeth.

"Hey, I thought you stuttered on *ch* and *st*," she teased him. "When did you start stuttering on *ay*?"

He mock-glared down at her. "I've got you-ou in my ar-arms," he said through the chatter-ing. "I'd be ni-ice if I were you-ou."

"Shore's that way," she informed him blandly, pointing back towards the shoreline. "You know you can get out, right?"

"And lo-ose m-my manly card st-st-status?" he asked, aghast. "I worked ha-hard for th-that."

"I won't tell anyone, I swear. It'll just be be-tween you, me, and the squirrels. Maybe an eagle or two."

"But I wa-was gonna dr-drop you in!" he protested.

"All the more reason for you to carry me back to shore." She settled in against his chest, accidentally pulling his t-shirt down his chest a little, and instantly decided to use that to her advantage. "After all," she murmured, leaning in and kissing his exposed collarbone, "I have much...*warmer* activities in mind."

He let out a growl of frustration. "You're ki-killing me," he moaned. She swirled her tongue over the collarbone and then breathed lightly on the damp spot, sending another shiver through him, but this time she didn't think it was from the cold.

With a groan that seemed torn from his throat, he splashed back towards the shore, Sparky barking and running along the shoreline, thrilled at the game they were playing. Her antics faded away as Troy let Penny slide down the front of him, one torturous inch at a time, finally depositing her in the warm, dry sand.

"I wasn't gonna—" He broke off, a pain-filled groan emanating from him as he covered her mouth and began kissing her as if his life depended upon it.

Wasn't going to what?

Which was the last coherent thought she had for quite a while.

CHAPTER 17

TROY

*D*AMMIT, this wasn't part of the plan. He was gonna make her fall in love with him, so irrevocably and totally that she would never dream of leaving him for the big city, and *then* he could make her his. He wasn't gonna let himself touch her before then.

Except right now, he was quite sure he would die if he didn't.

As he yanked his shirt off with abandon, tossing it to the side, he told himself that even if this wasn't part of the plan, it was still okay to do it. If he believed for one minute that she couldn't possibly be happy in Long Valley, in

Sawyer there with him, he'd let her go. More than anything in the world, he just wanted her to be happy. That was all that mattered to him.

So if he could bind her to him through sex, then all the better. It was just another form of persuasion, right?

He felt a smidge bit of guilt at that – it seemed...underhanded, somehow, to use sexual desire to get what he wanted from her – but then Penny groaned as she threaded her fingers into his hair and pulled his lips down to hers. "Please, please, please," she panted against his lips, and he wondered if she even knew what she was pleading for, or if it had simply become a mindless chant. He wanted to tease her by asking, but that would require too much breath, too much thinking, and quite frankly, there just wasn't enough blood north of the belt line for something like that.

He managed to lean over long enough to shuck off his jeans and then his hands were on her, stripping her bare to his gaze. A tiny part of his brain – really, almost too small to contain a whole thought – brought up the vague idea that there was something wrong here but as his hands stroked down over her lithe, slim body, it was hard to bring that thought into focus.

Outside.

The single word finally reappeared in his vocabulary, and he knew then that's what he was struggling with.

"We're…outside…" he murmured between kisses down the side of her neck, collarbone, and then to her small, pert, perfectly proportioned breasts. Their pink tips were begging to be suckled and who was he to say no? His tongue swirled across the tiny bumps and the proud nipple on one and then the other breast, and he was quite sure that he'd never in his life tasted something as delicious as this. He sunk ever farther into the abyss of desire, losing track of the world around them.

"We are," Penny confirmed, a hint of laughter in her voice, but he didn't know what she was agreeing to, or why she was laughing.

"We are what?" he finally managed to make himself ask as he pulled himself away from her body long enough to find the blanket he'd packed away in his backpack. He'd planned on them using it to sit on during their picnic, but...change of plans.

"We are outside," Penny said, and this time the laughter wasn't simply a hint in her voice but had become full throated.

Outside.

The word had reappeared in his vocabulary again. Right. They were outside.

He felt thick, miles thick, and his hands trembled with lust as he laid the blanket out on the ground. He stood and stroked his hands down her gently curving sides, the feel of her setting him on fire. It had been so damn long since he'd had any attention that wasn't self-ministered, he was a little terrified he was gonna unman himself in front of her like a randy teenage boy.

Hell, he *was* a randy teenage boy in that moment. His driver's license might put his age at 36, but his dick was saying he was at least two decades younger than that.

He made himself step back for just a moment, pulling his hands away from the softest, smoothest skin he'd ever felt, and *focus*. It was literally painful and he felt like he could use his dick to pound through concrete just then, but he made himself do it anyway.

"Penny," he said, looking her straight in the eye, her blonde hair tousled and wild around her face, her lips swollen from their rough kisses, and his resolve came within a hair breadths of dissolving into nothingness. In that moment, every word was a painful chore that he had to force out before his self control completely disappeared. "We're outside. Someone could come along at any minute and find us. If you want to go back, we can."

Please, please, please don't ask me to do that.

At that moment, he wouldn't even be able to zip up his jeans over the hard-on he was sporting, let alone walk with any sort of ease, but he would do it if she wanted to. He loved her that much, which was something he would not, could not tell her. Not yet. He could see it in her eyes – she didn't feel the same way. Not yet. She felt lust. She felt attraction.

But she didn't feel love.

And God help him, he was trying to use that lust and attraction to his advantage, so he could hurry along the process of love.

Which probably made him the biggest bastard to ever walk the earth, something he should totally feel guilty about, but didn't. Not just then, anyway.

Penny hesitated, nibbling on her bruised bottom lip, and Troy prayed harder than he'd ever prayed for anything in his life. *Please God...*

Finally, she shrugged. "No one's been up here since we started hiking the trail," she pointed out. "I think we're safe."

Thank you, God.

He swept her up into his arms and carried her the few steps over to the blanket, not wanting to waste a moment, not wanting to give her a chance to change her mind.

He was a good guy; he wasn't a saint.

He'd done the right thing. He'd asked her if she wanted to turn back. He wouldn't ask again.

What followed was a blur of lust and legs and lips, and the perfect harmony of their personalities. She shouted and whispered and moaned, babbling about what she wanted and how much she wanted him, or simply chanting his name over and over again.

He, on the other hand, didn't say a word but instead let his lips – dancing across her skin – say everything he felt. Words were difficult in the best of times; they were impossible now.

He followed the line of her body down to her tiny waist and perfectly flat stomach, kissing his way across her cashmere skin – soft and smooth and pale pink – and to her innie belly button that begged for a tongue swirl across it. "Troy," Penny panted. "Please, Troy."

He knew what she wanted. Even though this was their first horizontal dance together, he felt connected to her in a way that he hadn't felt with other women, even after sleeping with them dozens of times. This connection with Penny was primal and deep and way beyond words or understanding. It just *was*.

But he didn't settle himself between her thighs and push his way inside like he knew she wanted.

Instead, he moved further down her gorgeous body, to the apex of her thighs. He was surprised to find that she kept herself perfectly shaved and plucked to a billiard's cube of baldness. The previous girlfriends he'd had, had only trimmed their pubic hair short. It was a completely different sensation and feel to run his tongue across the supple skin, without a hair to get in the way.

Her eyes closed and she began panting. "Troy, Troy, Troy," she said, begging him for more. "Plleeaassseee…" she moaned, as he began to stroke up inside the folds of her and across her clit. Her hips were raising up in the air now, and she was pushing, arching, begging, and he couldn't hold back anymore. His self-control crumbled and he slid inside of her in one swift motion, her soft, warm body welcoming him and it was then that all thoughts, all reasoning, disappeared and he was only feelings and desire and an overwhelming drive to make her *his*.

He came then, his back arching and his whole body tensing and the world disappearing, and it was only the two of them and no one and nothing else existed...

He didn't know how long it was before he finally drifted back to reality. He was cuddled up to Penny, his arm wrapped tightly around her and as the world came into focus again, he realized he was probably smothering her. He pulled back to give her some breathing room, but she clutched at his arm, holding him in place. "Not yet," she whispered, and he pulled her tighter against him with a smile. He'd happily hold her all day long.

CHAPTER 18

PENNY

*W*ITH A BIG stretch of relief, Penny headed out to her Civic. It was Friday after work, and she fully planned on celebrating by…

Well, by checking in on her mother. Because she was a party animal like that.

It'd been a crazy week at work for her and based on the few texts she'd managed to trade with Troy, it had been just as crazy at the mill. Apparently, the very beginning of harvest was starting to hit, so they were ramping up to get ready for the fall. He'd already warned her that when harvest hit full swing, he'd be pretty much MIA for at least two months.

Well, I'll probably be gone by that point anyway. Somebody somewhere is going to need a graphic artist with more skill than experience. I just haven't found them yet.

She ignored the stab of pain at the idea of leaving. This was what she wanted. She didn't want to work at the newspaper for the rest of her life, chasing down leads on who said what at the chili cook-off. She had bigger dreams than this town could hold. She couldn't let herself forget that, no matter how sexy Troy looked in bed.

Actually, it wasn't just in bed that Troy was looking sexy. She grinned a little to herself as she took a left and headed towards her mom's.

There was their first time, out in the wilds of Idaho, of course – she *still* couldn't believe she'd done that and even more amazingly, no one had walked up that trail and caught them – but after that, they'd done it on the couch, over the railing of the mezzanine of his house, in the backseat of her car, and that time in his backyard under the stars.

Ooohhh yyeeaaahhhh…

Now that was something she'd never forget, even if she was 92 and couldn't name what year it was. There are some things that were quite literally unforgettable, and that night was permanently a part of that list.

After that first whoopsie where they'd both lost their minds and had forgotten to use a condom, they'd been careful ever since. She was not going to get trapped in this town. No how, no way. Hell, pulling into her mom's subdivision just now made shivers go down her spine, and not in a good way. Every house in the Moose Run subdivision was a cookie-cutter version of its neighbor, with the occasional resident getting especially creative and painting their front door a dark red instead of leaving it as treated wood.

Walking on the wild side.

This neighborhood represented everything she didn't want in life, and driving through it was a damn good reminder that no matter how sexy Troy was, this was not the world for her.

She opened the front door to her mom's house after a cursory knock. "Hey, Mom!" she called out, pulling the door closed behind her. "How's it going today?"

"Good, good," came her mom's muffled reply. "Be right there."

It sounded like her mother was rooting around in the attic or something. Penny sighed as she headed into the kitchen to find something to eat. Her mother was a self-described "organized hoarder," which just meant that all of the stuff stacked to the ceiling in the attic and spare bedroom was in neatly labeled boxes, rather than in open piles or garbage bags or something.

Someday, in the far distant future when her mother passed away, it would be Penny's job to wade through all of it and decide what to do. Honestly, a lighter and a can of gasoline had seemed like a perfectly valid plan to her, but when she'd jokingly mentioned that to her mom one time, her mom'd had a meltdown.

She'd never mentioned it again.

Penny pulled out the makings for a sandwich from the fridge and quickly slapped one together. She'd been so busy pouring over the proposed budget for the city of Franklin for the next fiscal year that she hadn't taken a break for lunch. She'd been trying to make sense out of it so she could report her findings in a coherent article that said more than, "Much money will be spent," which was what her first instinct had told her to do. Her stomach was audibly growling in anticipation by the time she took the first bite of her sandwich.

"There you are," her mom said in the doorway of the kitchen, dirt and dust and more than a few cobwebs strung across her.

Penny swallowed the bite – talking with her mouth full was *not* allowed in her mom's house – and said, "Mom, you look like a homeless orphan off the street. What on earth were you doing up there?"

Her mom shrugged and headed for the fridge for a big glass of milk. "Just rearranging and cleaning. It was getting awfully dirty up there, you know."

"It's an attic. That's what attics do," Penny pointed out and then took a large bite of the sandwich. *Food.* It was heaven to her aching stomach.

"Yes, well, not my attic," her mom sniffed as she poured out a glass of milk. "Want one?" She held the jug out towards Penny and she nodded. Her mom grabbed another glass from the cupboard and poured her some. "How was work today?"

"Mind numbing. My brain feels cooked." She leaned against the counter as she sipped the delicious milk. It was the one thing she could never drink too much of. She'd give up alcohol, water, soda, and every other form of liquid before she gave up milk. "It's budget season for both Franklin and Sawyer, and somehow, I've gotten the reputation that this is my schtick, so everyone happily dumps it in my lap. I've pointed out numerous times that I went to school for graphic arts, not accounting, but because I don't faint dead away at the sight of a spreadsheet, everyone thinks I'm some sort of financial genius."

"You've always been good at numbers, dear," her mom said mildly as she washed up in the sink. At least she was now clean up to her elbows, although her hair and clothes were going to need a lot more help. "You got that from your father, of course. After he passed, having to do the household bank account..." She sighed and shook her head. "That was a disaster, waiting to happen."

That *was* a disaster that had happened, but Penny said nothing. It was typical for her mom to ignore what was, and instead focus on what she wanted to believe, and Penny had long ago resigned herself to that truthitude.

As a kid, she'd just assumed that her mother knew what she was doing. What kid wouldn't? It wasn't until high school, when she started spotting *LAST NOTICE* in bright red ink across multiple bills in the mail that she started to ask questions. It'd taken her years to help her mom dig her way out of that mountain of debt. She'd come within a hair's breadth of losing the house; she had lost her new car.

Yup, that'd been a verifiable, horrendous, overwhelming mess of a disaster all right. Penny wondered for a moment what it would be like to have a mother who was more like a mother and less like an unreliable 16-year-old friend, but then shrugged the thought away. Her mother was who she was, and no amount of wishing would change her. If wishing could change her mom, Wanda Roth would've had a personality transplant a long time ago.

"When are you going to bring that boy of yours over so I can meet him?" Mom asked, leaning against the opposite counter as she finished off the last of her glass of milk. "The talk around town is that he's quite the looker."

"You know he is," Penny pointed out with a none-too-subtle roll of the eyes. "You've liked the pics I've posted of the two of us on Facebook. You've *commented* on those pics. You can't pretend you didn't see them."

"But, that's only his face," her mom

protested. "For all I know, he's missing a leg and three fingers from a car bomb explosion."

"Car bomb…?" Penny didn't know whether to laugh or cry over that one. "He's never been in the military, Mom. I promise you, he's in possession of all of his body parts."

"Well, I just won't know that for sure until I meet him," Mom said firmly. "Tomorrow afternoon? He can come over and we can watch the baseball game together. But," she held up a warning finger, "if he's a Yankees fan, well then, he can go back home and we can pretend like this never happened. You'll just have to start all over again."

"I'll be sure to inform him of that," Penny said dryly.

"Oh, don't tell him!" her mom said seriously. "He might pretend to be a Dodgers fan just to make a good impression. You can't let him know what's riding on this."

"Yes, Mom," Penny agreed dutifully, trying not to laugh. She loved her mom dearly, but there were days that her baseball obsession was a little out of control. She didn't even know if

Troy watched baseball. It wasn't nearly as big in Idaho as, say, football was. It was a uniquely Wanda Roth obsession, as far as Penny could tell. "I'm going to head out, now that I've eaten all your food and drunk all your milk." She went to press a kiss to her mom's cheek but made it an air kiss instead when she spotted the cobweb clinging to her mom's cheekbone. "I'll talk to Troy about tomorrow, promise."

"Tell him I make great tailgating food," Mom said, trailing her as they walked to the door. "No need to go to a baseball stadium — the beer is cold and the snacks are awesome here."

"I'll tell him all about it," Penny promised.

"But not which team to cheer for," her mom reminded her.

"I would never dream of it," Penny said solemnly, and closed the door behind her before she let the grin break out across her face. Her mom was something else. The important part was that she looked healthy. Other than the dusting of…well, dust across her face and hair, she had a healthy glow, a spring in her step, a sparkle in her eye. At least for today, she was still okay. Penny felt the weight ease off her chest.

Someday, she was going to stop worrying and hovering over her mom. Today wasn't that day, and honestly, tomorrow wasn't looking good, either.

She drove across town to the slums of Franklin – luckily, in a small town in Idaho, "slums" was a relative term and her neighborhood was certainly nothing like what a soul would find in the slums of Chicago or something – and pulled up in front of her rundown apartment complex. Before she even got out of the car, she pulled out her cell phone and texted Troy. She knew better than to call him; unless she was on fire, she knew Troy would only want to text.

I'm off work. Got any plans for tonight?

She stepped out of her car and swung her purse over her shoulder. First order of business – change into a shorter pair of heels. Her feet had had enough of the three inchers for the day.

Wanted to show you something. Wear comfy shoes; no skirt. Be there in 20.

She laughed a little at that. *No skirt?* she texted back. *All right, but I'm going to scandalize the neighbors.*

She unlocked her front door and began slipping out of her work clothes. There was a long pause with no answer from Troy, and then just an emoji showed up on her lock screen:

She laughed out loud at that.

She quickly changed into jean shorts, tennies, and a t-shirt. The shoes were covered in silver and pink sequins but they didn't have heels on 'em, so she figured Troy would approve. This was as practical as Penny Roth got.

It was when she was tugging her hair back into a ponytail that she heard a light knock on the front door and then, "Hello?" as Troy pushed the door open. With one final wrap of the band, she came hurrying into the living room.

"Hey, baby!" she said as she laid one on him.

What was supposed to be a quick kiss quickly became a lot more involved and she'd already started angling him towards the couch when he pulled away. Her eyes drifted open slowly as her mind struggled to figure out what'd just happened – *where did Troy go?* – when he popped a kiss on the end of her nose.

"C'mon, let's go," he said as he began pulling her towards the front door. She was shocked that he was turning down a clear invitation for sex in favor of…whatever it was that he was hell bent on showing her. "I've been meaning to ask you about this for a while," he said as he helped her into the passenger seat of his truck, then shut the door and hurried around to his side before continuing, "but I kept forgetting. I wanted to do it today before I forgot again."

Now she was *really* curious. What could this possibly be? Her mind raced through the possibilities but she was coming up with a big, fat nothing. Troy just didn't get excited about a lot of things. It was one of the reasons why their relationship worked so well. He helped counterbalance her when she got overly excited about the small stuff. He brought her back down to earth.

They were quiet for a minute as Penny idly watched the grazing cows pass, trying to solve the mystery as they drove. Between Franklin and Sawyer, the valley was almost as wide as it was long, and ranchers used the large open spaces to run beef cattle. The mountains that edged the valley were a ways off, hard to see through the light haze, but of course they were there. Long Valley may run short on entertainment and sophistication and clothing stores that sold something other than Wranglers, but it sure didn't run short on mountains.

Which reminded her – she needed to follow up on the ski resort thing. See if anything was happening behind the scenes. The rumors had quieted down and Mr. Toewes had been pushing her to focus on budgets instead, and she'd let that story drop. She made a mental note to make some calls on Monday.

"You've said before that I don't talk a lot, so you felt like you were dating a st-st-stranger,"

Troy said formally, almost like it was an announcement he'd been working on for a while, jerking Penny back from her wandering thoughts. She realized then that Troy had been using the whole truck ride thus far to think of how to broach this topic. Whatever he was about to show her meant a whole hell of a lot to him.

Don't screw this up, Penny.

"Yeah, I said that when we were on that hike up in the Goldforks," Penny said slowly. "But I haven't felt that way since then. At least, not as much, anyway."

"I want to show you something that is *me*. So that I'm not a st-st-stranger."

She reached out and squeezed his hand. "I can't wait," she said, and meant it. Whatever it was, it was a damn big deal in Troy's world, which just made the anticipation even stronger. She'd never liked being on the receiving end of surprises, and it took a real act of self-control not to reach out and shake his shoulders while yelling, *Just tell me what it is!*

"How was work today?" he asked, and, welcoming a distraction since moving Sawyer closer to Franklin wasn't an option and since shaking an answer out of Troy also wasn't an option, she launched into a rundown of how she'd become the financial guru at the newspaper.

"My dad was a CPA for years – it's why they named me Penny. My dad wanted to name me Hundred Dollar Bill because he wanted me to be rich, but my mother put her foot down over that one." She laughed. "My mom isn't always the most practical person on planet Earth and my dad was a good counter-balance to that, but there were times when she had to talk sense into him. Anyway, so numbers and spreadsheets and stuff just make sense to me, since I got that aptitude from my father, but I'm no financial wizard. But somehow, since I don't go running, screaming from the room in a panic because there are numbers printed on a piece of paper, I've become the lucky duck who gets to translate these budgets into stories that can be run in the newspaper. When I finally give my notice at the paper, I think they're going to try to chain me to my desk. Heaven forbid someone else learn how to read a spreadsheet."

She held her breath, waiting for him to respond to the idea of her leaving – not sure what she wanted to hear, honestly, but wanting to hear it anyway – but Troy simply pulled to a stop and cut the engine. "We're here," he said, and swung out to help her out of the truck. She peered up through the windshield as he was skirting the truck, and realized they were at the old Horvath Mill on Main Street in Sawyer.

He wants to show me a pile of blackened bricks? She nibbled on her bottom lip. There *had* to be more to it than that.

He helped her down and, holding her hand, he pulled her towards a side door. He reluctantly let go of her hand long enough to unlock the padlock and then grabbed it again to pull her inside. It took her a minute for her eyes to adjust to the gloom – there weren't any lights on, of course, so the only light in the building was filtering through the dirt-encrusted windows.

They walked quietly through, each lost in their own thoughts as they looked around. Perhaps it was because of the poor lighting, but the age of the building and the blackened bricks combined together with the dust in the air gave everything a washed-out look, like she was in a black-and-white movie. Wandering around, she felt a desire bubble up in her to bring the old girl back to life – to bring color back to it.

"Can you clean bricks?" she asked, breaking the silence between them. "Or are you stuck with the black from the fire?"

He grinned at her, clearly pleased that her mind had been working along the same lines as his. "I've done research-ch-ch, and you can clean them. It's hard work, but it can be done."

"So you're thinking of restoring this building…" Penny said, and waited for him to nod. "And then once you do, what are you thinking you can do with the space? You guys don't need a second mill, and anyway, it would just have all of the same problems that it did before – traffic, being too close to the high school, blah

blah. This is a hell of a lot of room – what would you put in here?"

"Come here," he said, grabbing her hand and pulling her back outside. He opened the cover on the bed of his truck to reveal the most elaborate saddle she'd ever seen.

"Whoa," she breathed, stroking her fingers over the leatherwork. The swirls in the leather, the glint of the silver... "Whoa," she said again. "Where did you buy this? I didn't know you rode." No wonder he was so excited to show this to her. To spend this kind of money on a saddle, he must be one hell of a horse lover. How was it that she didn't know that about him? He really did hide—

"I made this," he said quietly.

The air stopped. The world stopped. She just stared at him, mouth gaping open. She'd been able to – somewhat – accept the idea of him being a horse enthusiast without her knowing about it, but to *make* the saddle…that took so much more skill than just sitting in one.

And to make *this* saddle…

"No…way…" she breathed. "Are you being

serious right now? Tell me you're just pulling my leg."

He laughed a little at that. "I wouldn't kid about something like this. While in high school, a local ranch-ch-cher and friend of the family showed me the basics of leatherworking. I was fascinated by it, and in my free time, I began messing around with it. This will be the grand prize at the Sawyer St-St-Stampede this year — they've been using some guy out of Nevada to make the saddles before, but I pitch-ched them on using me inst-stead, and..." He shrugged. "They went for it."

"They went for it," she echoed, disbelievingly. "I'd say they did. Troy, this is absolutely gorgeous. I cannot *believe* you made this. You *made* this." She pressed a quick, hard kiss to his lips. "You are full of more surprises..." she murmured, but her mind was already skipping ahead, connecting the dots. "So you want to restore the mill and use it as your leatherworking shop?"

"I've been thinking about it. My uncle...he has to do something with it. The city is breathing down his neck to bulldoze it or clean it up or something. So I thought why not do my leatherworking here? I have a small shop behind my house but it's more like a glorified tool shed than an actual shop."

"I'm staying focused, I promise," she said with a small laugh, "but I just have to say that I can't believe how much you've changed since we've started dating. You're practically giving speeches over there."

He wrinkled his nose with a small laugh of his own. "I hadn't thought about it, but you're right. I'm not as worried about st-st-stuttering." He rolled his eyes at that. "A st-st-stutterer who can't say st-st-stutter. Hell, at least-st I can say my own name."

"You can say Troy?" She was totally confused by that topic change.

"You wouldn't believe how many st-st-stutterers can't say their own name. If I had a problem with T's, then of course 'Troy' would be very difficult for me."

"Oh." That made her head hurt a little. Having a stutter made life difficult enough; she couldn't imagine how much that would be magnified by not being able to say your own damn name. "Okay, so, back to your idea. Let's go inside and look around, now that I know what you're going for."

They walked back into the cool of the building and Penny began looking around – really looking. What she saw wasn't encouraging. Some of the huge, arched windows facing Main Street had broken panes, with graffitied boards covering them over. There was dust and dirt and cobwebs everywhere, along with copious amounts of bird poop, not to mention the blackened bricks along three walls. Luckily all four walls hadn't been affected in the fire, but because the structure was so tall, it was probably two or three stories worth of blackened bricks to clean.

That was mostly superficial, though. Lots of elbow grease, cleaning products, and disposable gloves, and it'd look a hundred times better. She should get her mom in here – give her something to clean that actually needed cleaning. As for the windows, she had no idea if it was possible to replace just a couple of panes of glass in a window instead of the entire thing, but if so, that'd help preserve the character of the building, not to mention would hopefully be cheaper than replacing these giant – and totally gorgeous – windows.

But it wasn't the superficial that worried her. "When was the mill built?" she asked, running her fingers along a dirty windowsill.

"1927, right before the Great Depression hit."

"Hmmm...I'm going to guess that wiring standards have changed since then?" she asked pointedly. "Did you guys update the wiring at any point?"

"Probably..." he said uncertainly. "I'd have to ask Uncle Horvath."

"My other worry is heating and cooling such a huge space. Unless there's something I don't know about leatherworking – which would honestly not be difficult – it doesn't seem like a space intensive hobby. This seems like a hell of a lot more space than you really need to do the work. Is there something I'm missing?"

His shoulders slumped a little and she instantly felt stupendously, terribly guilty. "I'm not saying it can't be done!" she rushed to say. "It totally could. I'm just—"

"No, you're right. Trying to rest-st-store a place like this in the evenings and weekends – it would take forever, all so I could have a huge building with lots of upkeep and wast-st-sted space." He sent her a grimace of a smile. "I don't know what I was thinking."

That did *not* help. She felt the guilt pressing down on her, smothering her. "I'm sorry," she offered weakly. "It really is a neat building – I love the patterns in the brick over those doors." She nodded down towards one end of the building, where a bricklayer had obviously spent a lot of time creating intricate patterns in what would have otherwise been a very utilitarian wall.

"Those bricks are some of my favorite parts of this building," he said, his face brightening a little. "I asked my uncle one time about that – if my great-grandfather had planned that or if the bricklayer just-t-t did it on his own recognizance, and my uncle asked me, 'What pattern in the bricks?'" Troy shook his head with a small laugh. "My uncle is not exactly a romantic kind of guy. He simply doesn't think about things like that. But this building means a lot to him, because of the family hist-sto-story, you know?"

"Have you talked to your uncle about taking the building over and doing something with it?" she asked. Maybe his uncle would have an idea that she and Troy were missing.

"No, I wanted to have a full plan in place before I went to him. He'd want to know what I was gonna do and how, and…" He shrugged. "It was simply an idea I've been kicking around. It's too busy at the mill to take this on and the running of the mill, too. My aunt is st-st-starting to get antsy – she really wants him to retire so they can move down south. Become snowbirds. She's sick of the snow and the cold. They've worked hard all their lives – I don't blame her for wanting to begin taking it easy now. Oh, speaking of, my aunt is becoming unbearable. Either I bring you home to meet her, or she disowns me."

Penny laughed out loud at that, even as her heart sank beneath the guilt of deflating Troy's dream. "My mom is getting worse by the day. She wants you to come over tomorrow and watch the baseball game with her."

They began heading out of the dusty mill, its echoing cavernous space giving way to bright sunshine and late summer heat.

"Baseball?" Troy asked, surprised, as he locked the padlock back up again. "I don't know a lot about baseball, truly."

"Baseball is easy. Remember one rule of thumb: The team from Los Angeles is *always* the best team. If you were going to pick one, that would be the one to cheer for." She stared straight into his eyes, trying to convey the important info without breaking her word to her mom.

"Los Angeles..." he murmured as he helped her into the truck. When he got around to his side and brought the engine to life, he guessed, "That's the Dodgers, right?"

She sent him a huge smile. "Just remember, I didn't say the name. I would never, ever tell you which team to cheer for."

"Of course not," he said mock-seriously. "Are there any cities I need to hate?"

"Any one but L.A. to be safe, but New York is definitely the worst. You might as well declare yourself a puppy killer."

Troy barked out a laugh of surprise. "Okay, got it. Your mom takes this seriously."

"You have *no* idea…So, tomorrow afternoon, my mom's place? Then she can stop making jokes about you being the victim of a car bomb."

"Car…" He trailed off, horrified. "She does know I live in Sawyer, right? Not Baghdad?"

"I've tried informing her of this fact, and her response to that is that she hasn't seen you with her own two eyes, and thus can't know for sure."

"But she's seen the pics on Facebook!" he protested. "She sent me a friend request-t-t two months ago."

"My mom is…uhhh…colorful. Different.

You'll see. You'll love her, even as you want to wrap your hands around her neck and squeeze. It's a particular talent of my mom's."

"All right, tomorrow afternoon. Root for the Dodgers; curse at the Yankees. Got it. But, my aunt is getting just-st-st as bad. She hasn't mentioned any car bombings to me, but since she isn't on Facebook, she's only seen the pics on my phone. She says she wants to fatten you up with some pie and coffee. Do you have time right now?"

She realized with a start that they'd just been sitting in front of the old mill, his truck idling, as they chatted. Yeah, this was a totally different Troy than she'd first met, for sure.

"Absolutely!" She looked down at her ripped jean shorts and sparkly shoes. "Ummm...I didn't exactly get dressed up, per your instructions."

"I'm sad to note that there are clothes on your lower half," he said solemnly, and then winked.

She laughed. "That would make a *great* first impression on your aunt and uncle," she said dryly. "Here's my half-naked girlfriend. Ain't she grand?!"

He was already driving the streets of Sawyer, apparently heading towards his aunt and uncle's house. "They'll love you no matter what you're wearing," he promised, getting back to the topic at hand. "Truly, they're just-st-st gonna be thrilled that I'm bringing a girl home."

She nodded and smiled her best carefree smile, even as a little bit of panic wormed its way into her. She was meeting his family; he was meeting hers…this was what serious relationships did. Not friends-with-benefits relationships did.

"I applied for another job last night," she blurted out. He knew this wasn't a forever kind of arrangement – she'd been clear from the get-go – but still…she felt she had to remind him. It was only fair. "Down in California. The pay isn't great, but they do a lot of promotions from within, so I'd be able to move up quick if I worked hard."

"You'll move up the ranks quickly then," he

predicted. "You're a damn hard worker." He pulled to a stop in front of a low-slung ranch house. "Ready?" he asked.

She sent him a bright smile, a little brighter than the last one she'd sent him, only because this time she didn't have the guilt hanging over her that he'd somehow forgotten their deal. He was a grown-up. He knew the rules. If he chose to ignore reality and then be heartbroken when she moved, it wasn't on her conscience.

"Ready," she said, and together, they walked towards the Horvath house.

CHAPTER 19

TROY

"WEELLLLCCCOOMMEEEE to the Sawyer Stampede!" Kurtis Workman's voice boomed out into the arena, and the crowd let out whoops and cheers in response. He was the local go-to guy for all events that required an emcee, and was well liked because he brought a big-time feel to their small-town events. Troy cheered and clapped along with everyone else, and grinned down at Penny at the excitement in the air.

The big event for them was something most other attendees wouldn't think twice about: The showing off of each of the prizes, including the saddle he'd made. He'd originally asked the rodeo committee not to mention his name while displaying the saddle to the crowd, but Penny had pointed out the obvious flaw in that plan – then no one would know he'd made it.

"You can't make new contacts for work if no one knows you do this stuff," she'd pointed out.

But it was beginning already – he was tensing up with dread for the moment when the crowd packed into the grandstands would all turn to look at him.

Looks can't kill. It'll be fine.

"Up for grabs this year," Kurtis' voice boomed, "we've got a huge array of prizes for the lucky son of a gun – and daughter of a gun, I suppose," everyone laughed, "who wins their event. We've got everything from gift certificates for Betty's Diner, to a delivery of premium horse hay in two-string bales, to a year of free stabling of your horse out at the Goldforks Riding Center. I do believe there's even some cash prizes to be found on this here list."

More laughter and cheers as the crowd began to relax and really get into the swing of things. "But this year...this year we have a special treat. In years' past, we've given away a hand-tooled saddle – gorgeous as could be. We've been bringing it up from Nevada and although the gentleman down there who's been making it for us is a real good guy, well...he just ain't local. This year, we discovered a local leatherman – leathermaker? I'm not sure what to call him – but anyway, he's from right here in Sawyer and boy howdy does he do some fantastic work."

Penny gripped his arm in excitement, grinning up at him. He felt his stomach flip-flop even as he kept a straight face. No reason to show how nervous he was.

"Hey Mike, bring this year's saddle out, will ya?"

Mike, the local mechanic and one of the men who helped put the rodeo on each year, came walking out, leading a dainty all-black horse, the light tan of the saddle a stark contrast to the mare's coat.

"Now, this mare is actually one of Dawson Blackhorse's out at his breeding ranch – she ain't part of the prize package, although I suspect that if you give Dawson an offer he can't refuse, you might be able to take her home anyway. No, that gorgeous saddle on her back is what you oughta be admiring." Mike turned and walked lengthwise across the arena a few steps, the hitch in his get-along a little more pronounced in the deep dirt and sawdust of the arena. Many, many moons ago, Mike had been a bull rider himself and had his hip stomped to pieces by an angry bull. Now, he participated in the rodeos as an organizer – a slightly less dangerous profession.

But turning lengthwise meant that the side of the mare – and thus the saddle – was now facing directly towards the stands, and in response, gasps and murmurs of appreciation swept through the crowd at the sight. Troy sought Penny's hand and gripped it in his own, not daring to look at her or look around but just stared forward into the arena like any other spectator would. No reason to bring attention to himself one second sooner than he had to.

"I do believe," Kurtis continued, "and I think y'all would agree, that this is the best-lookin' saddle we've ever commissioned for the Sawyer Stampede. Suitable for a lady or a gentleman, every bit of this was done by hand by our very own Troy Horvath. Troy, stand up and wave."

The gasps of the crowd at the sight of the saddle only grew louder when they heard his name. Even as he pushed himself to his feet to wave and acknowledge the whooping and hollering of the crowd, he could hear the whispered conversation behind him. "Troy? Troy Horvath? I had no idea! I thought he just worked out at the mill."

"He's also a firefighter, just like his uncle," someone else replied. "But there ain't no one in the Horvath family who does leatherworking."

"There is now!" They both laughed.

Troy sunk back down onto the wooden bench, trying not to see how off-balance he felt at being on the receiving end of so much attention. "You're going to get a lot of work from this," Penny whispered to him, her smile so brilliant, it rivaled the bright August sun. "Just you watch. You impressed a lot of people just now."

He nodded and squeezed her hand again. She was right. It was worth the 90 seconds of pure terror to launch this career off the ground.

But…it's not a career. Only a hobby.

Reality was intruding, like an unwanted and intoxicated great-uncle at the Thanksgiving table.

Aunt and Uncle Horvath are counting on me to take over the mill. I've seen how hard Uncle Horvath works year-round, but especially during harvest time. If I'm the new owner, that'll be me. No more taking time off to attend the Sawyer Stampede on a Friday afternoon. The mill will always *have to come first, if I'm gonna make it succeed.*

He felt a bit of the excitement in his chest begin to deflate, much like a balloon the day after a kid's birthday party. He was still a *little* excited – the idea of being able to do this professionally on the weekends hadn't lost its appeal – but he wanted more than that.

He couldn't hurt his aunt and uncle by refusing the mill; he also couldn't run the mill and a full-time leatherworking business at the same time.

There are too many couldn'ts in this.

After a few rounds of women's barrel racing, Penny began making pointed hints about how they should go find some yummy fair food to eat, so they made their way from the stands and over to the merchant area. Person after person came up and congratulated him on a job well done, and more than a few told him that he shouldn't be "hiding his light under a bushel."

He wasn't sure how to react to the effusive praise, but Penny didn't miss a beat. She dryly told Mr. Maddow, who'd been a customer of the Horvath Mill for a good six decades or so, that "Troy hasn't been hiding his light under a bushel – he's been hiding it under a saddle!" Mr. Maddow let out a rusty laugh and slapped his knee.

"You've got a live one here, Troy!" he chortled before doffing his hat and tottering off.

Troy shook his head in amazement. Penny had this enviable ability to always know what she should say in any given situation. It was hard not to be a little jealous at that talent. It was surely not ever gonna be a claim to fame for him.

"C'mon," she said, tugging on his arm again and pulling him out of his reverie, "I can smell the elephant ears from over here. If I'm going to get fat on carbs, elephant ears are the way to go."

Troy tried not to snort – too loudly, anyway. Penny looked like she'd just stepped off the pages of a fashion magazine, but only if the fashion magazine was geared towards chic country gals. She had her hair in short braids and was wearing a sparkling cowboy hat, jean shorts, bright red cowboy boots, and a plaid shirt tied just above her tiny waist. She looked delicious enough to eat and Troy had half a mind to drag her underneath the stands and show her the popular make-out spot for high

schoolers – you were never too old to neck underneath the bleachers – when he caught a
whiff of Mexican food. He turned and spotted
Carmelita manning a booth selling homemade
tamales.

Luckily, a popular event was going on at the
moment – calf roping, men's division – so the
line wasn't forever long. He tugged Penny to a
stop. "What are your thoughts on tamales?" he
asked.

"Never had one. Why?" she asked.

He gaped at her, and then without another
word, headed for Carmelita's booth with Penny
in tow. There were some travesties that simply
had to be remedied.

They made it up to the front of the line,
where Jennifer spotted him first. It was just her
and Carma working the booth; Stetson must
have been watching Flint. "Troy!" Jennifer said,
a huge smile lighting up her face. "I saw that
saddle you made – I had no idea!"

Carmelita looked up and a wide smile
creased her face, too. "Troy," she said happily.
"All this time, and you never told me how tal-

ented you are. You should make many more saddles. You have a gift from God." She crossed her ample chest. "Not everyone can do what you do. Are you going to open up a saddle store now?"

"I'm…looking at it," he said evasively.

"Well, my Declan, he has horses, so if you open up a saddle shop, I will let him know. Now, who is this?" She turned to Penny with an expectant look on her face.

"Carmelita, this is Penny. Penny, this is Carmelita and this is Jennifer." He felt a sweat break out across his face. He was embarrassed to admit it, but he had no idea what Carmelita's last name was. She'd always just been Carmelita, or Karma, if one of the Miller boys was feeling snarky that day. Hopefully, no one noticed that he'd skipped the last name's part of the introduction.

"So good to meet you, Penny," Jenn said effusively, giving Penny a one-armed hug across the table. "I'd heard that someone had snagged Troy's heart, but no one told me how *gorgeous* you are. It's so lovely to put a face to the name."

They began to chat about babies and small towns and how different Sawyer was from the outside world as Troy gulped, turning back to Carmelita with a forced smile plastered on his face. What did Penny think about being the woman who'd "snagged" his heart? Those were awfully permanent-sounding words. Would she go running for the hills?

I better give her a nutritious lunch to help her on her way.

"Four tamales, please," he said to Carmelita. As she efficiently wrapped them up for him and handled the cash, he asked her, "So, does this mean that you're gonna open up a Mexican place in town after all? Did he talk you into it?"

He hoped she could infer who "he" was, because there was roughly a 0% chance or so that he could say "Stetson" without getting stuck on the name for a good five minutes.

See, it could've been so much worse. What if Mom had named me Stetson instead of Troy?

He felt a bolt of panic shoot down his spine at the mere thought.

She laughed heartily. "No, no. My Stetson…he is a dreamer. I am too old to run a restaurant every day. But I can make many tamales and bring them to the fair, and feed people here." She shrugged. "It gives me something to do, so it is a nice compromise. But no restaurant for me." She handed the brown paper bag over with a big smile. "Enjoy."

"We will," Troy promised, and grabbed Penny's hand. "Ready?"

"We'll have to chat more!" Jenn said and gave Penny another quick hug. "I'm on Main Street – my partner and I run Miller & Nash Accounting. You should stop by and we can go get some coffee and muffins from the Muffin Man Bakery. Gage makes you forget the words 'low-carb diet' were ever introduced into the English language."

They both laughed and it took everything in Troy to keep from openly rolling his eyes. Penny was tall but skinny; Jennifer was short but skinny. If there were ever two women who didn't need to go on a diet, it was these two.

They began wandering up the dirt path that meandered between the stalls, heading for the large open area reserved for eating. On the way, they passed more merchant booths, and he noticed that several were run by local businesses that had recently been started. Before he knew it, Penny was chatting up Iris Miller and snapping pictures for the newspaper of the handmade canes that Iris carved. Ivy, Iris' younger sister, was there at the booth too, and Troy recognized a few of the paintings from the wine and arts festival in Franklin. Looking at Iris and Ivy, both with thick dark red hair, bright blue eyes, and gorgeous smiles…they could've been twins, although he knew Ivy was the younger of the two by a couple of years.

"This is Ivy McClain, the painter from Once Upon a Trinket," Troy said, once he could get a word in edgewise between her and Iris.

"You're Ivy?" Penny gasped, turning to Ivy and shaking her hand. "I should've known – I saw your picture at the arts festival. I just wasn't expecting to see you here. You've got such talent! I just loved all of the paintings down at Once." And then they were off, chattering away like old friends, and Troy simply shook his head as he grinned.

Just like he'd thought – Penny would love it in Long Valley if she found the right group of friends. She'd been living a pretty lonely existence since moving back to take care of Wanda; of course someone like Penny would struggle with that. She was a social butterfly who'd gotten lost in the proverbial desert.

The conversation just kept going and going, though, and finally he had to interrupt them. "Our tamales are getting cold," he reminded Penny, holding the paper bag up.

"Oh, did you get some tamales from Carmelita?" Iris asked reverently, like they'd been blessed with the Holy Grail of food. "You must go enjoy them. She is one of the best cooks in the valley. Come back later and we can chat some more!"

"Sounds great!" Penny said enthusiastically.

"What about under that shade tree?" she asked Troy, pointing to a large oak tree just behind the row of merchant booths. They made their way back there as Penny chatted up a storm. "Such awesome people here in Sawyer. I think I was born in the wrong Long Valley town!"

Troy contented himself to simply nod, when he really wanted to take her by the shoulders and yell, "EXACTLY!" at the top of his lungs. His self control was top-notch, if he did say so himself.

They settled onto the ground in the blessed shade from the heat of the August sun as Troy pulled the tamales out of the bag, handing her one. "Did you catch that Jennifer and Iris are sist-st-sters-in-law?" he asked as he began unwrapping his tamale. "Jennifer is married to St-st-stetson, the youngest Miller boy—don't do that!" he shouted.

Penny paused, the fully wrapped tamale partially inside of her open mouth, about ready to bite down…right through the corn husk.

"You really never have had a tamale before, have you," he said, and then started laughing.

"Sorry, I don't mean to laugh. I…" He bust up laughing again.

She glared at him, looking less and less amused by every passing second of laughter, and the look on her face…it just made him laugh harder. "I'm not laughing at you!" he finally gasped out. "I'm laughing *with* you!"

"You'll notice I'm not laughing, though," she said sarcastically, and that made him feel terrible enough to straighten up.

"No, you're not. I'm sorry," he said seriously. "Ummm…tamales are cooked in a corn husk. A really *tough* corn husk. You don't eat that part. You peel it back." He took the tamale and showed her. "Now eat that part," he said, pointing at the inner corn tortilla and filling.

Doubtfully, she took a small bite, and then her eyes widened with pleasure. "Oh, this is delicious!" she exclaimed. "No wonder everyone is always talking about tamales!" She happily took another bite. "Where have you been all my life?" she asked the Mexican food in her hands.

"To be fair," Troy said, "Carmelita is a superb cook, so don't expect all tamales to be this delicious. I'd hate for you to be disappointed if you have one by somebody else."

"What were you saying before saving me from my *faux pas* and then laughing uproariously at my ignorance?" Penny asked before taking another bite of her tamale.

"Ummm..." he said, thinking back, gladly wanting to discuss any other topic that didn't involve tough corn husks. He really shouldn't have laughed that hard at her. "Oh! Right. Jennifer is married to the youngest Miller brother, St-st-stetson. Iris just got married to the middle Miller brother, Declan, earlier this summer. And then Carmelita is St-st-stetson's housekeeper. Oh, and Ivy is the younger sister to Iris, and is dating Austin, one of Declan's closest-st friends."

Penny gave him a wide-eyed look. "Is there going to be a test later?" she asked. "I might need a family tree. Or a diagram."

Troy pulled out a second tamale and began unwrapping it. "Isn't it like this in Franklin?" he asked. "Everyone related to everyone else?"

"Yeah, kinda. I guess." She thought for a moment as she chewed. "Hmmm…Franklin is larger, first off, so it isn't quite that same small-town feel, you know? Also, it's a tourist town, so it's a perpetual revolving door of strangers staying there for a vacation and then heading back home. Here in Sawyer, it seems like everyone knows everyone else; in Franklin, because of all of the tourists, that just isn't true." She shrugged. "I can tell you this, though – I attended Franklin School District schools for twelve years, and no one in my graduating class was anything like Jennifer, Iris, or Ivy."

It was on the tip of his tongue to say, "You think you could be happy here if you had friends like them to hang out with?" but he couldn't be that transparent. He couldn't push Penny that hard. He had to let her learn to love the community, and choose to stay there of her own volition. If he pushed and nagged and finagled her into staying, she might resent him in five years, and then where would they be?

Divorced, that's where.

Once they were done eating, they ditched

their trash into a trash barrel and then Penny pulled him towards the merchant area again. "I saw a soap booth that I wanted to check out. C'mon."

He wanted to laugh – they were supposed to be there for a rodeo, not for a day of shopping – but he realized that of course Penny would be more interested in the booths than the arena. Despite how gorgeous she looked in her country girl outfit, he knew it was just outer trappings for her. She wasn't a country girl at heart, and watching a bunch of guys wrestle steers to the ground just wasn't going to keep her enthralled.

Honestly, he didn't care – being with Penny was all that mattered. If she wanted to go window shopping from here until next year, he'd be happy to do it, as long as she was holding his hand through it all.

"So tell me about your products," Penny said, pulling Troy's attention back to the matter at hand. He realized they were standing in front of Kylie VanLueven's booth, her boyfriend – Adam Whitaker and the local vet –

sitting beside her. Adam and Troy shook hands and chatted about the weather that summer, about how dry it had been and how out of control the fires had been, while Penny and Kylie swapped soap and lotion tips. He heard Penny ask Kylie if she would mind being featured in the newspaper, and Kylie gushed happily that it'd be a big boon for her business if she could.

Troy nodded towards the two girls chatting. "I heard about Kylie's ex showing up, and what happened down at the clinic," he said in a low voice to Adam. In a small town where not much happened, the attempted abduction by Kylie's insane ex-boyfriend the previous week had certainly been the focal point of the local gossip mill. "I'm glad she's okay."

Adam nodded, his mouth twisting with pain at the memory of what could've been. "Thanks for not mentioning it in front of Kylie," he said just as quietly. "I know she doesn't show it, but that really threw her for a loop. She's been getting bad nightmares ever since." He blew out a breath. "It's been tough."

Troy looked between Adam and Kylie for a

moment, marveling at what an unusual pair they made. He had to be a good decade and a half older than Kylie—

"Sixteen years," Adam said.

"What?" Troy said, startled.

"There's a sixteen-year difference between us. I could see the calculator running in your head, and thought I'd spare you the arithmetic."

Troy laughed heartily. "Thanks," he said, mortified but trying to hide it. He nodded towards Kylie's swollen belly. "When is she due?"

"Another three months." They stood in silence for just a moment, listening to Penny and Kylie discussing the advantages of using goat's milk over cow's milk. Penny was probably about eight years older than Kylie, and yet, there didn't seem to be a chasm between them because of that age difference.

Just like with Adam and Kylie. She must be something special, to relate to people of all ages so easily.

He didn't know Kylie well – she was probably still in diapers when he graduated from high school – but looking at her now…

He could see the attraction. She wasn't for him, of course, but for Adam – he was a lucky guy.

"Where's Sparky today?" Adam asked.

"Home. Crowds are too hard for her. She'd spend the whole time trying to keep from getting cornered by someone she doesn't know, which is practically everyone here...I couldn't bring her to the fair." It was tough to acknowledge that despite Troy's best efforts, Sparky still didn't trust most of the human race. She probably never would.

"A real good call," Adam said approvingly. "She's been through a whole hell of a lot. You can't expect her to deal with crowds at this point, or maybe not ever."

"Kinda what I figured." They stood silently for a moment, both lost in their own thoughts about the bastard who hurt Sparky, and at least for Troy, hoping karma was a real thing.

"Did you ever hear that the owner showed up at the firehouse?" Troy asked. Surprised, Adam shook his head. "A real asshat. Came in demanding Sparky, claiming I'd taken her." He laughed humorlessly. "He picked the wrong night to come to the firehouse; Abby was training with us that night, and after she told him what kind of money he'd be on the hook for, since he was the one who caused that fire out in the hills, he decided that maybe he didn't know who Sparky was after all."

Adam grinned at that. "Good. Someone like that doesn't deserve a sweetie like Sparky."

"You ready?" Penny asked, turning to him. He nodded and shook Adam's hand and waved to Kylie, but instead of heading in to check out more merchant stalls or to go watch the rodeo itself, Penny began dragging him past the bathrooms and dumpsters, towards a quiet corner of the fairgrounds where the occasional cowboy walked by with his horse, but was otherwise deserted.

"Ummm…where are we going?" He was completely confused. Unless she wanted to tour temporary metal corrals and pet some horses, there was nothing out there for them.

"I. Have. The. Best. Idea. *Ever.*" Penny's whole face was alight with excitement as she looked up at him. "I don't know why we didn't think of this before!"

"What?" He couldn't imagine what would get Penny this excited. She looked like she was about to burst out of her skin from the sheer excitement of it all.

"A farmer's market!" she exclaimed, and then waited for his response, as if that was supposed to actually be an answer to…well, anything at all.

"Farmer's market?" he finally responded, when it became clear she wasn't gonna elaborate if he didn't nudge her in the right direction.

"In the old mill! Look at everyone here today – Carmelita. Iris. Ivy. Kylie. And then there was that metal art booth that I spotted – we totally need to go check that out. Anyway," she waved her hand dismissively, "they're all selling items they're making, but there isn't one place to go to find them all, other than the fair this weekend."

She began pacing back and forth in front

of him, like a lecturing professor in front of a class.

"Carmelita – she doesn't want to open up a restaurant, right? Too much work. But what if she only had to make tamales to sell once a week? And Iris. Her canes are *gorgeous*, but you can't have a whole store of nothing but canes in Sawyer, Idaho. There's no way to sustain enough sales to make it worth it. But if she just has to be there every Saturday, or her and Ivy switch off weekends…then it's not such a big deal. Having the old mill to hold the market in means that no matter the weather, it would happen every time. It could be open year-round. And then you could sell your saddles and bridles and belts and purses…Troy, *this is it!*"

She was practically shouting at this point, she was so thrilled. She began ticking it off on her fingers. "It would use all of that space rather than wasting it; there's *plenty* of parking because it was originally built to accommodate large trucks; it's right there on Main Street so the location is perfect…I can't believe we didn't think of this before!"

Troy stood there and just stared at her, mouth gaped open in shock. It was the most blindingly obvious solution on the face of the planet, and he never, ever would've thought of it himself. He was the one from the small town. He was the one who knew all of the talented people who comprise Long Valley. And yet, it completely escaped him.

He pressed a hard kiss to Penny's lips in celebration. "Perfect, totally perfect. It's exactly what this town needs to grow…"

He trailed off.

"What? What's wrong?" she asked. "You look like someone just kicked a puppy. You know this is perfect, Troy — I can't believe we didn't think of it before." She was talking faster now, almost as if she were trying to keep him from saying whatever his doubts were, not wanting to admit that there could be faults with the idea. "Adam could come down and do animal vaccinations and—"

"When, Penny?" Troy broke in. "When

would I have the time to remodel the old mill and bring it up to code? You're the one who pointed out that the wiring is probably crap. It would need heating, new windows…I don't have time to do all of that, *plus* run the Horvath Mill."

She'd fallen silent by now, her jaw set stubbornly as she stared up at him, defiant, unwilling to admit defeat.

"I *can't* do all of that and take over the mill. I'm—"

"Can't or won't?" Penny asked, interrupting him. "Someday, you're going to have to start living your own dreams instead of your family's. Running that mill isn't what *you* want to do."

"Like you living in Franklin and taking care of your mom?" Troy retorted back, a little pissed at her high-horse attitude. "That wasn't your dream, and yet you've been doing it for *years*. Why is it okay for you to take care of your family, but it's not okay for me to take care of mine?"

"Because my obligation has an expiration

date to it!" she shot back. "I'm going to be moving out of this place and living *my. dreams.*" She stabbed her chest with every word. "You're going to be at the Horvath Mill for the rest of your life because it's what you're *supposed* to do. I'm willing to sacrifice for a little while, but not forever. I'll be working towards my goals in life while you're still grinding up wheat for Old McDonald and wondering where your life went."

They were breathing heavily, glaring at each other, neither one willing to give an inch. His anger only grew in size the longer the silence stretched out. It was so easy for Penny to spout all of that off – she didn't have a four-generation legacy to uphold. City people never understood. He didn't know why he thought she was any different.

Penny broke first.

"I'm sorry. I shouldn't have said that. It's good that you're loyal to your family. It's just hard for me to see…you're not happy. Not really. Not out at the mill. I just want you to have it all."

He nodded abruptly, not trusting himself to say anything. He wasn't sure if he was ready to move on; to pretend like nothing had happened. Her words were too harsh. Too rough. They stung too much.

"Let's go get an elephant's ear and watch more of the rodeo," Penny said, looping her arm into his and pulling him back towards the fairgrounds. "We can watch some idiot get up on a bull and almost get killed while gaining ten pounds from sugary carbs. You know, typical fair activities."

He grimaced in her direction, trying to pretend like she was being funny; that he was fine; that there was nothing wrong.

I'll be working towards my goals in life while you're still grinding up wheat for Old McDonald and wondering where your life went.

No, the sting of that wasn't gonna disappear any time soon.

CHAPTER 20

PENNY

HERE WAS A KNOCK on the front door, and Mom turned to Penny, her face lit up with excitement. "Go, go," she said, shooing her daughter towards the front door. "Your handsome man awaits!"

Penny wondered as she went if that were even true. After the rodeo last weekend, there'd been a definite…cooling off between them. She probably shouldn't have said what she did – it was her greatest failing, for sure. Always opinionated. Always happy to tell other people what to do and how to do it. But here, she wasn't in charge of Troy's life, and she sure as hell shouldn't stick her nose in where it didn't belong. She knew that. She just...

Dammit all, it was hard to watch him dedicate his life to something he didn't love, simply out of family loyalty. All of these months, and any time he mentioned the new Horvath Mill or work in general, he was just...flat.

There, but not engaged. Not excited.

But the *old* mill...his eyes lit up and he almost sparkled with excitement at the challenge of it – if a burly, quiet cowboy could sparkle, that was.

Watching him choose against his own self-interests to please family members hurt her heart, honestly.

She opened the front door to find Troy there, bearing not one but two bouquets in his hands, and wearing a Dodgers jersey. Penny's eyes went wide and she clapped her hand over her mouth to hold back the bark of laughter threatening to bubble out. "Just wait until my mother sees you!" she said, dragging him inside and shutting the door behind him.

"What beautiful flowe...what is that you're

wearing, young man?" Mom demanded from the doorway of the kitchen, her hands planted on her hips. "Don't tell me you bought that jersey to impress *me*." Her tone was at exact odds to her words – honestly, she couldn't have sounded more thrilled at the idea.

He handed the smaller of the two bouquets over. "Not at all, ma'am," he said in a deep drawl, and Penny narrowed her eyes at him. It was almost like he was trying to sound more...*country cowboy* than normal. She'd mentioned one time that her mom adored the thick country accent – was he laying it on thick to impress Wanda?

Troy avoided her gaze even as he continued, "Why, I just pulled this outta the back of my closet."

That was it. He *was* trying to impress her mom, and he knew just what he was doing. Mom would love the flowers, but the jersey and the accent was what would put her over the edge, and right into heaven territory.

But *why* did he care so much about what

her mother thought? Was he just one of those people who wanted to impress everyone? Or was he trying to impress her mom because he wanted something more than just a temporary relationship with Penny?

Her eyes narrowed as she stared thoughtfully at Troy. In her experience, if you weren't planning on marrying someone, there wasn't much point in impressing their family. It wasn't like you hung out with that family every Friday night after you broke up with their child. So this focus on what her mom loved…

"And for you," he said to Penny with a tiny bow as he handed over the gorgeous bouquet – an exact copy of the one he gave to her mom, except bigger.

"I better get these into some water," her mom fussed after drawing in a deep breath of their scent. "They're just too gorgeous to have them out in the air without anything to water 'em. Penny, do you want me to grab a vase for you, too?"

"That'd be great – thanks, Mom," she

tossed over her shoulder, not breaking eye contact with Troy now that she had it. "What are you doing?" she hissed at Troy. "Flowers for my *mother?*"

"Every pretty lady deserves flowers," he told her with a wink and a smile.

She wasn't charmed.

Okay, she was a little bit charmed. But she hid it well, and that was what counted.

"So I applied for another job last night," she said bluntly. She took a deep, appreciative sniff of the flowers — it was only appropriate to admire them, right? No reason to be rude about them — even as she kept her eyes glued on Troy. "Down in Houston. I would be working for an oil drilling firm, creating their ad campaigns for them."

"They'd be dumb to pass you by," he responded with another easy smile.

She studied him, looking for a crack in his composure. There was no way that he was okay with her leaving, and she just needed proof of that so she had an excuse to break things off with him. It was better to break things off and save him from himself. It was kinder. More thoughtful. She shouldn't let him hurt himself like this.

But without a care in the world, he pressed a kiss to her cheek and headed into the kitchen. "Is there anything I can do to help?" he asked as Wanda arranged finger foods on a platter.

"Grab that bowl of dip right there," her mom said, nodding towards the bowl on the counter, "and follow me into the living room. The Dodgers are playing the Houston Astros today. Houston…can you even imagine living down there? Humid, hot…I just don't understand being an Astro fan at all." She said it like Houston fans were on par with murderers.

Troy looked at Penny, his mouth curling up in silent laughter and she scrunched up her face with a silent *grrr*.

Promptly, she decided that there was no reason at all to look at him. Not one. "Mom," she said, scooping up the plate of sliced cheeses and following them into the living room, "I just applied for a job in Houston, actually."

Her mom froze and then slowly straightened to stare in horror at her only daughter. "There are days I don't know who you are," her mom said mildly.

"Mom!" Penny cried, exasperated. "It's a *job*. Houston is a perfectly fine city. And anyway, Los Angeles is hot, too. I don't see why you think the Dodgers are still a good team."

"Because it's a *dry* heat," Mom said, as if explaining a simple concept to a four year old. She turned to Troy and shook her head mournfully. "I just don't know where I went wrong."

This time, Troy's laughter wasn't so silent and Penny glared at the two of them. She was *quite* sure she didn't appreciate them ganging up on her.

"C'mon," Troy said, holding out his hand to Penny to pull her down onto the couch next to him. "The game is about to begin."

She took his hand, slightly mollified both by him wanting to sit by her, and by the fact that she knew The Secret about him that her mom didn't.

He didn't say, "The game is about to *start*," because then he would've gotten tripped up on the *st* and stuttered his way through *start*.

Whether he even thought about it consciously at this point, she had no clue, or maybe he'd long ago wiped all *ch* and *st* words out of his vocabulary whenever possible. But because she knew to listen for it, she could catch the thousand different times that he chose *just* the right word when no one else would even notice it.

As she snuggled down beside Troy, listening to him and Mom banter about who was the best player in the Dodgers lineup, she frowned at herself. She wasn't sure why she was so out of sorts about her mom and Troy teasing her. It wasn't a big deal. It was cute that her mom adored Troy so much. It was cute that Troy had taken the time to not only buy a jersey to impress her, but even study up on baseball so he could relate to her.

It was cute. It was all cute. She liked it, she really did.

Just like she liked the idea of moving down to Houston, where there were…

Her thoughts hit a brick wall just then. Thinking about it now, she had absolutely no idea what was in Houston. Oil rigs, cowboys who lassoed women for practice, and cow skulls on every wall?

Why did I apply for a job in Texas, of all places? I'm trying to get away from hicks, not move in with them. Houston isn't any better than Franklin; it's just bigger. More Wranglers doesn't equal civilization.

"Are you okay?" Troy asked, interrupting her internal debate. "You seem…upset today."

"I'm fine," she said, plastering a smile on her face. "It was just another long week at work and I'm not looking forward to everything that I need to get done this next week."

Troy squeezed her against his side. "I hope the newspaper appreciates what a hard worker you are," he said loyally, and pressed a kiss to her forehead.

"Thanks," she said, but she didn't feel thankful. She felt grumpy and out of sorts and on edge and…

Totally not her.

And she'd be damned if she had any idea why.

CHAPTER 21

TROY

HE WAS EATING BREAKFAST with Aunt and Uncle Horvath, listening to Aunt Horvath discuss which vegetables she needed to get canned out of the garden before the first freeze hit, when there was a knock at the back door. They all just froze and then looked at each other, waiting for someone else to know what was going on, but it was clear by the expression on his aunt and uncle's faces that they were just as much in the dark as Troy was. He stood up to go answer the knock when the door creaked open, and who but Bryce stuck his head around the corner of it.

Troy just gaped at him. He would've expected to find Santa Claus on the other side of the door before finding Bryce.

"Surprise!" Troy's cousin said, a huge grin on his face.

"Bryce!" Aunt Horvath scolded, her hand over her heart with the shock of it all. "You're going to kill an old lady off by doing that. Come here and give your momma a kiss."

Uncle Horvath, normally a fairly taciturn man, looked positively stunned and more than a little emotional. "Bryce," he said, but his voice cracked, giving the depths of his feelings away. "Son…what are you…I can't believe you're here."

Bryce gave a bone-cracking squeeze to his mom, a full-body hug to Troy, and then a manly one-arm squeeze with his dad. Uncle Horvath wasn't much for hugging people, not even his own child who he hadn't seen in two years.

"Surprise!" Bryce said again, his grin even

bigger, if that was possible. It was clear that he'd been looking forward to shocking his parents for quite some time, and now that he'd done it, was more than a little pleased with himself. "I'm on leave with the Air Force and wanted to come home to visit for a bit. I figured you guys still had my old room made up, or at least a couch for me to sleep on."

"Of course you've got your own room," Aunt Horvath said, dabbing the edges of her eyes with her apron. "It will always be there for you. I may've moved a bit of sewing into it, but it's still your room. Let me…uhh…uncover the bed. I was just working on some Christmas presents and had everything laid out."

"Christmas?" Bryce asked. "Mom, it's September."

"It takes a long time to make handmade presents. You know that. I'll be right back." She disappeared down the hallway, muttering under her breath about old women's hearts not being made to withstand this kind of shock.

Uncle Horvath gestured Bryce to the fourth,

and usually unused, chair at the breakfast table. "Come, sit. Mom can rustle up a plate for you when she gets back. How long are you planning to stay?" There was hope in his voice that Bryce would give an answer that wasn't, "A week." Uncle Horvath didn't always get along with Bryce – they'd butted heads more than once, and if they were being honest about it, Bryce had joined the Air Force to escape his father's overbearing attitude – but he was still his son, and Troy knew that Uncle Horvath would love to have him there in Long Valley again, for however long Bryce was willing to stay.

"Not real sure at the moment," Bryce said. "I…well, I'd better wait for Mom to come back."

Uncle Horvath's bushy eyebrows went up at that and a gleam of hope in his eye appeared that could've been seen from the International Space Station. "Sounds good," he gruffed out. They began chatting about the unseasonably warm weather and how the crops were this year – both fail-safe topics for any male Idahoan looking to avoid emotions – as Troy sat and watched his cousin quietly.

The close-cropped haircut was flattering on Bryce – still a little weird to see after years of him wearing it long in defiance of his father.

Just to piss him off, if they were gonna be honest about it.

Bryce had only been home once since joining the Air Force, and it hadn't been a real long visit that time. He'd made some excuse about needing to go catch up with some old military friends of his and disappeared before his two-week leave was even halfway over.

"This town is gonna suck me dry," Bryce had told Troy more than once. "It's just...soul destroying. Everything pressing in on you; everything right in your face. Everyone knowing everything about you..."

Troy had listened because that's what Troy did, but inwardly, he couldn't have disagreed more. Sawyer was warm and welcoming and comfortable. It was filled with people who cared about one another, and didn't expect something out of you that you weren't willing to give…like long speeches.

No, in Troy's estimation, Sawyer was just about perfect.

"I got everything cleaned up in there," Aunt Horvath said, bustling back down the hallway and over to the breakfast table. "Are you hungry? Of course you're hungry," she replied, not giving Bryce a chance to say a word. "You always could out-eat Mitchell and Jessie combined together. Let me just put a little something together."

"Bryce here had something he wanted to discuss when you got back," Uncle Horvath told his wife, and just the fact that he'd brought it up spoke volumes to Troy. His uncle was on tenterhooks about whatever it was that Bryce wanted to talk about. Troy could only hope it wasn't something like, "They're sending me to the Middle East for the next ten years and I'm here to say goodbye." It would just kill them to have their boy gone that long.

"Oh?" Aunt Horvath said, looking up from her mixing bowl. "What's going on, dear?" She looked straight at Bryce, her face a combination of terror and hope. Terror at the idea that it was news about some far-off place that the Air Force was gonna be sending him next; hope that Bryce was gonna announce he'd be sticking around for a while.

"The Air Force is struggling with recruitment quotas," Bryce said quietly, "and is asking people who are nearing the end of their term to re-up. I'd been planning on leaving, but they're offering a $15,000 bonus to anyone who signs on for another four-year term."

The tempered excitement in his parents' eyes quickly began to fade away. It was the worst possible news they could've heard, but they were made of stout Hungarian stock and wouldn't dream of dissuading their son from serving their country.

Aunt Horvath recovered first. "Fifteen thousand dollars is a lot of money," she said with a nod, eyes focused on the mixing bowl, not looking up at her son. "You could do a lot with that much money."

Uncle Horvath said nothing, his face inscrutable. Troy knew he'd shut down to avoid showing emotions at the announcement. It wouldn't be fitting to beg his son not to do it. Life was about sacrifices, and the Horvaths weren't about to shirk their responsibilities in bearing some of those sacrifices.

"I have two weeks before I have to report back to Nellis Air Force Base," Bryce said quietly. "I wanted to spend it here, if that's okay."

"You know you're welcome here for as long as you want, dear," Aunt Horvath said, a forced smile firmly planted on her face as she poured pancake batter on the griddle. No one said the words out loud, but they were all thinking it – it was no problem for him to stay for two weeks. It was the leaving at the end of it that was gonna be damn difficult.

Troy watched the devastated faces of his aunt and uncle in silence, their pain reinforcing his duty once again. No matter what Penny thought, he couldn't just turn his back on his family and choose a different profession on a lark. He owed his aunt and uncle almost everything he had, and to hurt them like this, after all three of their children hurt them...

It was unthinkable. Troy was the Horvath child who would continue the family legacy. It was up to him, no matter what he might wish otherwise.

The next few days sped by in a blur of hard work, now that the harvest season was in full swing. All thoughts of trying to woo Penny into staying, all underhanded schemes of making Mrs. Roth happy to further his cause, were pushed aside. His cousin stayed home with Aunt Horvath, helping her bring in the harvest from the garden and get the food into jars in preparation of the upcoming winter.

More than once, Aunt Horvath mentioned how lovely it was to have help this fall, and how she was speeding right through what normally took weeks to get done. Bryce would simply pop a kiss on his mom's cheek and say something like, "Helping my mom is what any good son would do."

Yeah, but you never have, Troy wanted to point out. When Bryce was at home before he joined the military, he hadn't exactly been what one would call a hard worker. He'd fought his parents every step of the way when it came to doing chores, and would often disappear for hours at a time just when an extra pair of hands would've been the most appreciated.

When Bryce had first announced he was gonna join the military, it'd taken every bit of self control that Troy had not to bust up laughing. Bryce, being forced to get up before noon every single day? Bryce, being forced to push himself physically and mentally?

He hadn't said a word, of course, but internally, he'd been laying bets on how long it'd take before Bryce was pushed out of the Air Force. Two months, tops.

And yet, here it was, six years later, and they were begging him to stay in for another four.

Will wonders never cease.

It was on day four of Bryce being home that he pulled Troy off to the side. "Hey, what would you think about me coming with you to the mill today?" he asked after breakfast.

There he was.

There was his old cousin back in full force. He wanted to come to the mill so he could sit in Troy's office and play on his phone, far away from vegetables and hot canning jars and hard work. He'd lasted a full three days of real work before crumbling in the face of it.

It's a damn good thing you didn't join the Marines. I think boot camp would've killed you.

"Sure," Troy said with a shrug. He wasn't Bryce's keeper. As operations manager of the mill, Troy had his own office, dusty and dirty and uninspiring as it was, and there was a real piece-of-shit couch against one wall that Troy sometimes snagged a bit of shut-eye on during the height of the harvest season, rather than wasting the energy of driving home at night. Dollars to donuts, Bryce would be snoring away on it by two that afternoon.

I guess the Air Force wasn't a miracle worker after all.

It wasn't until they got to the mill and Bryce didn't plant his ass on the couch that Troy realized something was up.

"What do you want me to do first?" Bryce asked, looking around the office as if searching for something to do.

"First-st?" Troy echoed, wincing at the stutter but Bryce didn't seem to notice.

"Yeah. What do you need help on here at the mill? I might not have much experience running specialized machinery, but I do have a good back and two strong hands."

Troy simply stared at his cousin, too shocked to say anything. His cousin was asking for something to do? He *wanted* to work hard?

And then the idea came to him, and he felt a tiny, minuscule, itsy-bitsy bit of guilt for the sheer assholishness of it, but mostly, he just wanted to laugh at the sheer genius of it.

"C'mon," he said, pushing the endless paperwork away for a moment and standing up. He could work his way through buyers and price per tonnage in a little bit. Right now, he had a cousin's life to make miserable. "Grab that hard hat and coveralls there," he said, nodding towards his own pair of work clothes hanging from a hook. "You'll need it."

After his cousin pulled the coveralls on, Troy led the way through the mill and towards a back storage area where a stockpile of wheat had gone rotten when the roof sprung a leak that no one noticed for two weeks. The smell of fermenting wheat was enough to knock a grown man on his ass. Troy had been avoiding the task of cleaning it out because it was one of the worst jobs in the mill, and honestly, not even a masochist would enjoy the task. Which was why he didn't just assign someone else to the job – if Troy wasn't willing to do it, he couldn't ask someone else to.

Unless they were *asking* to do it, in which case of course Troy would agree. Who was he to tell his cousin no?

Yup, this would cure Bryce of whatever in- sanity had grabbed a hold of him right quick like. An hour of shoveling putrid, rotting wheat, and Bryce would be begging for a ride back to his parents' house.

CHAPTER 22

PENNY

*P*ENNY SKIMMED DOWN the list of help wanted postings, looking for that magical unicorn where the employer wanted someone with little advertising experience, lots of unhoned potential, and were located in a big city with decent-enough pay that Penny could actually afford to eat on a semi-regular basis.

Definitely a magical unicorn. Maybe even a technicolor, time-hopping magical unicorn. When she'd graduated from college, she hadn't realized how difficult it would be to actually get a job in her field. Everyone would want to hire her, right? But taking a six-year break from it to take care of her mom had hobbled her in ways she just hadn't imagined at the time.

Hobbled. Such a nicer way of saying completely screwed me over.

She spotted it then. PRESTIGIOUS AD-VERTISING FIRM IN SEATTLE WITH RARE GROUND-FLOOR OPENING. She clicked on the listing and began scrolling through it, on the hunt for the usual verbiage that would throw her out of the running from the get-go: Five year's experience required. Or sometimes, even ten year's experience was being demanded. It was definitely an employ-er's market, not an employee's market.

She got to the end of the listing, and slowly scrolled back up again, in shock. She had to have just missed it. She'd look again. The pay was too high, the benefits were too good, for them to not have strict requirements in place.

It wasn't until she'd read through it another two times before she really started to believe it was a possibility for her. *I could actually work in Seattle!* With a deep breath, she began tailoring her resumé specifically for this job. She didn't do that with every job, but she did with the ones that she really, really wanted.

And she really, really wanted this one.

The memory of Troy's intense green eyes and short, spiky eyelashes popped into her mind, unbidden, but she pushed it away just as quickly. Now was not the time to go soft. This was her chance – she could feel it in her bones. She couldn't let a cowboy get in the way of making her dream come true, no matter how stunning his eyes were.

CHAPTER 23

TROY

IT WAS THE END of week one of Bryce's stay at his parents' house, and as far as Troy could tell, his cousin had had a personality transplant while in the military. There was nothing else to explain the miracle away. Despite Troy giving him every dirty, disgusting job he could think of, Bryce never once complained, tried to hide, or even looked grumpy. The harder he was working, the happier he seemed to be.

Definitely a personality transplant.

They were driving home late on Saturday night, both of them yawning and feeling more than a little worn down at the pace required by the mill, when Bryce turned to Troy. "Do you work this hard all the time?" he asked around another yawn.

"No, only during harvest-st." He hated the stutter, but as usual, his cousin passed it on by without comment.

"That's good. I was starting to think you were some sort of Superman, to keep this up week after week. I haven't pushed myself this hard since boot camp. I think the Air Force should send its recruits to work at the mill for a month. They'd come out the other side hardened warriors. Or at least in a lot better shape."

Troy laughed a little at that. It was true that during harvest season especially, the mill wasn't for the faint of heart. Which was why he was still more than a little stunned that his cousin hadn't wimped out yet. Troy was used to the brutal pace, and always knew that at the end of the season, he had normalcy to look forward to. Bryce, on the other hand, was doing this on his vacation.

Troy felt a slightly larger sliver of guilt work its way through his soul at that thought. Come Monday, he'd take it a little easier on Bryce, if he was still up for helping out.

"Harvest-st season is always rough. You picked a good time to come help out." His cousin snorted with laughter at that, and Troy turned to him for just a moment, daring to take his eyes off the road so Bryce could see how serious he was being. "No, honestly. Having your help this year has made this the easiest fall I can remember in a real long time."

He kinda felt like he was having an out-of-body experience, saying something like that, but it was true nonetheless. He was gonna miss his cousin when he went back, something he'd *never* expected to have happen. He'd liked his cousin all right growing up, but it was hard not to resent him when he'd caused so many problems and heartaches to his parents. Maybe Aunt and Uncle Horvath weren't perfect, but they deserved respect from their son, and that wasn't something Bryce had ever bothered to give them.

Until now.

After Troy's little speech, he could tell there was something Bryce wanted to say in return, and it was important. It was there in the air of the truck – an expectancy. Since Troy spent a lot more time listening than he did talking, he'd become quite the observer of people and no matter how much of a personality transplant Bryce'd had, he was still human. Something was up.

"I know the mill is yours," Bryce said in a rush as Troy pulled into his regular parking spot at the house and cut the engine, "and I'm not trying to take that away from you. But do you think there's a job for me there, too?"

Troy stared at his cousin in the darkness, trying to read his expression in lighting an owl would struggle in. There was no moon tonight, and living far out in the countryside like they did, the only light was from the dim stars overhead.

"Let's go inside," Troy said finally, wanting some light to be shed on the subject – literally.

Sparky jumped out of the bed of the truck

and trotted to Troy's side, following them inside where she made a beeline for her food bowl.

"You're wanting to work at the mill?" he asked Bryce, once they were settled down on the couch. "For how long? You're leaving again in a week."

Bryce shook his head. "When I told Mom and Dad about the bonus, they just assumed I was gonna take it. I didn't say anything because I didn't want to get their hopes up, but these two weeks are for me to figure out what I'm gonna do. I haven't signed the re-enlistment papers yet. I love the Air Force and all it's done for me, but I'm ready to move on. The money is a big enticement, but I've been saving for a while, so actually, it's not nearly as big of an enticement as you might think. I've got quite a bit more than that in savings." He shrugged.

Troy nodded, trying to keep his face flat as he thought through what Bryce was saying. He hadn't realized it at the time, but Bryce was right — he'd never actually said he'd re-up. Everyone had just assumed it when he'd told them how big the bonus was.

"You want to work at the mill, though?" Troy asked, not bothering to hide his surprise. "You may not want to re-up but that doesn't mean you have to come back to Sawyer and work in the Horvath Mill." Maybe all this was, was a failure of imagination. Maybe it just hadn't occurred to Bryce that there were other options. As nutty as that seemed, it seemed less nutty than Bryce wanting to work at the *mill*.

Just then, Sparky laid her head on Troy's lap, apparently done with her evening meal. She closed her eyes in blissful repose as Troy stroked her head. She wasn't real comfortable around Bryce yet – she was sitting on the far side from him, almost like she was using Troy as a shield between them – but pettings were worth venturing this close.

Bryce chuckled a little at that. "I think I deserved that," he said ruefully. "As hard as I tried to get out of work as a kid, I imagine it seems more than a little bizarre that I'd suddenly be developing an interest in it."

Troy didn't say a word; he was sure his face said it all.

"Joining the Air Force was the best thing I ever did. Taught me how to think about others before myself. Taught me how to get my lazy ass out of bed, and work hard. But the longer I've been away, the more I've come to miss Sawyer. At first I thought I was just romanticizing it, you know? Remembering the good stuff; forgetting the bad. And I'm sure there's some of that going on. But that's why I wanted to work this past week at the mill and with Mom at home, without the pressure from you or Mom and Dad knowing what I was thinking about. Otherwise, you know Mom would've spent the last week dropping hints the size of nuclear bombs about how much she misses having her children around, and whatever did she do wrong that her kids all left home and moved far away. If she thought she had even a smidgen of a chance of convincing me to stay here, she would've used every ounce of guilt she could muster on me to make me do it. And Mom can muster a *lot* of guilt."

Troy laughed at that. He didn't know if his cousin was romanticizing anything else, but he sure had a clear-eyed view of his mother. They both loved her dearly, but guilt was one of her favorite trips to send others on.

"You've been here for my parents, unlike any of us three kids ever were," Bryce said seriously. "When the rest of us were running for the hills, you were working your ass off at that mill and taking care of Mom and Dad through it all. Some might think it's nepotism that you're the operations manager of the mill, but it isn't. You work as hard as my dad does, and that's really saying something. You deserve that mill when Dad finally retires. But I'd like a place there too, if you'll have me. I don't want to start at the top – I'll start as the shop boy, pushing a broom. Work my way up the ranks, if I ever do. I trust you to be fair and treat me like you would any employee. I just need to know if I have a place before I turn down the Air Force."

Troy sat and stared in silence at his cousin for an eternity, stretching into two. Bryce didn't shift on the couch, or get antsy, or demand an answer. He just waited quietly for Troy's verdict. He probably knew as well as anyone that rushing Troy into a decision just didn't work. Troy didn't do rushed.

But in this instance, it was all coming together so perfectly, it hurt a little. There was an ache in Troy's chest – a hope that stung from its perfection. If he tried for this and it didn't work out, it'd devastate him. It was so much safer not to give it a shot, not to ruin what little he knew he had.

But if he could make it work, he could have so much more…

"Bryce, I've got an idea."

CHAPTER 24

PENNY

S HE HUMMED as she put her lipstick on and then dabbed her lips with a tissue. There – perfect.

Troy had insinuated that tonight was going to be a special night, and whatever he had in mind, she wanted to look damn good for it. She had good news of her own – she'd just finished the final round of interviews via Skype with Edge Advertising, Inc, and was waiting to hear back on whether she got the job. It was down to her and two other finalists. She had a damn good feeling about this one. Everything had just seemed to click together.

I'll have to leave Troy behind, though.

The pain of that lanced through her and she nearly groaned out loud at the thought. If only he'd come with her – they could both start over fresh in Seattle. She could work for Edge Advertising while Troy could…

She heard his knock on the front door before she managed to come up with a job for him. Well, something, anyway. Seattle was a big place. Lots to do. He could find something. He'd enjoy it more than working at the mill, for sure. No matter what he tried to tell himself, working there seemed to be sucking the soul right out of him.

"You here?" Troy called out as he walked in.

"Coming!" she said, and headed down the hallway and into the living room. She came to an abrupt stop when she saw Troy. "Handsome" didn't even come close to describing him. That was a bit like describing the sun as "bright." Well, yeah, of course, but there was so much more to it. He was wearing a charcoal-colored suit, light purple shirt, and eggplant-colored tie. He looked downright debonair.

Citified, even.

Stunning, that.

"Wow," she breathed. "Troy…you've been holding out on me! All this time, you've had me convinced you're nothing but a country boy."

"I am a country boy," he said with a boyish grin, "but I also know how to find upscale shops on occasion."

"Color me impressed," she murmured, and slipped into her sparkling spiked high heels. Now with his height advantage reduced, it was easier for her to wrap her arms around his neck and pull him down for a quick kiss. "I could stand to see this city boy a little more often," she murmured against his lips.

Of course, she wouldn't be seeing him much if she got the job and moved to Seattle, but she chose to ignore that problem. She'd gotten pretty good at blocking that fact out of her mind over the past several months and was now a certified pro in Avoidance Behaviors.

Hmmm…too bad that wasn't a skill she could market on her resumé.

Troy helped her into the truck and then hurried around to his side, pointing the truck towards Sawyer, or maybe Boise. He still hadn't told her where they were going, and despite her rather blunt hints over the past couple of days that he really ought to give her something to go on, he hadn't let out a peep. She thought about pulling her skirt up her thigh a little and showing some skin; see if she could get him to break then, but decided that waiting to find out wouldn't *actually* kill her. She should behave herself. It'd be embarrassing to explain to the sheriff that they'd ended up in the ditch because she'd been doing her best to seduce the truth out of Troy.

"Any follow-up on the new resort?" he asked as they drove, passing the ever-present fields of Black Angus cows. The deciduous trees dotting the fence lines were all a brilliant red and orange, and she wondered for a moment what the train ride would be like now that it was fall.

I won't find out because I'm leaving. Probably.

Which I'm happy about. Definitely.

"No, not at the moment. The developers are looking for some deep-pocketed investors so they're sort of stalled out until they get the funding lined up." She shrugged. "The letters to the editor have died off; there for a bit, that's all we were running on the opinion page. It seems like everyone has an opinion, and a strong one at that. Either this is the best thing to ever happen to Long Valley, or the worst idea in the history of mankind. There doesn't appear to be an in-between."

Troy chuckled a little at that. "I guess I'm the odd ball out, then," he said with a shrug of his own. "I can see the good and the bad. I'm not sure how to feel about it."

"So how are things going with your cousin Bryce?" she asked. "You haven't said much since he got home and you started working his ass off. Is he still working hard, or has he started wimping out on you?"

"Would you believe, he's turned into a damn hard worker. Never would've guessed."

He shook his head in wonder. "I keep wanting to feel his head for a fever. Doesn't seem a damn thing like the same guy I've known all my life. The military sure does work miracles."

She reached over and intertwined her fingers into his. "Sounds like the Air Force is the best thing that could've ever happened to him. Is he heading back soon?"

"I'm…I'm not sure," he murmured, but he seemed…off. Like he was holding something back. Before she could ask him what he was thinking about, he lifted her hand to his lips and pressed a kiss to it. "How's your mom taking that loss to the Cleveland Indians? I bet she was a bear to be around after that. Going into an extra inning and then st-st-still losing against-st *Cleveland*…"

Penny laughed. "Two days. Two days of mourning. Wore all black. I was just sure she was going to dot ashes from the fireplace on her forehead." She shook her head as she chuckled again. "I don't care about baseball, which makes her just nuts. What I'm thrilled about is the clean bill of health from the doctor that she got just yesterday. Said she's healthy as a horse and will probably outlive me. Which, considering how stubborn my mom is, is probably true. If the Grim Reaper came knocking at the door, I think she'd just tell him to buzz off."

"I'm pretty sure she already has," Troy said softly. "Twice."

"Hmmm…Good point. My mom is tough as nails. The Grim Reaper is probably scared of her at this point."

They both laughed, but again, Troy seemed…stiff. Hesitant. They came in the far side of Sawyer, but instead of passing on through to Boise, he took a left into the parking lot of the old mill, where he cut the engine.

The old mill?

He grinned at her, a boyish excitement mixed with nerves that practically vibrated off him. She opened her mouth to ask him what was going on – this was an awfully dirty place to wear such fancy clothes – but he shook his head. "You'll see," he said mysteriously, before hurrying to her side of the truck to help her out.

Her arm through his, they made their way across the parking lot, the intrigue growing by the minute. The sliding doors on the side of the mill were already open, and draped above the doors were twinkling lights, casting a warm, soft glow into the twilight of the evening.

"Oh, pretty!" she exclaimed, and he squeezed her arm.

"Wait until you see inside," he said, and again, the boyish excitement was practically radiating off him.

As they took the last few steps and she could finally see inside of the old mill, she realized that he had every right to be excited and proud. "Troy," she gasped, somehow making his one-syllable name sound like two. "I... wow...who helped you with this?!"

There were strings of lights crisscrossing overhead, making the cavernous room feel more intimate and cozy than it would otherwise. Old, decorative doors were set up, blocking off the rest of the mill from view, bringing everything in close. The flickering of the candles, the bouquets of flowers, an old farm table set for two…

It looked Instagram ready.

Truth time: She thought the world of Troy, but she'd seen his office at the mill. She'd seen his house. Décor was *not* his strong suit. There was *no way* he did this himself.

And then she peered closer at the shabby chic doors.

"Just a minute here," she gasped, realization dawning on her, and then she broke out laughing. "My mother! I'd recognize those doors anywhere. She's been storing them up in the attic for years. I kept telling her that there wasn't a damn place to fit them in the house and she needed to get rid of them, but she kept insisting they'd be used one day, and here they are." She shook her head. "No wonder Mom's been so happy this week, even with the Dodgers losing. Give her a place to decorate and she just goes crazy. Wait!" She turned and glared at him, hands on her hips. "You *knew* my mom wore black and was in mourning this week! If you two were working on this together…"

Troy grinned, totally unrepentant. "I couldn't let the cat out of the bag too quickly. It would've ruined the surprise."

"Shit," she groaned. "Do you realize that now I have to listen to my mother say 'I told you so!' for the next ten years, at least? She's going to point to her using these doors as a reason to hoard even more."

"Honestly, it wasn't only the doors," he admitted freely. "Look around, and I'm sure you'll recognize more. I bought the flowers from Carla at Happy Petals. Otherwise, this was all your mom."

Penny glared at him in mock anger. "This meal we're about to eat better be damn tasty to make up for all of the trouble you just caused," she warned him. "Otherwise, I might make you kiss me to make up for it."

"And that'd be simply tragic…" he murmured, pulling her up against his broad chest and giving her the thorough hello kiss he'd skipped when he'd picked her up. She realized now that he'd been so nervous, he hadn't been able to properly kiss her, and she'd been so curious about where they were going on this mysterious date, she hadn't even noticed the oversight.

Well, she noticed it now. She felt herself melting into him as the fire roared stronger between them. The world narrowed to just the two of them and their lips and she dug her fingers into his shoulders, holding onto him as the world spun around them…

In a daze, she finally registered that he was pulling back, and off balance, she pulled back a bit also, blinking as the world swam into focus. "Whoa," she breathed.

"Yeah," he murmured, and brushed a stray curl out of her face. "We…uhh…better eat." His voice was cracked and trembling a bit and even in the romantic, dim lighting, she could tell his pupils were blown. She wondered if she had that same look of naked desire on her face, and then cursed where they were. No matter how cutesy her mother had managed to make it in here, it still wasn't overly clean, and there certainly wasn't a bed in sight. "Carmelita will be very upset if we let her food get cold," Troy added.

"We definitely can't make her angry!" Penny said with a forced laugh, smoothing down the front of her shirt, trying to regain her equilibrium. "Not if we want tamales again."

"Exactly my thoughts." Troy escorted her over to the farm-style table set for two, floating white candles in a glass bowl adding to the ambiance. After she was settled in her chair, a posh affair with a linen slipcover that draped to the cement floor, Troy unzipped something – it was too dark for her to see what it was – and pulled two plates out, already loaded up with food. Carmelita had apparently gone Western tonight, with roast beef, mashed potatoes, green beans, and rolls on the plate, along with small salads in hand-carved wooden bowls.

"You guys really thought of everything, didn't you?" Penny said when Troy uncorked a bottle of wine and poured a glass for her, and then some water for him.

"It's the same wine that we drank at the

arts fair in Franklin on our first-st date," he told her. "I tracked it down. You'd seemed to really like it…" He trailed off and shrugged, apparently a little embarrassed by his sentimental gesture.

She took a sip of the pink moscato and let out a happy sigh. "I can't believe you did that," she said softly, the dancing flames setting his green eyes ablaze. The warmth of the wine was already beginning to spread through her veins. "I can't believe any of this."

He picked up her hand and kissed the back of it. "A beautiful date for a beautiful lady," he murmured.

A little bit of panic prickled the back of her neck then. Even as they picked up their silverware and began to chit-chat about life and how upset Sparky had been at being left at home instead of coming on this date, and how Wanda had struggled to keep this whole thing a secret, Penny worried.

She didn't want to. After all, who complained about a handsome man – who kissed better than Fabio – setting up a date like this, going through all of this work and expense?

Answer: Penny Roth, that's who.

Even as Troy laughed, showing off his pearly white teeth and she smiled back, she was feeling…unsettled.

Why? What's wrong? Why can't I just enjoy this?

Because no man does all of this for someone he doesn't love, that's why.

Sure, some guys might do this in order to "score" and get a girl in bed, but she was already a willing participant there. No reason to wine and dine her just to make that happen.

They'd been floating along in this happy, blasé world, no commitments, no strings attached, and then he started impressing her mother, which made her worried. And now he was trying really hard to impress her, which made her even more worried.

He isn't going to ruin this. Not after all this time. He's too smart for that. I've been too straightforward. He knows better.

"So, big news," he said, breaking into her thoughts.

"Oh?" she said, taking a small bite of the rare roast beef. *Heaven.* She wondered for a moment if she could get away with kidnapping Carmelita and taking her to Seattle with her.

"Bryce wants to st-st-stay here in Long Valley. He's turning down the bonus and getting out of the Air Force."

She stared at him, mouth agape, fork halfway to her mouth. "No way," she finally whispered.

"Yes way," he said, laughing, the joy lighting up his whole face. "He asked me if I'd hire him on at the mill, and—"

Please tell me you did it. Please tell me you did it.

"—I told him I'd do one better than that. I offered him the mill."

"Yes! I'm so proud of you!" Penny hollered, practically launching herself across the table at him. "You did it – you really did it!" She was covering his face with kisses as he laughed and settled her further down onto his lap.

"I did," he said when she finally quit squealing with joy long enough for him to speak. "I talked to Aunt and Uncle Horvath and we made a deal. For all of my work at the mill over the years, I get my inheritance now, and nothing later when they pass away." He looked slightly ill at the idea of discussing his second set of parents dying, and hurried on. "They're deeding this mill over to me, and a $50,000 loan at no interest-st, and no pay- ments for the first-st five years, to give me time to make a go of it. I want to do what you suggest-st-sted – a farmer's market every Saturday in here. People can rent booths from me – it's an indoor space so it'll happen no matter what. No worrying about the weather. It'll double as my leatherworking shop during the week. Oh, and my house on the back forty of my aunt and uncle's property – they're splitting it off along with five acres and giving it to me. It's the other half of my inheritance."

"I cannot believe it," Penny breathed, her mind spinning. "Honestly, I'm just in shock. Bryce wants to take over the mill?! The military really did change him!" She hadn't known him before he joined, of course, and had only met him once on this visit home, but Troy had told her plenty of stories of him growing up.

"I kinda want to send the Air Force a thank-you letter," Troy admitted with a broad grin. "I never would've guessed it."

Penny finally slipped off his lap and sat back down in her chair, staring at Troy across the table. "You've been a busy little bee," she said, a little wounded that he'd kept such huge news from her. "Working all of this out with your aunt and uncle and cousin, and then cleaning and decorating the mill...what do your parents have to say about it?"

Troy shrugged. "My parents know Long Valley is my home. I visit them in Boise when I get groceries and things, but they never expected me to move back there, especially since I was supposed to take over the mill. So I don't think they really care one way or the other, except that they want me to be happy. It's been so long since I lived with them, they feel more like my aunt and uncle, and my aunt and uncle feel a lot more like my parents. It's...weird, I know."

"I have a mother who wears black when her baseball team loses, and hoards old doors in her attic. I wouldn't know how to relate to a normal family, honestly." Not to mention Penny doing the books for her mom and making sure she didn't spend her way into bankruptcy.

No, her family was definitely not "normal" in the least.

She settled into her chair and took another bite of her potatoes, savoring the homemade gravy drizzled on top, when she felt a little deflation in her joy bubble. She'd been pushing Troy to do something with this old mill and not take over the new one for what felt like months, but now that it was really happening, she realized a fatal flaw in her plan:

This meant he wouldn't be coming with her when she left.

Somehow, without really thinking it through, she'd believed that he should take over the old mill and make it his, *and* also follow her wherever she ended up. Now that reality had slapped her across the face, she felt a little

stupid for not putting those two thoughts together and realizing that they wouldn't both
work. *Duh.* He was going to be living his dream,
and that meant staying right here in Long
Valley.

Right in the area that made her feel smoth-
ered alive. Panicked. Overwhelmed.

*Well then, it's a good thing I knew the rules from
the beginning and made sure not to fall in love, right?*

She felt slightly ill. She didn't know why;
she should be thrilled. But her stomach was
twisting and turning and tying itself into knots.

"Are you okay?" Troy asked, reaching out
and taking her hand. "You look a little pale."

"Oh, I'm fine," she reassured him breezily,
taking another sip of her wine.

Or at least that's what she liked to pretend
happened. More likely that the tremble in her
voice and hand was noticeable from the moon
and Troy absolutely knew that she was full of
shit, but ever the gentleman, he didn't push it.

"There's one more thing…"

"Yeah?" she said brightly, staring down at
her plate, spending forever picking just the

right green bean to spear with her fork. So many choices. So hard to choose. Whichever one was she going to eat?

"Penny?" Troy whispered. "Are you—?"

"I'm great!" she announced forcefully and speared a green bean at random. "What else is there?" she asked politely, staring at Troy's nose, not quite brave enough to look him in the eye, as she chewed the bean into paste. She really needed to just take another bite but that meant making a choice – again – and suddenly, she felt oh-so-overwhelmed by the idea of choices.

"I want you to st-st-stay here."

The words hung in the air between them, almost visible, like a brick wall that had slammed down out of nowhere.

"I've been thinking," he rushed on. "You could open a graphic arts company here. In this mill. It's perfect. Then you don't have to work for someone else. You would own your own business. There isn't another graphics company in the whole valley." The words were spilling ever faster out of him now, like a dam that had been breached, spilling over, smothering her alive. He could tell she was going to say no, and she knew he could tell she was going to say no, and he was fighting with words to keep it from happening. "You're good with finances and anything you need help on, Jennifer Miller could be there for you. You don't have to leave."

"I can't stay here!" she cried, trying to push back against the wall of words, to stop him before he did something he'd hate himself for later, like beg her to stay. "You've always known that. I've never lied. I've never kept that from you. I have to leave. Don't you understand? This town will smother me alive. I can't *breathe* here. I can't breathe…"

She was hyperventilating then, gasping in the air but not getting any oxygen and she was going to die, literally die, and it was Long Valley that was going to do it to her. The world began to spin around her, and then Troy was shoving her head between her legs and telling her to take a deep breath, hold it, breathe out, breathe in, hold it, he was counting for her, and finally the tightness began to fade away, and the world began to come back again, and ashamed, she pushed herself upright.

"Do you need some water?" Troy asked quietly, his eyes searching her face even as he held his glass out to her. Ever the gentleman. Ever the thoughtful guy she'd fallen in love with.

No! She had *not* fallen in love with Troy Horvath. She knew better, dammit. She knew not to do that, so she hadn't. She clung to that thought with all her might.

"I'm good," she said woodenly, shaking her head. "I think I'd like to go home."

Quietly, he stood up and helped her out of her chair, escorting her to the door. "You don't have to decide right now," he said quietly. "It will be a lot of work to bring this mill back to life—"

"You don't get it!" she spat out, yanking her arm out of his and storming towards the truck. "I. Can't. Stay. Here. Do you want me to draw you a diagram? Tattoo it across your forehead?

The only reason I haven't gone stark-raving mad was because I knew I was leaving! I always knew I was leaving. And now you're trying to take that away from me." She yanked the passenger door open and struggled her way inside, realizing how much harder it was to get into his giant truck in heels and a skirt when Troy wasn't helping her. All these months and she'd never once gotten in or out without his helping hand.

He was such a gentleman. Such an Idahoan cowboy down to his well-worn boots.

Everything she didn't want in a man. Well, other than being handsome and kind and a hard worker and a good man, that was.

The tears were blurring the world around her, and there was a part of her that was grateful for that. Then she wouldn't have to see Troy's face and the pain sure to be written there.

He got into the truck silently and began heading back to Franklin. "I just-st thought you'd eventually warm to the idea if you could see how to be a graphic artist-st *and* stay in

Long Valley," he finally said in the painful silence. "I didn't think—"

"That everything I told you was actually *true*?!" she said snidely. "Yeah, I can see how that could be confusing for you. How many times, Troy? How many times have I said that I *had* to leave here?"

She wanted him to hurt. She wanted him to be in pain like she was in pain. It was too dark in the cab of the truck for her to see his expression, but what she did know was how the pain of it all was radiating through her like a stab wound. She too had had a dream of him coming with her, and that dream too had died tonight. It was a dream that didn't make much sense on the face of it, but that didn't make its failure any less painful.

"My mom…" she groaned suddenly, the full implication of what had just happened hitting her anew. "My mom knows all about this plan, doesn't she? That's why she helped decorate. Well, and because my mother loves to decorate. But she was hoping that I'd stay here, and you made her believe that it was a possibility and now I'm going to have to hear about it for the rest of my life, that I *could* have stayed in Long Valley if only, but no, I'm too stupid and rebellious to, and…do you have any idea how miserable you've made my life? She will *never* let this go."

"Only as miserable as you've made mine!" he shouted, cutting her off. She gaped at him. He didn't have much of a temper but when it lit on fire, things got nasty. She remembered the last time it had, and the name he'd called her. "I'm sorry, okay?" he said bitingly. "It's a terrible crime I committed, of falling in love with a gorgeous, funny woman who pushes me to live up to my full potential. I don't know what in the hell I was thinking! St-st-string me up from the nearest tree for that crime."

"I told you not to!" She was fighting back for her life, then, because surely this amount of pain would kill her. "I told you and told you and told you. Don't take it out on me when you're finally forced to deal with reality. I never lied to you, Troy Horvath. Not once. Don't lay this at my feet!"

"No, what I laid at your feet was my heart," he said calmly. It was a strange, painful calm, like he'd just shut himself down. Like they were strangers passing in the street. "You used one of your high heels to crush it. I hope you've enjoyed yourself."

He pulled into the parking lot in front of her apartment, threw the truck into park, and then sat there, not moving. Waiting for her to get out of his life.

It was strangely painful how much that hurt, she mused as she pushed herself out of the truck and to the pavement of the parking lot. She listened to the squeal of his tires as he peeled out and onto the street. She didn't know what she expected – he wasn't going to gently escort her to her door and kiss her goodnight. But still, he'd been such a gentleman all this time, helping her in and out of the truck every time, to the point that it was just natural. She'd thought it smothering and quaint at first – she was a grown woman and could walk on her own, thankyouverymuch – but now...

He was done with her.

She got the front door open and leaned against the wall once she got inside, trying to take deep breaths, trying to…

She sank down the wall and dropped to her ass on the floor with a thud, the pain pouring out of her in waves. She'd wanted to keep him at arm's length, and she'd wanted him to move with her when she got a job, and she'd wanted him to take over the old mill to make a go of it, and she'd wanted to remain friends no matter what happened…

It was a big jumble now, a big mess in her mind of conflicting desires and thoughts and all she knew was that somehow, she'd screwed this all up. Despite her very best efforts, she'd made a muck of things beyond any sort of repair.

She let the tears flow out of her in the darkness. There was nothing else to do.

CHAPTER 25

TROY

Six weeks later...

THE BURN FROM THE CHEMICALS made Troy's eyes sting and his arm was aching from days of scrubbing but still, he kept at it. Moose and Levi, fellow firefighters on the Sawyer City Fire Department, were hard at work on the wall opposite him. Being both best friends and of the male gender, they were of course flipping each other shit incessantly as they worked. It was difficult to suppress the pang of jealousy as he listened to them razz each other. He'd never really had the kind of relationship that Levi and Moose shared, that deep friendship where you could tell each other anything, at least not until—

He forced himself to stop there. No reason to go down that road. Again. It was well worn and full of dangerous potholes that could suck him in for days.

Instead, he listened quietly as the two started in on a contest to see who could clean the most bricks in five minutes. Not surprisingly, the trash talking started as quickly as the competition did. Troy gave them six minutes before they started asking him to be the judge — six minutes thirty on the outside. They were too competitive to let the other one win without a fight.

On the other hand, Troy had no doubt that either one would lay down their life for the other without blinking. It was just who they were.

After the training session down at the fire station had ended last night, Jaxson had asked him about the old mill and how the progress was coming along. Troy had instinctively tensed up – Jaxson didn't know it, of course, nor did anyone else, but the new fire chief had to be one of Troy's least favorite people on the planet. He seemed all right when it came to having a work ethic – at least he had one, anyway – but still, all of the snide comments that Jaxson had made over the past 11 months about what a shitty job Uncle Horvath had been doing as the fire chief before Jaxson took over…

It'd been hard for Troy to bite his tongue and not say anything. His uncle had been doing a damn fine job of it, considering his time restraints. He hadn't been a full-time employee like Jaxson was. Uncle Horvath had had a mill to run in his "spare" time. Of *course* he hadn't gotten as much done as Jaxson did, and it was a real assholish move for Jaxson to badmouth his predecessor like that. Jaxson didn't get what it was like to live in a small town and have a hundred different commitments, because everyone had to wear two or even three hats at a time. He was *just* the fire chief and in a town this size, that was a real luxury. The way Troy saw it, he had the quintessential city slicker outlook on life.

What is it with city slickers in this town, anyway?

The thought sent pain lancing through him again but he grimly pushed it away, choosing to simply scrub harder instead. If he just worked hard enough, he was sure he could scrub a certain city slicker right out of his mind.

But Jaxson's question after the firefighter training had been innocuous enough, and so Troy had tried to answer casually, not revealing his inner turmoil about Jaxson's presence in Sawyer. He'd told the group that the mill was "coming along" but apparently hadn't been convincing enough that he was actually making progress because before he knew it, the guys were all volunteering different times that they could come on down and help out.

Being a Saturday and all, today was a prime time for most of the guys to show up, and Abby, Wyatt, and Juan had already made their appearance that morning. They'd had to leave at noon for a family event, but Moose and Levi showed up just about that time, so it worked out pretty well in Troy's estimation. He only had one full wall left to scrub clean of the soot and damage from the fire, and two partial walls.

Okay, so that wasn't a cheerful thought after all. One whole wall *and* two partial walls?! It was such a slow and painstaking process to clean these damn bricks, the project just seemed to stretch out in front of him, endless and daunting, not to mention smelly as hell. If he never saw a can of oven cleaner again, it'd be too soon. The way he was tearing through the cans of the stuff, he really ought to be buying it in a giant vat from Costco. He had visions of pouring gallons on the wall and just letting it cascade down the dirty bricks. He'd have to wear a full body suit but it'd be worth—

"Hey, Jaxson!" Moose called out in greeting, and surprised, Troy used the excuse to drop the green scrubber into the bucket and turn to the open doorway. There stood the new fire chief, his wife's Great Dane by his side along with his two boys. "I didn't know you were coming today."

Jaxson shot them all an easy grin. "Sugar is in the nesting stage of her pregnancy, and she's informed me that I either leave the house and let her work, or she Spartan kicks my ass out the door. So, I thought I'd come down and bring some helpers with me."

"Wow," the older boy said as he looked around. He appeared to be maybe seven or eight years old. Troy had met him a few times, most memorably at Jaxson and Sugar's wedding, but couldn't remember his name at the moment for the life of him. "This place is *huge*."

Troy moved his way down the ladder, thrilled to have an excuse to take a break from scrubbing. At this point, he'd take almost any excuse to step away from the project. Honest to God, he wasn't sure if he'd ever be able to lift his left arm above his head again. Before he could say anything, though, the younger boy moved towards Sparky that'd been busy greeting the Great Dane, each of them sniffing each other's asses in true doggy greeting style.

"What's your dog's name?" the little boy asked, reaching for Sparky.

"Don't—" Troy barked out…just as Sparky licked the boy's hand.

Okay, so Sparky clearly didn't find this kid to be a threat. Good to know.

"Um, Sparky," Troy said, instantly deciding that if he ignored his outburst, everyone else would follow his lead. "Moose was the one who found her. Up in a wildfire."

"Really?" the little boy gasped, his eyes wide as he looked at Moose. "Did you have to carry Sparky out of the fire?"

"More like drag her," Moose said with a laugh. "She doesn't like everyone, and wasn't too fond of me being close to her." He watched the younger boy who was in the process of getting a dual face bath – one from the Great Dane, one from the setter. "I think she's your friend, though."

"Dogs like me," the boy said confidently and as Troy looked at him, packed between the two dogs, both of them loving on him, he had to agree with the kid. He wasn't boasting, but simply stating the truth.

"Well, we're here to help, not get face baths from the dogs," Jaxson said firmly. "Troy, what can we help with?"

Troy froze, not sure of what to say. It was hard to know what jobs to give to two little boys. Having them scrub walls with caustic oven cleaner didn't seem like a great idea.

"What about back there?" Jaxson asked, pointing towards the far end of the building, apparently realizing that Troy was in need of some help in coming up with suggestions. "It looks like it could use a good sweeping, and the windows are low enough that the boys could wash them – at least the bottom part."

"Good idea," Troy said, grateful for the help. It really was too bad Jaxson was a know-it-all prick. He could be a nice guy at times.

"We brought our own supplies just in case," Jaxson said. "Aiden, Frankie, go get the stuff out of the Explorer. We've got some cleaning to do."

With raised eyebrows, Troy watched the two boys obediently head towards the open doors without complaint. Getting kids to listen like that was impressive. The only other time Troy had seen Jaxson with his sons was on the day of Jaxson and Sugar's wedding, and they'd been a real handful then. It'd been another mark against him in Troy's book – for heaven's sakes, Jaxson couldn't even keep his kids under control, how was he supposed to run a fire department – but watching them now, he wondered if it'd just been the excitement of the day that'd caused them to be…less than well behaved. Although the audience at the wedding had thought their shenanigans were cute and had laughed along at them, Troy hadn't been impressed.

His parents and his aunt and uncle…neither set of parental figures would've allowed him to act like that without a paddling in public over it.

"How's the pregnancy going?" Levi rumbled, his deep voice echoing in the cavernous mill. "Is Sugar sick a lot?"

Jaxson shrugged a little. "Some," he said. "The bakery is hard because of all of the smells. She's suddenly decided that sugar is a terrible, terrible thing and won't bring donuts or cakes home anymore." He looked mournfully down at his perfectly flat stomach. "I've already lost ten pounds. She's only six months along, and I already can't wait for this pregnancy to get over with. Hopefully her insane stance on sugar will disappear once she's had the baby."

"Sugar doesn't like sugar?" Moose asked incredulously, and laughed.

"Believe me, that's a joke you don't want to tell around her. I may…uh…have already mentioned this observation to her, and she didn't find it *nearly* as funny as I did."

The boys reappeared just then, the brooms and dustpans knocking against their heads as they struggled with the adult-sized items. "Thanks, boys," Jaxson said. "Okay, we need to get to work. Maybe if we work hard enough, we'll have enough time to stop at the bakery on the way back home to talk Gage out of some donuts."

"Yeah!" the two boys shouted in unison and ran, brooms swinging wildly, towards the far end of the mill.

"I better go after them and keep an eye on them," Jaxson said with another easy laugh. "I'd hate to see them somehow destroy this building when a fire didn't do the trick. My boys are...talented, shall we say, in destruction." He followed his boys, the Great Dane on his heels. Sparky flopped back down on the floor next to Troy's ladder, snuggling back down for a nap now that her buddy was going elsewhere to hang out.

Moose, Levi, and Troy all drifted back to work. More damn walls to scrub. Troy was just sure the blackened bricks were multiplying when he wasn't watching. He'd known in a theoretical sense that it'd be a lot of work to clean them, but if he'd known beforehand just how *much* work...

Ignorance was bliss and all that.

Just like I knew Penny was gonna leave Long Valley, and I fell in love with her anyway.

Shit. So maybe ignorance wasn't bliss after all. He'd been damn ignorant to think that he could change who Penny was at her core. Ignorant, stupid, willfully blind, dumb…

All of those things and probably a few more besides.

He hadn't heard from her since That Night. He'd only found out that she had moved to Seattle for a job when someone had asked him how she was liking it up there. He had been careful not to touch Facebook since That Night, not wanting to see the crazy happy pictures of her, enjoying her new exciting life.

He wanted her to be happy, of course; he just couldn't handle seeing it for himself.

A saint, he was not.

A howl of little-boy laughter pealed out, echoing off the bricks, and the sheer joy of it made Troy smile, just a little. It was surprising how the atmosphere of the mill changed now that there were kids in it. Moose and Levi had kidded around and teased each other while working, but that wasn't the same.

As Troy worked, he couldn't help but watch Jaxson at work, too. Not surprisingly, he was spending most of his time supervising his boys, making sure they stayed on track and didn't just turn their brooms into swords.

The Great Dane had patiently lay down on the sidelines, not kicking up a fuss or wanting attention but just waiting for his humans to be done so they could go do something fun together. His placid, waiting nature also surprised Troy. The day of Jaxson and Sugar's wedding, the beast had caused a ruckus with his thick, heavy tail, knocking everything over in sight as he'd joyfully jumped around. Troy'd had to hurry to take the beast outside before he caused even more damage, and all he could think at the time was that he couldn't *begin* to understand why they'd wanted this dog in the ceremony.

Now, though, watching his sweet nature around the two boys and Jaxson, Troy could see the attraction.

His heart twisted a little in his chest.

Maybe he'd been too quick to judge that day.

Maybe he'd just been in a sour mood because he'd felt pushed into being a groomsman for Jaxson when he really hadn't wanted to be. No one then or now knew his true thoughts about the new fire chief, and so when Jaxson had asked him, Moose, and Levi to be his groomsmen, Troy hadn't felt like he could say no. For hell's sakes, who said no to a request like that?

Consequently, he'd spent the whole wedding in a pissy mood, just wanting it to be over and done with so he could escape outside and hurry to the peace and quiet of his home.

Maybe I'm not such a nice guy after all.

That thought hurt a little. He'd spent his whole life with that integral belief about himself – that he was one of the good guys.

Well, most of his life, anyway. There was that fighting stage he'd gone through as a young teenage boy when he'd been kind of a shithead, which had landed him in Sawyer. He hadn't exactly been a paragon of patience and kindness at that point.

That aside – which to be fair to himself, could be chalked up to teenage hormones mixed with a natural reaction to fight back against bullying – he'd tried his best to always be a good guy.

Now, he wondered if he had been a judgmental prick at the same time. Was it possible to be both of those simultaneously?

"Hey you two, less sword fighting, more sweeping," Jaxson said. "I'm pretty sure Gage doesn't give out donuts to little boys who play around instead of work."

But Jaxson had made so many snarky comments about what a terrible job Troy's uncle had done as fire chief. Didn't that make him a judgmental prick, too?

It was true that there were a lot of things that had been left undone while Uncle Horvath was chief, but Troy'd had a front-row seat to it all, and knew what a struggle it was for him to run the mill *and* be the fire chief simultaneously. Troy'd seen the long nights, the bags under his eyes as his uncle had pushed himself to the very limits.

Aunt Horvath had been supportive in her own way by keeping supper warm on the stove for them when they came home late from a bad fire, but she'd also bluntly informed her husband that if he didn't cut back on something – and sooner rather than later – his heart was gonna give out and this town would find itself without a fire chief *or* a mill owner. She'd never been much for biting her tongue and didn't hesitate in telling her husband that he was well on his way to making her a widow.

Still, his uncle had hung in there, trying to serve his community that he firmly believed needed him...right up until the city decided that what they really needed was a full-time fire chief instead. It'd been a slap to the face, but Troy could tell his uncle had also been relieved. He could finally stop trying to balance the two equally important demands on his time.

If only Jaxson had stepped up to the plate and been a little less of a jackass about the things Uncle Horvath had let slide, it might not've been such a bad handover from one chief to the next.

"Looking good!" Jaxson said encouragingly. "Frankie, maybe a little less enthusiasm. If you swing the broom around like that, you throw more dirt into the air than you sweep up into a dustpan. Here, let me show you."

Troy slowed a little, his scrubbing circles becoming smaller and smaller as he stared sightlessly at the blackened bricks in front of him.

Did he *really* believe that?

He knew his uncle. He knew how much pride he had. He knew that being replaced, even if it had been by James (his right-hand man), would've been hard for Uncle Horvath to swallow. He'd spent so many decades of his life dedicated to the department, Jesus Christ himself could've taken it over and his uncle would've found something to be pissed about.

After all this time, maybe he needed to let the anger go. Troy continued to scrub unseeingly, his mind going around in endless circles as he went. He'd read enough hippie, kumbaya bullshit articles in his aunt's women's magazines to know that anger and bitterness only hurt the person who was angry and bitter; the focus of that anger and bitterness was rarely affected at all.

Except, it wasn't bullshit in this case. Hell, Jaxson didn't even know that Troy was pissed at him, let alone allow it to somehow affect him or change his behavior. Troy'd been carrying all of this around, and for what? Just because his uncle was a good guy and had done the best he could under the circumstances, didn't mean he'd actually done everything that needed to be done.

As much as Troy hated to admit it, Jaxson had been right about needing good radios, and the new fire truck having more bells and whistles than usable features, and—

He dropped his green scrubber into the pail and climbed back down the ladder to go watch the Anderson family at work. Jaxson casually came over to stand by him, watching together as the two little boys worked to sweep dirt and wrappers and trash into the dustpan.

They weren't perfect, but they were also kids, so…

"You've got good kids," Troy said softly. He could see that now.

"Thanks. They can be a handful, especially when they've just come back from their mom's house. Lately, she hasn't been much for watching them, and instead lets them run wild…they're picking up some real bad habits in Boise. I'm just glad that the judge finally awarded me primary custody over them. That was a hell of a court battle." He shook his head. "The court system can be rough."

Troy nodded. He couldn't say he'd been through anything like that, but he could imagine it'd be tough to have an outsider tell you how often you could see your own damn kids.

Then Troy drew in a deep breath and said what he should've been saying from the get-go. "I'm glad you moved up here so you could fight for them. They're worth fighting for, and the town is better off for having you here."

It was a freakin' speech in Troy's world, and

he held his breath, wondering how Jaxson would react.

"Thanks, Troy." Jaxson clapped Troy on the back, the maximum level of affection that two straight males were ever willing to show each other. "It wasn't an easy transition, but I'm damn glad I'm here. Aiden!" he hollered, moving forward and grabbing the broom handle that he'd been swinging around in the air. "Not a toy. We're here to clean. You two need to sweep up that last spot over there," he pointed to the corner where a pile of dirt was still left, "and then we'll be done and it'll be donut time. I want to see you two do your best."

Over his shoulder, Jaxson sent a laughing shrug towards Troy that clearly said, *Boys. What're you gonna do?* and stayed where he was so he could keep a firmer grip on the two.

Troy watched the three of them working together for a moment, and then turned back to watch Moose and Levi working together. Even here, in this moment when he had five people there specifically to help him out, he still felt like the outsider.

When he'd been out at the Miller's place, helping Abby and Wyatt move into their new house, he hadn't felt like a sore thumb sticking out. He'd been having fun; laughing and enjoying himself, even if he wasn't talking much. What was the difference? Why'd he been so happy there, and so miserable here?

Penny. It all came back to her. She'd been gone six weeks and still the pain was as fresh as the moment he'd dropped her off at her apartment building that last time. He'd thought that if he just had the perfect moment set-up, the perfect atmosphere, he could knock down those last walls around her. For a long time there, he'd known that he was more in love with her than she was with him, and he'd been okay with that. He'd been willing to wait; to give her the time to make her way to the truthitude, as she'd call it, that they belonged together.

But she kept talking about getting a job elsewhere, and that combined with the opportunity to make this old mill a reality…he had to make his move.

And what a disastrous move that had turned out to be.

As the Andersons left, and then Moose and Levi left, Troy just continued to scrub and work, work and scrub. Maybe, just maybe, he could scrub it all right out of his mind, soul, and most importantly, his heart.

CHAPTER 26

PENNY

*L*IFE SUCKED DONKEY DICK.

Her boss was terrible, her apartment was tiny, the weather was depressing, and the work was uninspiring. Oh, and it was almost Christmas, and here she was, hours away from home, with no chance of being able to make it home for the holidays. Rent was eating up more of her paycheck than she'd hoped it would, and she was barely hanging on by her fingernails. The gas and time off to go home…those were luxuries she just couldn't afford with her new "glamorous" job.

Oh, it was glamorous, all right. Who didn't look forward to being ridden like a rented mule by an asshat of a boss who still hadn't bothered to learn her name? The first fifteen times she'd corrected him – *It's Penny, not Peggy* – he'd been snippy and rude, and had continued to call her the wrong name anyway. She'd finally given up on being called the right name earlier that week, and consoled herself that at least HR knew how to spell her name on her paychecks, and wasn't that what mattered?

She was, to put it bluntly, miserable. Why oh why had she ever, in a million years, thought that moving to Seattle was a good idea?

She peered down the aisle between the tan, soulless cubicles and past the copy machine squished up against the coffee pot, squinting to see if the rain had stopped yet.

Ugh. Either a giant was spitting on the window yet again, or it was *still* raining outside.

Wranglers are starting to take on a whole new appeal.

At least, dry ones were. *Anything* dry was appealing, actually.

Coming from an Intermountain West state where water was a precious commodity, and whether or not they were going to get enough this year for the crops was an ongoing topic of discussion, the interminable rain had been a novelty at first. Everything was so painfully, overwhelmingly *green*, despite the fact that not a soul had a sprinkler system in their yard.

There were still fights over water like there were back in Idaho, but here, it was a fight over who was going to get stuck with it. Redirecting a rain spout into someone else's yard was practically an act of war.

The farmers of Long Valley would sell their mothers off to the highest bidder to have access to this much water. The grain would grow so well, Troy would never be able to come home from the mill—

She sighed and propped her chin on her hand as she stared sightlessly down at the newest proposal she was supposed to be working on.

"Supposed to be" being the operative term. Try as she might, she just couldn't figure out how to get excited about selling vegan water.

"But...but *all* water is vegan," she'd pointed out to her boss when she'd been given the assignment.

"Hippies are idiots," he'd told her bluntly. "Put happy smiling cows on the bottles, and it'll sell like hot cakes."

How on earth was this one of the most prestigious advertising firms in the west? They used to be so exclusive. Companies begged them to run their advertising campaigns for them. When she'd been in college, they'd been *the* place to work, and all of the students dreamed about someday joining their ranks.

Something had happened to the firm between her graduation from college and now, and Penny was too damn tired from the grayness and darkness and eternity of rain to figure out what. Greedy management? Incompetent management? Greedy, incompetent management?

Dammit all, she'd wanted this. She had. She still wanted this. She couldn't give up and go crawling back to Long Valley with her tail tucked between her legs. She wanted to live in a big city with all of the culture and opportunities to be found there. When she and Troy'd had that last big blowout, she'd woken up the next morning to an email in her inbox, congratulating her on being hired. She had felt like it was a sign from God – finally, the job she'd been searching for for months, coming right on the heels of what could only be considered a break-up with Troy. Not that they'd discussed that specifically, but yeah…

She'd been so sure that this was what she was supposed to be doing. It had worked out so perfectly. And then…

The papers swam in front of her eyes as she stared down at the paperwork. This couldn't be what she'd been dreaming of and working for, for so long. She refused to believe it. There had to be more to the big city and living the dream than this.

"Peggy!" her boss barked as he strode by, his black leather shoes squeaking with every step. "I need that draft by noon tomorrow."

She nodded numbly. She could totally come up with something by then.

Right?

Smiling cows. Happy cows. Why are we associating cows with water? Has no one ever seen a watering hole for a herd of cows? They piss and shit wherever they're standing. The mud is usually churned up so much that they're up to their knees in it. It's disgusting. Cows and water shouldn't go—

"Well?" he barked, and she realized belatedly that he'd stopped and was standing right next to her cubicle. "Are you going to do something? I've been watching you do nothing but stare off into space for the past hour. Edge Advertising isn't paying you to admire the rain."

Her mind sort of blanked out, though, after everything past the "do something" part of his question.

Was she going to do something?

He was right. Dear God in heaven, her boss from hell was right!

She *hadn't* been doing something, unless throwing a one-person pity party counted as "something." She'd been so miserable ever since she moved up here, she'd really been doing nothing but hiding from the world.

"You're right," she breathed, staring up at her boss but not really seeing him.

She was seeing Troy's eyes, crinkling at the corners when he smiled. She was seeing his pupils blown wide as he stared down at her with pure lust in his eyes. She was seeing the Goldfork Mountains, framing the sky, their snowy peaks comforting and beautiful. She was seeing her mom, wearing black and prattling on about the Dodgers chances this season and cleaning the attic yet again, but at least Penny knew she was okay. She could see that her mother was thriving and happy, unlike now where her mother wasn't talking to her at all. She'd told Penny she was being a certifiable idiot by telling Troy no, and then had hung up on her.

"You're right," she repeated, and it was only then that she realized her boss had been talking. He stopped and stared at her, his scowl only deepening.

"Are you listening to me?" he demanded. "You need more cows—"

"No," she said simply.

"No what? No, you don't need more cows? I'm the boss here, and—"

"No, I'm not listening to you, and no, you're not the boss here. Well, you're not the boss of *me* anyway, because I'm quitting. I'm quitting this firm and this damn awful weather and the humidity and I'm going *home*."

She snagged her purse off the hook on the cubicle wall and realized with a start that she had nothing else to take with her. It'd been almost two months since she'd started here, and she hadn't brought in so much as an extra tube of lipstick or a framed picture of her mother or *anything*.

"I won't give you a reference if you walk out like this!" her boss yelled, his cheeks turning a brilliant red as he glowered angrily at her. "Good luck ever finding a job in advertising again!"

"That's okay!" she told him cheerfully. "My next boss will be me, and I'm pretty happy to say that I'll hire myself. Good luck with your vegan water client."

She walked towards the elevator, practically

skipping as she went. Every step, she grew lighter and happier. She was going to go back to her hovel of an apartment, pack up her belongings, and head for home.

She wouldn't call her mom ahead of time; her mom loved surprises and she was about to give her mom the surprise of a lifetime. And once she was done being loved on and could take a shower to freshen up – after all, it was eight or nine hours by car from Seattle to Franklin, not to mention all of the packing she still had to do – she could go give Troy the surprise of a lifetime, too.

She walked out into the cold drizzle of the ever-present rainstorm and laughed out loud, ignoring the stares of the passerby's who probably thought she had a screw loose…or seven.

For the first time in two months, she felt happy again. Finally, *this* was what she was meant to do.

CHAPTER 27

TROY

TROY STRIPPED OFF HIS SHIRT, wincing at the pain of the twinging muscles that were sending lightning bolts through him. He'd always thought he worked hard at the new mill, but now that he was working on restoring the old one, racing against the clock to get it up and going and thriving before his money ran out, he realized his previous pace was child's play.

Before, harvest had always been a crazy time but then it would end and life would go back to normal. This new pace was like living through one harvest after another with no break in sight.

He toed his boots off, shucked his jeans, and crawled into bed wearing only his boxers. He really ought to take a shower, but that would require so much energy, there was just… no…wayyy…

His radio went off, jerking him awake. "Franklin Fire Department requests assistance with a residential fire in the Moose Run subdivision," the radio crackled. "There is a residential fire in the Moose Run subdivision."

Troy was fumbling and shoving his arms into his shirt, trying to get his clothes on but his shirt was strangling him and he couldn't figure out why until he realized he had put it on backwards. He yanked it off and flipped on the lamp next to his bed, squinting into the bright light.

Let's try this again, shall we? Nice and slow. Killing yourself with your own damn shirt isn't gonna help anyone.

The panic was hard to push down, though.

The Moose Run subdivision was where Wanda lived. Of course, lots of people lived there. The chances of it actually being Wanda's house were pretty small.

That sane and rational thought didn't do a damn thing for his panic levels.

What if…

He wouldn't let himself finish that thought.

He wouldn't know until he got there, and until then, there was no reason to worry.

Hurry, hurry, hurry.

Finally dressed, he ran out into the cold winter night, the icy air stealing the breath from his lungs, and pushed himself up and into the cab of his truck. He groaned aloud when he heard the thump of Sparky's paws landing in the bed. He really ought to order her back inside, but he started the engine instead. She wouldn't go out with him to the fire, of course, and arguing with her right now would take too much time. She could go for a joyride over to the fire station – it wouldn't hurt anything.

He listened to the radio chatter as he drove,

men reporting in that they were on their way. He waited for a quiet moment, and then thumbed the radio call button himself. "This is Troy Horvath. Coming up on Main now."

"Acknowledged," Jaxson radioed back.

It sucked that he had to drive into town to get geared up before he could head back towards Franklin. His house was on the Franklin side of Sawyer; Wanda's house was on the Sawyer side of Franklin. It was only a 20-minute drive from his house to Penny's mother's house, but not if he took a detour to the fire station first.

Of course, he couldn't go into a house fire without his gear or oxygen tanks. That was suicide. It wasn't called Personal Protective Equipment because it was a "nice" thing to have.

And anyway, it was quite possible it wasn't Wanda's house. There had to be fifty houses in that subdivision and as of yet, no one had reported out the address. There seemed to be some confusion on the topic, which was strange, to say the least. How could they not know which house was on fire? Usually the dancing orange and red flames gave it away.

His truck vents had just started to push out heat, warming the cab up, when he pulled to a stop in front of the station and cut the engine with a regretful sigh. It was Murphy's Law for Winter Travel – your destination was always about sixty seconds past where your engine had finally started putting out heat.

He could only hope someone had thought to flip on the heaters inside of the station. He hadn't checked the weather but based on the bitterness of the cold, it had to be sub-zero temps tonight.

He hurried in through the man door of the station, Sparky streaking in behind him. Poor girl was probably freezing her tail off after that bone-aching cold ride in the bed of the truck. If she'd just ride upfront with him, she'd be much better off, but no matter how much re-laxing she'd done since spring when he'd first gotten her, the cab of his truck was still the one place she absolutely refused to go.

"Hey, Troy!" Jaxson called out, sliding the

last of his turnout gear into place, and Troy pushed himself to catch up. Levi was there and also getting ready, but Moose hadn't arrived yet. No big surprise there; he'd moved to Franklin that past summer, so he was gonna be driving past the house fire in question to get to Sawyer to get geared up, just so he could take a ride in the fire truck right back to Franklin.

Ah. The joy of small towns, where everything is at least a 30-minute drive away.

Luke and Dylan were there, sliding into their gear, Dylan's hair sticking up every which way, clearly tousled from sleep.

What time is it, anyway?

Belatedly, Troy thought to check the clock on the wall and realized it was just after two in the morning. Damn, no wonder he felt so thick. It was almost like he was caught in a dream, wandering aimlessly around, pushing himself to register sounds and turn them into recognizable words.

And the panic sure as shit wasn't helping, but instead was adding another layer of stupidity to his brain.

If it's you, Wanda, I promise I'll get you out.

It was why he was a firefighter − to help others. He just hadn't expected to help a woman who he'd grown to love and admire, and who'd already fought and won against two bouts of cancer.

Surely God knows what she's already been through, and won't put her through this also. No reason to panic. Just get your turnout gear on and what comes, comes. Worrying beforehand isn't gonna make it any better.

Moose came in then, looking just as rumpled and tired as everyone else, but his strides were purposeful as he hurried into his gear. Jaxson had already started both fire trucks − the engine and the water truck − letting them heat up as they idled.

"Why is Franklin requesting our help?" Levi asked. "Moose Run is on our side of Franklin, but they're still a lot closer than we are."

"They're already out on a fire on the north side of Franklin. Tonight's the night for fires in Franklin," Jaxson said grimly. "Ready?"

"Ready!" the firefighters responded in unison. They split off into the two trucks, Troy grabbing the bucket seat directly behind the driver's seat of the engine. He wanted to see the flames as quickly as possible, so he could stop panicking. As soon as he knew for sure it wasn't Wanda, he could breathe again.

He felt the cold, wet nose of Sparky before he saw her in the darkness of the wailing fire truck.

"Sparky?"

She thumped her tail against the floor of the truck, whining as she nudged his hand again.

"What's that?" Moose asked from the passenger seat. He turned as he heard her whine again. "Sparky? What's she doing in here?"

"I don't know," Troy said, dumbfounded. "I forgot to pay attention to where she was at. She hates being inside of vehicles and confined spaces." He stared in shock at his loyal dog, even as he scratched her behind the ears. "I guess I figured she'd wait for me back at the firehouse."

"Well, now she can be a proper fire station

mascot," Jaxson said over the wail of the siren. "Didn't Georgia think she was a Dalmatian when she first saw her, because of the black spots and white fur?"

"Oh yeah, I gave her shit about that for days." Moose stared at Sparky for a moment longer and then turned back in his seat to face forward. "After living through that wildfire up in the mountains, I doubt she'll want to go anywhere near the fire itself, but you'll keep an eye on her, right?"

"Of course," Troy agreed, narrowing his eyes as he glared down at his way-too-faithful dog. Now he had Wanda *and* Sparky to worry about. Grand.

As they got closer to the Moose Run subdivision, Troy peered through the inky darkness, trying to figure out if the flames were coming from Wanda's house. It looked like it was about the right spot. *Dammit.* He'd been hoping the fire would be in some far-off corner of the subdivision and he'd be able to tell on arrival that it wasn't her house.

Sirens wailing, Jaxson maneuvered the

truck around tight corners, cursing the people parked on the street, making it difficult to squeeze the engine through. "C'mon, c'mon," he muttered under his breath. "We gotta hurry."

In the bucket seat, Troy felt helpless. Riding to a fire was the worst part of a call-out, in his book. All he could do was sit and watch and wait to arrive. The helplessness of the situation grated on his nerves.

They turned down Elkindeer Street and Troy sucked in a quick breath.

Shit.

It was Wanda's house.

Actually, it looked like it'd started originally in her neighbor's house, because both structures were now ablaze, the neighbor's house far worse than Wanda's. The picket fence between the two houses was also on fire, flames shooting up as it licked its way along the top of the railing.

They screeched to a stop in front of the two homes and piled out, Jaxson immediately assessing where to focus their efforts. Troy was scanning the yard, looking for a cloud of gray hair on a petite woman, but heart sinking, he only spotted a dark-haired woman in the yard of the house that was a goner. Part of the roof had already caved in. There was no way they were going to be able to save that house now.

And there was no sign of Wanda.

"Thank God you're here!" the neighbor wailed, standing out in her front yard in her bathrobe. "I knocked on Wanda's door but I didn't get an answer and I didn't dare open the door. I've watched *Backdraft*, you know. But she's almost died twice, you know. Breast cancer." She gestured to her chest. "Her daughter moved to Seattle, you know. Left Wanda by herself. You have to help her!" She was bawling again, clutching her yowling cat to her chest. Levi moved over to her side.

"Ma'am, let's step over here," he rumbled in his deep, soothing voice. "Out of the way of the firefighters. Now, tell me how you think this started." The rest of their conversation was lost in the roar of the flames.

Troy, Jaxson, and Moose all exchanged nervous glances. The roof of Wanda's house was starting to look scary – in danger of collapse at any moment. Usually the house fires they responded to were not this far along, and Troy wondered for a moment if this one had gotten this bad because they'd had to drive all the way from Sawyer to Franklin to respond to it. The extra 30-minute head start was great news for the fire; not such great news for the house.

Or for Wanda.

"Troy, you lay line. Moose, you and I go in through—"

"I know Wanda, and this house," Troy interrupted. "It's Penny's mother's house. I should take the lead. I know where Wanda's bedroom is."

"Oh, shit," Jaxson breathed and for a moment, the world just seemed to freeze around them as Moose and Jaxson took the information in.

Hurry, hurry, hurry. They didn't have time for this. Jaxson needed to start making decisions, or Troy was just gonna make a run for the front door and protocol be damned.

"Troy, you're on point. Moose, lay out the hose. We gotta move fast. Dylan, Luke!" he called out, and the two men came hurrying over. "Troy and I will go through the front door; you search the backyard and garage to make sure there are no small animals hiding somewhere. Does she have a pet?" he asked, turning back to Troy, the dancing flames of the fire lighting and then hiding his face. Troy shook his head. At least, she hadn't two months ago when he'd last seen her. "Good. Moose, once the hose is laid, start spraying and praying. Let's go."

They all pulled their masks into place and after a quick radio check on their new in-helmet radios, they headed for their assignments, Jaxson on Troy's heels as they pushed the front door open and stepped inside.

Troy paused for just a moment, recalling the layout of the house in his mind. It was a dark, inky, swirling blackness in front of him, the smoke blocking out any light they would've gained from the flames. Troy's stomach boiled with lava at the tension – he couldn't remember if the hallway was to the left or to the right. It was so disorienting, being there without any light. Jaxson waited, not saying anything, giving Troy the seconds he needed to think through it, and there was a small, distracted part of Troy's brain that was thankful for that. He'd tell him thank you later.

Left.

Without saying a word, he began feeling along the wall until he found the corner with his hands and turned down the hallway. Jaxson was right behind him, hanging onto a strap on his pack to keep from getting separated in the eternal darkness.

Right or left? One was the bathroom, one was her bedroom. Oh, and a linen closet in there too. Dammit all, he hadn't expected to be quizzed on the layout of Wanda's home like this, obviously, and now he was cursing the times he'd spent drooling over Penny's smile or her laugh instead of studying the inside of Wanda's home. Now a woman's life was in his hands – a very special woman – and she could pay for this with her life.

Although he couldn't recall any specific memory that made him sure of the choice, it just felt right to turn left. He pushed through the door and immediately came into contact with her dresser. *Thank you, God.* He'd chosen correctly. He felt his way past the dresser and over to the bed.

The empty bed.

"Dammit," he said into the radio. "Not here."

"Let's check under the bed and in the closet," Jaxson radioed back. "Maybe she's trying to lay low under the cloud of smoke."

Troy dropped to his knees and began feeling underneath the bed while Jaxson started to search the closet, but immediately, he knew Wanda wasn't under there. He could feel boxes and tubs filling every square inch of space, and Penny's laughing comment about her mother being the world's most organized hoarder popped into his mind. She'd apparently used the space under her bed for yet more storage.

"Not here," he said into the in-helmet radio, and slammed his hand down into the mattress. *Shit.* Where could she be?

Maybe she'd crawled into the bathroom? Shuffling their feet along the floor, feeling for her body as they went, they crossed the hallway to the bathroom, and then even checked inside of the damn linen closet.

Hang in there, Wanda. I'm gonna find you. I'm not gonna let you down. Not this time.

"It's getting hot in here," Jaxson radioed. "We need to head out."

Of course it was getting hot in there, but that wasn't really what Jaxson meant. He meant that it was getting dangerous, and Troy knew, even as he ignored his fire chief, that the man was right. The creaking of the lumber was only getting louder as the house began to strain under the weight of flames and ash and water from the truck.

Still, Troy shuffled towards the living room, using his feet to search as much as he was using his eyes and hands. There was one more place he could look—

The low oxygen alarm sounded in his helmet.

"We're running out of air," Jaxson shouted. "We gotta head back outside."

Still, Troy pushed forward. He just needed to check Wanda's La-Z-Boy. It was her favorite place to sit while watching the ball games on TV. Maybe she'd fallen asleep that night in her chair.

"We have to go, Troy!" Jaxson yelled. "That's an order!"

"Almost there!" Troy shouted back. The panic that'd been pulsing through him ever since he'd heard the words "Moose Run" was only getting stronger, drowning everything else out. He couldn't let Wanda die on his watch. Not if he could help it. Not if he had to die trying to save her.

He reached the chair, and her body. He could've wept with relief as he slid his arms under her frail body, noting even as he began shuffling for the front door that she'd lost weight in the last two months. She was so tiny now. Had she quit eating? Or was the cancer back?

She couldn't die. Not after all she'd been through. She couldn't.

The low oxygen alert switched over to a no-oxygen alarm, louder and more obnoxious. He couldn't think. He had to get outside. Nothing else mattered. *Outside, outside, outside.* He was swimming through gravy, pushing himself, couldn't breathe no matter how much he sucked in. His chest was tight and somehow, the darkness around him was getting even darker.

He stumbled out onto the front porch, tripping over something and then he was on his knees, scrabbling at his mask, trying to get it off his face, and then he felt Sparky's cold nose on the nape of his neck which just couldn't be right, and then a growl of exertion, and hands were there, pulling him and Wanda − *thunk, thunk, thunk* down the porch steps − and then pulling at his mask, yanking it away from his face and he could breathe again but it hurt, it all hurt.

It was in that moment that he discovered that he'd died, because Penny, his angel, was hovering over him and holding him and telling him that everything was gonna be okay. It was strange, because he thought he'd hurt less when he was dead, but then the world went black and he knew no more.

CHAPTER 28

PENNY

*W*HEN SHE'D PASSED the open bay doors to the Sawyer Fire Department station, the warm lights spilling out into the cold winter night, she'd said a quick prayer for whoever was affected. She realized then that Troy was probably out on that call, and sent up a quick prayer for him, too.

But it wasn't until she got to the outskirts of Franklin and realized that the dancing flames she'd seen through the dark winter night was in her mom's subdivision, that she got really worried. Troy would be fine – he'd had many years of training. He was practically born with a hose in one hand and an axe in the other. But her mom's subdivision…

What were the chances? Minuscule, probably. But the further she'd driven into the maze of streets, the harder her heart had pounded in her chest. It was either her mom's house on fire, or her neighbor's.

Turned out, all of the above.

She'd thrown her car into park and had sprinted across the street, hellbent on running inside and finding her mom, but before she made it up the front sidewalk, Moose had tackled her to the ground.

It was an appropriate name for him, honestly, because as far as she could tell, he was about the size of a moose.

"Oof," she'd grunted when she'd hit the ground, every bit of air having been expelled from her body.

"You can't go in there," Moose'd yelled over the crackling of the fire.

"My mom—" Penny had gasped as the edges of her vision had gone black. "She's…"

"We know. Troy is in there and so is Jaxson.

You gotta promise me you'll stay out here before I let you off the ground."

The frozen, snow-covered ground. Already, her teeth had started chattering from the full-body contact with the icy surface.

"Agreed," she'd grunted.

And now, she was just standing there, watching the flames dance, panic swirling, dancing, fighting to roar to the surface. It had been a long car ride and she'd taken her coat off hours ago so she should've been cold in the sub-zero temperatures, but of course, the heat from the flames made it feel like she was slowly going to roast alive instead.

She wanted to make another run for it — every cell of her body was screaming that something had gone wrong, that they were in there too long, that they were all going to die and it would be all her fault because she hadn't been here when the fire had started to pull her mom to safety and she didn't know if she wanted to scream or cry or yell or pound the ground with her fists but she wanted to do something — anything at all.

Anything—

And then she saw movement at the door and damn well didn't care about her promise to Moose – those were just words but this was Troy and her mom's life on the line – and so she went running, Moose and the other guys just inches behind her.

A streak of white darted in front of her, easily beating her to the front porch, and began pulling at Troy and her mom, trying to move them away from the heat of the flames.

The acrid smoke burned her eyes and lungs and the heat singed her skin but she didn't care, she too had to help pull them to safety. Troy was tugging at his mask, as weak as a newborn kitten attempting to stand for the first time, Sparky by his side, frantic and barking.

Penny debated for just a split second of whether to take his mask off first or move him away from the fire, but then Luke was picking up his arm and yelling at her to pick up the other one, so together they pulled him down the front steps and onto the lawn, Moose and Dylan carrying her mom over to the waiting ambulance. She heard someone radio for a second ambulance even as she pulled the mask off Troy, looking for signs of life. Had he died trying to save her mom?

Please God, don't let him die. Don't let my mom die.

She was torn between Troy and her mom, her gaze flickering between the two, not knowing who to go to, when Troy's eyes fluttered open for just a moment. She stroked his hair away from his face, crying and laughing hysterically and yelling, "I came home for you. You can't die on me now!" but his eyes were already closed again and his body was limp against her.

"He needs help!" she screamed. Moose pushed her hands away for a moment and she fought him until she realized that he was trying to put his own breathing mask on Troy. She quickly moved out of the way, letting him give Troy the precious oxygen he needed. She looked around frantically as she heard the ambulance pull away, the sirens wailing, and spotted Jaxson sitting on the ground, holding someone's mask to his face as he took deep breaths.

"What happened in there?!" she yelled across Troy's prone body, even as she stroked his hair away from his face. "It's okay, it's all right, just hang in there," she murmured to him.

Dylan spoke. "Based on the radio chatter while they were in there," he said quietly, "they couldn't find your mom. She wasn't in her room. They found her in the La-Z-Boy out in the living room, but by that point, they were out of oxygen. Troy refused to leave until he found your mom."

"You idiot," she said lovingly to the unconscious Troy sprawled across her lap. "If I live to be 102, I'll never deserve you. But, you have to live to 102, too." She started yelling, "You hear me, Troy Horvath? You live to 102, dammit, or I'll be pissed!" Her moods were swinging wildly and there was a tiny part of her brain that was telling her that she wasn't in control and she needed to calm down, but it just wasn't possible. Not with Troy lying there in her arms; her mom in an ambulance on the way to the hospital.

"The second ambulance is almost here," Dylan said quietly. "Listen – can you hear the sirens?"

She paused for a moment and listened. In the distance, she could hear the wail of the sirens as they grew closer.

"They're almost here," she told Troy. "You get to hang on now. That's your only job. Just hang on. You don't get to die, my mom doesn't get to die – nobody dies tonight. You got it? Nobody."

She felt a slight change in the air and she looked up to find that they were gaining on the fire. The flames weren't as brilliant or bright. There were more pockets of fire still left, but at least to her untrained eye, it was almost under control.

The sirens came to a stop, and numbly, Penny realized that EMTs were running a stretcher towards them. Hands were pulling her away from Troy and she tried to stand up, to tell the paramedics what had happened to Troy, but her legs had frozen into the kneeling position and no matter how hard she tried, she couldn't get her legs to cooperate; to hold her weight underneath her. And then her whole body was wracked with convulsions, the pain of the cold and ice and snow finally registering in her mind.

"This lady doesn't have a coat on," someone said. "What the hell was she doing kneeling in the snow?"

She told them not to worry about her – that she'd be fine, that they needed to get Troy to the hospital.

"What language does this woman speak?" someone asked. "Can anyone translate for her?"

English, you idiot. I'm speaking English.

But this time, she couldn't vocalize the words at all. They just hung in her mind, taunting her, as she drifted into the blackness.

CHAPTER 29

TROY

TALKING. So many people talking. Why were they so loud? Didn't they know he needed to sleep? He'd never been so tired in all his life. He wanted to tell them to shut up and let him sleep.

Then the sounds disappeared and he was drifting again. Drifting on a cloud that buoyed him along, no pain, just warmth, warm, warmer, too warm, why was he so hot? Squares of cold were being pressed to his skin. So cold right there. Why were they making him cold? He tried to tell them to stop, but still, the cold and hot continued, twisting around inside.

Pain.

It was everywhere. It was trying to nibble in around the edges and make him crazy. Couldn't he take a Tylenol, or seven? He tried to tell the voices he wanted Tylenol or Advil or Aleve or *something* but no one seemed to understand. They were all right there, but no one was listening.

"Troy, it's okay," she whispered. Someone was talking to him. Who was it? He knew that voice. He liked that voice. She was someone special. Who was she?

"Just relax and sleep, okay?" This time, there were fingers stroking across his forehead and through his hair. Such a lovely, soft touch.

"Mom?" he whispered, his voice cracking and straining. It hurt to talk – damn, it hurt. What was wrong with his throat?

"Hi, baby," Mom whispered.

"How are you feeling?" Dad asked.

"Water," he whispered.

A straw appeared at his lips, pushing against them, and he wrapped his lips around it and sucked in deep.

"Thank you," he finally whispered as he lay back. "Throat. Hurts."

"You were in a real bad fire," Mom said, and her voice sounded shaky. "Dear, why don't you call your brother and tell him that Troy has woken up? He'll want to know."

"Sure. Be right back." A quick squeeze of Troy's hand and then footsteps were fading away.

"Are you in pain?" Mom asked anxiously. "I can tell the doctor to up the morphine."

"No," he whispered. His throat was on fire and his body was on fire but even then, he knew he didn't want to become hooked on painkillers. "Tylenol or something?"

"I'll ask the doctor. Oh Troy, I can't believe you're awake." Her hand was shaking and Troy knew she was crying. He squeezed her hand, too tired to say anything. He was drifting again, catching snippets of words but none of them made sense. People were trying to ask him questions but he had no answers.

"Hey, Troy." A girl's voice. He knew this voice. Who was this? He loved this person, he knew that much. "I know you can't hear me, so I'm going to have to say this all over again when you wake up. Maybe we'll consider this to be a practice run." She laughed a little.

It was right there – her name. Pamela? Penelope? Polly?

He was trapped – he could hear but couldn't talk. No matter how hard he commanded his mouth to move and his lungs to expel air, nothing happened. Just drifting, like a piece of wood on the current of a river.

"...okay. They said because she was asleep, she didn't breathe as deep, so her lungs are better than they would be otherwise. You saved her life, you know..."

The words went away then, and he was drifting along, pain and heat and cold and calm all mixed together. It was peaceful here, and he didn't want to leave, not ever. But a tugging came along and began to pull him to the surface. He had to wake up. He couldn't ignore it any longer. The voices wouldn't allow him.

His eyes fluttered open, feeling like sandpaper scraping along his eyeballs as he squinted up into the bright light. A face into view and then she leaned over and she came into focus.

"Penny?" he whispered.

Nothing made sense. If he were dead, he wouldn't ache all over like this, right? Something was wrong. Why was she there? Angels didn't appear to live people – at least, he didn't think so. Actually, he'd never been dead before. Maybe they didn't appear to dead people, either.

"Hiya, handsome," Penny whispered, and leaned over to press a kiss to his forehead. "Welcome to the land of the living."

"Water," he whispered. His throat hurt so damn bad. Maybe if he could just cool it down some, then he could think. He could figure out why he was dead and alive at the same time.

She held a little cup up and angled the straw into his mouth. He greedily sucked down the liquid and then laid his head back on the pillow with a happy sigh. He felt so much better.

He still didn't know why he was dead and alive at the same time, though.

"Are we in heaven?" he asked, his voice cracking and rough. For some reason, this made Angel Penny laugh.

"No, we're in a hospital in Boise. But I can see how you'd get the two confused," she said teasingly.

If he could open his eyes up again, he'd totally glare at her for that one.

"Do you remember what happened?" asked heavenly-earthly Penny.

He searched back through his memory, but there were just a jumble of words and flashes of movement and he didn't know what any of it meant.

"No," he whispered.

"You saved my mom's life, that's what happened. If I wasn't so thankful, I'd beat you over the head with this pillow. Any sane person would've escaped long before you did. Jaxson told me you wouldn't leave, and your damn stubbornness is what saved my mom's life."

He creaked one eyelid open to peer up at her. "You don't sound grateful," he rasped out.

"That's because I haven't decided yet if I

want to strangle you for putting me through the last week."

"Week?" It hadn't been that long since the fire that he only vaguely remembered. Why, that was just...earlier today? Last night? None of that seemed right, actually.

"Yeah, week. You've been drifting in and out for about that long. The doctors even medicated you pretty heavily at one point because they wanted you to sleep so you could heal, and all you were doing was arguing about sticks in the water."

"Argue?"

"Yeah, argue. You were very adamant that there were sticks in the water, and wouldn't go back to sleep until I agreed to collect them all for you."

He was so dazed, he couldn't decide if she was kidding or not. He decided to leave it alone for the moment. "Sparky?" he whispered. It seemed like she'd been there the night of the fire, but of course that couldn't be right. She would've been at home, safe and sound.

"I don't know if you remember or not, or

even realized it was happening, but when you got to the front porch with my mom in your arms, you collapsed there, and Sparky darted forward and began trying to drag you to safety. I can't believe she was willing to go that close to flames again, but she was – for you. I missed it at the time, but they told me later that the embers fell on her at one point and Moose'd had to smother the flames, which she did *not* appreciate, but she still wouldn't move. She was so worried about you."

"Mom?" he whispered. It seemed like she'd been there at the hospital, or maybe that was just part of the delusions, too.

"I finally met them – your parents, I mean. Your mom and dad have been here all week, and so have your aunt and uncle. Bryce has popped in and out, based on time he could get off from the mill. All of the Millers have come by, Jaxson and Sugar and the boys, Levi and Moose and Dylan, Luke and his wife Bonnie... I kept telling them that you weren't awake to appreciate their coming, but of course, you can't keep the people you love away in a time like this."

People I love…

It was true that he did love all of those people. He was sure lucky in the friends and family department. But more than anyone else…

"Did you come home from Seattle after the fire?" His throat felt like it'd been set on fire again after such a long question and even without him asking, Penny brought the straw of liquid life back up to his lips. He gulped it down greedily and then sank back against the pillows.

"No," she finally whispered, and then was quiet for so long, he forced his eyelids to open so he could look up at her. Her normally perfectly styled hair was a rat's nest, her signature red lipstick was gone, but in his eyes, he'd never seen anyone as beautiful as she was in that moment.

"I was already driving back to Idaho when the fire broke out. I had no idea any of this would happen when I left Seattle. I was coming back home because…"

She drew in a deep breath and then slowly released it.

"Troy," she whispered, "I love you. I love Long Valley. I love living here. I think I even like Wranglers. At least, Wranglers on you. They make your ass look amazing. But that's not the point." She waved her hand in the air dismissively.

"It's not?" he croaked. Honestly, he could handle hearing a little more about how she thought his ass looked amazing, in or out of Wranglers, but she kept going.

"No, it's not. I was an idiot."

This just kept getting better and better. He decided on the spot that he was a-okay with her veering off the topic of his ass, if this was what she was gonna talk about.

She ran her fingers through his hair. "For so long, I clung to this idea that I needed to leave this valley to really be *me*. Nothing else mattered. I had to escape as soon as possible. When I met the Millers and your aunt and uncle and the guys at the fire department and I started to fall in love with Long Valley for the

418 | ERIN WRIGHT

first time in my life, it scared the shit out of me."

He snorted with laughter at that, which set off a coughing fit. After another gallon of water or so, he snuggled back against the bed, except somehow, she was now behind him and his pillow ended up being her chest and side instead.

It was *almost* worth feeling like his whole body had been set on fire.

"I didn't want to admit that, even to myself, and so I fought it tooth and nail. I *wanted* you to break up with me. I was safer that way. It was less scary. I kept trying to push you away, but you didn't budge. And then, the dinner at the mill." She shrugged, which did delicious things to the parts of her body that were pressed against him, and despite enjoying every moment of that, he was even more sad that he was too broken to do anything but appreciate it. Maybe being set on fire wasn't worth it after all.

"I hated Seattle. Dreary rain All. The. Time. It's just this wall of green, everywhere you look. I felt claustrophobic. The buildings were close, the trees were close, the bushes were close, the clouds were close – it rained for 33 days straight. And what did I get for 33 days of misery? Not even any white fluffy stuff covering the ground. It was just wet – everything was wet."

"So you decided to come back to me," he said hoarsely, pushing the words out past his raw throat, "because it rained too much in Seattle? What if you'd moved to LA or San Diego?"

He peeled his eyes open again and shifted to lie against the pillows propped up at the head of the hospital bed, so he could glare at her. If her whole *mea culpa* was gonna simply be, "I don't like the rain, so let's date!" he wanted none of it. She'd eventually figure out that there were warm *and* dry cities other than Seattle that she could move to, and would destroy his heart again.

And he just wouldn't be able to live through a second round.

She bit her bottom lip. "Sorry," she whispered. "I've had a whole week to practice this speech. You'd think I could do it better than this."

She took another deep breath. "I love you with all my heart and soul. Seattle being the wrong climate for me just helped me realize that a little faster, is all. But loving you has always meant loving Long Valley too, and that wasn't something I was ever going to allow myself to do. I've spent my whole life trying to escape this hellhole. But now I know the truth – I can stay in Long Valley and still be *me*. I don't have to give up high heels and sparkles on my tennis shoes and lipstick in order to live here. I don't have to give up who I am, or what I care about. It just took me a while to figure that out."

Content with her answer, he let his eyelids slide shut again. "I love you too," he whispered, "and someday, I'm gonna feel well enough to show you just how much."

"I already know, babe, I already know." She kissed him on the forehead. "Now sleep. You've got a lot of fans who will want to talk to you now that you've woken up."

He wanted to laugh at that – *fans*. It made him sound like some sort of superstar, instead of just an Idaho farm boy who happened to fight fires when his community needed him.

But he was too tired to laugh and so instead, he closed his eyes and began to drift again.

EPILOGUE

October, 2019

*I*T WAS ONE OF THOSE rare fall days where the weather was simply post-card perfect, with the golds and reds of autumn leaves swirling to the ground with each light whisper of wind, and fat, fluffy white clouds stretching across the brilliant blue sky. It put Penny in the mood to design a logo for a forestry company, or maybe a home décor store.

But, no design work for her today. Today was Grand Opening Day. She felt a thrill of excitement run down her spine. After all this time, it was a little insane to think that it was *finally* happening.

It had been a risky move to hold the grand opening for the Long Valley Business Co-op during harvest – prying farmers away from their tractors long enough to come on down for the celebration was a big concern. But Penny had pointed out to Troy that their primary de-mographic was the wives anyway; the husbands were just bonus. As she peered out from behind the drapes, hiding her from the crowds milling about, she noted with satisfaction that she was right. More than a few farmers were out there, but it was mostly farm wives and tourists.

Perfect.

After the grand opening was over with, she was planning on sleeping for a week. Maybe even two, but only if she could convince Troy to sleep with her. She grinned to herself, her hand caressing her perfectly flat stomach. Al-though there hadn't been nearly enough time lately for them to simply cuddle together in bed, they had managed a few fun times, and now, she couldn't *wait* to give Troy the news, hopefully that night. He was gonna be the best—

"Hey Penny, the mayor says he's ready," Kylie Whitaker called out, popping her head around the corner of the curtain, her adorable one-year-old baby girl propped on her hip. "We're just waiting on you two." Even with a baby underfoot, running the veterinarian clinic, and getting married, the ever-efficient and cheerful wife to Adam Whitaker had been a big part in getting the co-op off the ground. Penny was sure her goat soaps and lotions were going to fly off the shelves now that she had a good place to sell them.

"Thanks. I'll go find Troy," Penny said with a wave, and began the search for him. In the last week, he'd been bitten by the one-more-thing bug, and at this point, Penny was a little worried there was no cure for it. He was going to one-more-thing himself right into an early grave.

"Hey, babe!" she called, opening and closing doors as she went. *Not in the utility closet. Not in the storage closet. Not in the—* "There you are!" she said when she opened up the door to his workshop. The comforting smell of leather embraced her and she paused to take a long, deep breath of it. Leather and pine trees — old Penny would've died laughing at the suggestion that those would become her two favorite smells in the world, but new Penny...

They were the smell of Troy, and thus the smell of love.

"Oh, hey," he said distractedly, sorting through his pile of leather scraps as Sparky stood and stretched, padding over for some loving. "Where did I put that..." he mumbled to himself.

"Babe, the mayor is waiting for us," she said, sliding her arms around his waist and popping a kiss on his mouth while also scratching Sparky behind the ears. "Along with the rest of the town."

"Dammit, is it really that late?" He looked up at the clock on the wall and let out a few choice swear words. "Where in the hell did the morning go?" he asked rhetorically. "I was gonna get one last-st thing done…"

"It'll all be here when this is over with," she promised him, threading her fingers through his and tugging him towards the door. She absentmindedly stroked her thumb over the scarred and rippled skin on the back of his hand – the worst of the damage still remaining from the fire. His left hand would never be the same again, which as a left-handed artist, had been a huge blow to him. Over the past ten months, though, he'd done countless hours of physical therapy and had been able to regain most of his mobility, along with strengthening his right hand to compensate.

She thanked the heavens again that it wasn't worse than this, at least for Troy. The doctors had said his relative youth and health had been his saving grace – the reason why he was able to recover as fully as he did. Still, every time his radio went off, it was hard for her to quell the pure panic that roared through her veins. What if he wasn't so lucky the next time? What if he went back for a dog or kitten or child, and died? What if—

Just thinking about it was making her heart try to pound its way out of her chest. Him continuing to serve as a volunteer firefighter was one of the few rip-roaring fights they'd gotten into since she'd come back from Seattle. She'd finally caved, realizing that it was a part of who he was – how he gave back to the community.

Firefighting and this business co-op, that was.

"How's my hair?" he asked gruffly, just before they stepped out onto the temporary dais together. She quickly ran her fingers through it and then pressed a hard, quick kiss to his lips.

"I love you," she murmured, "and I'm so damn proud of you."

"I couldn't have done it without you." He shot her a nervous grin. "Let's do this, eh?"

Hand in hand, they stepped out from behind the curtain and up onto the platform, waving to the crowd as the mayor moved onto the platform from the other side.

"Thank you, everyone, for coming today,"

the mayor said into the mic, the sound echoing through the large building via the sound system they'd paid stupidly good money to install. They had plans of playing music every Saturday during the open hours of the farmer's market, and if they could swing it, even bring in some bands and hold a concert or two.

One major event at a time, Penny.

She focused on the mayor, only to realize that he was rambling on and on about how wonderful this new venue was...making it seem like he'd been an integral part every step of the way. She tried not to roll her eyes too hard. He was a typical politician – he didn't want to be out in front in case an idea fell through, but once it was a clearly viable plan, he hurried to the front of the parade to make sure he received his due in helping bring it to fruition.

She glanced over at Troy, who had the same bemused smile on his face as he attempted to politely listen to the mayor claim most of the credit for this idea coming together.

Everyone here knows the truth.

She didn't know if her telepathic powers were up to snuff or not, but just in case, she'd repeat that truthitude to him that night as they got into bed. Because everyone in Long Valley *did* know the truth – this was the brainchild of Troy Horvath, and the product of many hundreds of hours of volunteer labor from the community.

Finally, the mayor wound down his speech and received a light smattering of applause for his overblown bluster.

"And now, I present to you, Troy Horvath!" the mayor said, gesturing for Troy to take centerstage. Troy kept his hand wrapped around Penny's as they walked over together, the applause and whistles of encouragement almost a wall of sound coming straight at them. Troy's mental telepathy skills seemed to be working just fine, and he was currently screaming, "DON'T LEAVE ME UP HERE!" nice and loud, straight at her.

She squeezed his hand that had been burned by love. She wasn't going anywhere.

The mayor handed the mic over to Troy

and reluctantly stepped off the dais. Troy did his best to smile at the crowd even as he was handed a mic that he handled much like he would a live snake. She squeezed his hand again.

You're gonna do great, babe. Just talk slow, think about what you're gonna say, and you'll make it through.

Just in case her mental telepathy powers weren't up to conveying such complex ideas, she changed it to mentally chanting *I love you, I love you, I love you* over and over again. Even her pathetic powers would be able to transmit that much, right?

"Welcome to opening day of the Long Valley Business Co-op," Troy rumbled into the microphone, and the crowd burst out into cheers again. Penny scanned the crowd, searching for her mom, finding her just a few feet back from the stage. She had burns all the way down the right side of her body and was now walking with a cane – a beautiful creation hand-carved by Iris Miller, of course – but as always, her spirit was unbreakable. When they caught gazes, her mom threw her a kiss and a wink.

"It's been a long time coming," Troy continued, once the cheers died down. "Every one of the founding members of the co-op helped make this happen. When I say your name, please wave so everyone can see you. Carmelita Juarez. Iris Miller. Ivy Bishop. Kylie Whitaker. Tennessee Garrett." Each woman waved, their husbands cheering the loudest for their spouses. "And of course, my Penny Roth. I couldn't have done this without her. Which is why—" he took a deep breath and stared into her eyes, "I would like to ask her to be my wife."

The room as a whole gasped, sucking all of the air out, leaving none for Penny.

At least, that's how it felt to her.

She stared at him as he dropped to one knee right there on the dais and pulled a ring box out, holding it up for her to see but she couldn't see a damn thing from the tears filling her eyes.

"Yes!" she shouted, and threw herself at him. Sparky, clearly delighted with this new game, came bounding over and was licking their faces, barking happily in agreement.

The crowd was laughing and cheering but still, she knew Troy heard her when she whispered, "Always."

AUTHOR'S NOTE, PART 2

THIS WAS AN ESPECIALLY poignant book for me to write. As long-time readers of mine might recall from other Author's Notes, I tend to pick topics based on experiences that family members have gone through, and *Burned by Love* is no exception.

I have a nephew who is in his early 20s, who has been stuttering since he was a toddler. For the longest time, everyone just assumed that he'd grow out of it, since that's a fairly common thing to happen. Unfortunately for my nephew, that wasn't the way the cookie crumbled. In fact, by time he got into high school and went to a special speech therapy company that specializes in stutterers, the doctor who ran the clinic told my sister that my nephew's case was the worst he'd ever seen in over twenty years of working in the field. His stutter is much, much, *much* worse than Troy's.

But if you look past the fact that there are only a couple dozen words that my nephew can *say* without stuttering (and sadly, no, his own name is *not* on that list) and focus on what he can *do*…well, that list is long.

He has an artistic ability that just shines when he's on the computer (much like Penny); he has a wicked sense of humor; he is incredibly intelligent; and he is a terrific listener. (I bet you didn't see that coming! 😀)

In fact, because of stuttering, he became everyone's best friend (who doesn't want a friend who listens to everything you have to say?!) and was voted Prom King his senior year. His high school classmates adored him, and for good reason. He has a wonderful, caring, loving heart. He's tall (well over 6'0"), broad-shouldered, muscular, blond hair, blue eyes, handsome as sin...

He just can't talk, or at least not easily.

With *Burned by Love*, I set out to create a story where someone like him could be the hero.

Growing up, I read romance novels under the covers with a flashlight, and I loved them all. Romance meant happily ever after. It meant kisses and love and two people who *belonged* together, no matter what.

But the more I read, the more I felt like the people in them were just *so* unrealistic. Do you remember the violet-eyes phase? It seemed like every romance novel I picked up there for a while had a heroine with violet eyes. Have you ever met someone in real life with honest-to-goodness purple eyes? I know I haven't.

But their waists were always tiny and their boobs were always big and their voices were like angels and the men were oh-so-perfect in every way...

I eventually realized that I had nothing in common with any of them. When I started writing my own romance novels, I wanted to write about *real* people with *real* struggles. People who are so real, you can reach out and touch them…or at least feel like you could.

Troy and Penny's story is part of that. I wanted to show what it was like to be trapped inside of a body that sometimes betrays you. I wanted to show what it was like to be trapped in a world that you thought would kill you if you stayed in it one more moment, and then realize in the end that it's all you've ever wanted.

In other words, I wanted to show real life. I hope I succeeded.

For anyone who is curious about stuttering, and specifically facts and info about how it afflicted B.B. King and Elvis in particular, you can check that out below:

B.B. King's story – https://www. stutteringhelp.org/content/bb-king

Elvis Presley's story – https://www. stutteringhelp.org/content/elvis-presley

There's a lot of info on that site about stuttering that you should check out if you're wanting to know more. There are many more famous people who stutter who I didn't even mention in the book (James Earl Jones, Marilyn Monroe, Marc Anthony, Joe Biden, Samuel L. Jackson...the list goes on. You'll be amazed by the people you find who're afflicted!)

So, here's to the *real* people of the world.

~Erin

ALSO BY ERIN WRIGHT

~ LONG VALLEY ~

Accounting for Love

Blizzard of Love

Arrested by Love

Returning for Love

Christmas of Love

Overdue for Love

Bundle of Love

Lessons in Love

Baked with Love (April 2019)

Bloom of Love (September 2019)

Banking on Love (March 2020)

Sheltered by Love (October 2020)

Holly and Love (December 2020)

Forged by Love (August 2021)

Conflicted by Love (April 2022)

Dishing Up Love (September 2022)

Gift of Love (December 2022)

~ FIREFIGHTERS OF LONG VALLEY ~

Flames of Love

Inferno of Love

Fire and Love

Burned by Love

~ MUSIC OF LONG VALLEY ~

Strummin' Up Love (July 2019)

Melody of Love (May 2020)

Rock 'n Love (March 2021)

Rhapsody of Love (February 2022)

~ SERVICEMEN OF LONG VALLEY ~

Thankful for Love (November 2019)

Commanded to Love (August 2020)

Salute to Love (June 2021)

Harbored by Love (November 2021)

Target of Love (July 2022)

ABOUT ERIN WRIGHT

USA Today Bestselling author Erin Wright has worked every job under the sun, including library director, barista, teacher, website designer, and ranch hand helping brand cattle, before settling into the career she's always dreamed about: Author.

She still loves coffee, doesn't love the smell of cow flesh burning, and has embarked on the adventure of a lifetime, traveling the country full-time in an RV. (No one has died yet in the confined 250-square-foot space – which she considers a real win – but let's be real, next week isn't looking so good…)

Find her updates on ErinWright.net, where you can sign up for her newsletter along with the requisite pictures of Jasmine the Writing

Cat, her kitty cat muse and snuggle buddy extraordinaire.

Wanna get in touch?
www.erinwright.net
erin@erinwright.net

Or reach out to Erin on your favorite social media platform:

facebook.com/AuthorErinWright

twitter.com/erinwrightlv

pinterest.com/erinwrightbooks

goodreads.com/erinwright

bookbub.com/profile/erin-wright

instagram.com/authorerinwright

CPSIA information can be obtained
at www.ICGtesting.com
Printed in the USA
LVHW030330210120
644179LV00011B/748